PULASKI'S

REDEMPTION

BY

ROBERT F. LACKEY

Heron Oaks, Murrells Inlet, SC
Copyright © 2019 Robert F. Lackey
Heron Oaks
ISBN-13: 9780692091487

Other Pulaski books by Robert F. Lackey:

Pulaski's Canal

Blood on the Chesapeake

Raven's Risk

Kingdoms in the Marsh

Brazen Deceit

Serpent's Compromise

Despot's Heel

Bloody Ground, Shallow Graves

Brutal Peace

DEDICATION

TO SANDI

*It is most fitting to dedicate my last book in this series
to my wife,
Sandra Marie Nelson Lackey
She was my greatest supporter in this endeavor,
and to whom the first book, Pulaski's Canal,
was dedicated.
She has always been my inspiration for Sonja,
and the reason why the character has so much life and
charm, as does she.*

Robert F. Lackey

ACKNOWLEDGEMENTS

No book can make its way to print without the hard work of many people.

I wish to acknowledge the valuable assistance of
STALWART BETA READERS
and thank each of them for their contributions:

James Cameron, Havre de Grace, Maryland

Judee Cooper, Edgewood, Maryland

Linda Cross, Avenue, Maryland

Kathy Cullum, Havre de Grace, Maryland

Lori English, Las Cruces, New Mexico

Diane Bassette Nelson, Interlaken, New York

Patti Paulus, Elkton, Maryland

Ken (Buddy) Quade, Westminster, Maryland

Marian Stokel, Leonardtown, Maryland

Michael J. Webb, Newport News, Virginia,

who aided significantly in finalizing this manuscript.

DEVELOPMENTAL EDITOR

Amber Wheeler Bacon
Surfside Beach, South Carolina

COPY EDITOR

Jennifer Cosham
Mount Airy, Maryland

FURTHER ACKNOWLEDGEMENTS

*The supportive members of the
Surfside Writers Group,
Surfside Beach, South Carolina,
Of the South Carolina Writers Association*

*The generosity and friendship of
Perry Baldwin Stewart
Owner of the historic A.P. McCombs House
(The Pink House)
Descendent of the real-life Mamie Stewart.*

*Karen and Ed Garono,
Owners of the historic Sawyer Building (C.1838) in
Havre de Grace, for the private tour during its
renovation. I continue to use this memory as
Nixon's Hotel.*

FURTHER ACKNOWLEDGEMENTS

I offer my appreciation and recognition for the wonderful generosity of

---

The Susquehanna Museum at the Lock House, Havre de Grace, Maryland

---

The Havre de Grace Maritime Museum, Havre de Grace, Maryland

The Friends of Concord Point Lighthouse, Inc., Havre de Grace, Maryland

---

The Chesapeake Bay Maritime Museum and the St. Michael's Museum, St. Michael's, Maryland

---

The Havre de Grace Decoy Museum

And that exquisite gem at the head of the Chesapeake Bay:

Havre de Grace

Where today whispers in your ear of yesterday.

PULASKI'S

REDEMPTION

BY
ROBERT F. LACKEY

THE FLOOD OF 1870

The highest tide known then to any living resident of Havre de Grace, Maryland, occurred on Sunday, January 2, 1870. Massive flooding swept the shores of the Upper Chesapeake Bay causing catastrophic damage within towns and villages. The historic flood tide even overpowered the current of the mighty Susquehanna River, pushing it back over a mile within the river's historical domain, up to a place known then as Watson's Island.

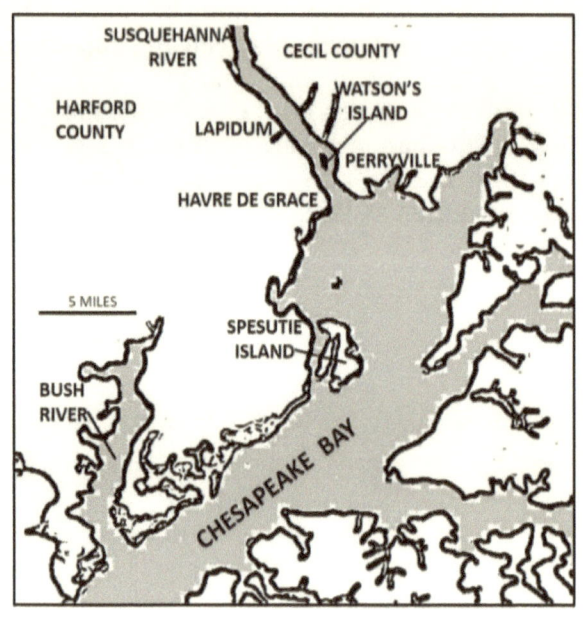

SUSQUEHANNA
RIVER

CECIL COUNTY

WATSON'S
ISLAND

HARFORD
COUNTY

LAPIDUM

PERRYVILLE

HAVRE DE GRACE

5 MILES

SPESUTIE
ISLAND

BUSH
RIVER

CHESAPEAKE BAY

OYSTER TONGING – Using hand tongs, long scissor-like tools with metal rakes on the ends, the waterman stands on the side of his boat, opens the tongs, and reaches to the bottom of the river to pull up oysters.

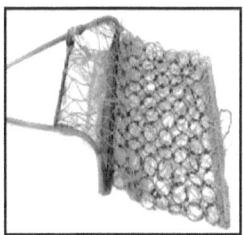

OYSTER DREDGING- A large clawlike metal scoop, called a dredge, towed along the bottom of the river by a sail boat scraping the oyster beds in far greater quantities than tonging, thought to damage the oyster bed.

PUNT GUN – A rifle shaped cannon mounted on a low-profile boat. The gun fired hundreds of pellets in a single shot, capable of killing several dozen ducks with each firing, for selling large numbers of ducks to restaurants.

of

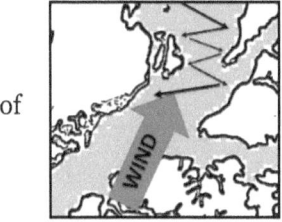

TACKING – Time-consuming sailing back and forth, zig-zag, across the front a contrary wind, gaining only modest distances toward the sailing ship's destination with each effort.

LAPIDUM, MARYLAND.
MONDAY, DECEMBER 27, 1869.
SIX DAYS BEFORE THE FLOOD.

Low pewter clouds tumbled on their journey north over a gritty river galloping south, and a mist roiled in the troubled space between them. A Great Blue Heron dipped from the sky to skim above the empty canal bordering a snow-covered slope. Ben Pulaski gazed from the livery buggy, out beyond the canal towpath to the Susquehanna River, ice lacing its edges as it raced down to the Chesapeake Bay. He paid the driver and sent him back to Havre de Grace, five miles south, where the train had brought him and his wife, Sonja. They stood together, sighing in shared satisfaction to be home in Lapidum once again. The misty view between the pair of massive oaks before their house reluctantly showed Port Deposit on the opposite shore. Like Lapidum, Port Deposit was in its winter slumber of white-capped roofs and black coal-fire plumes feather-brushed from chimney tops by the wind. The Heron squawked as it pulled itself higher into the air and turned south toward the bay where it hunted in the shallows. Ben put his arm around Sonja.

"Sounds like he wasn't happy to find the canal still just mud," Ben said.

His eyes were dark from sleepless travel since leaving the Virginia mountains on long jolting train rides east. Gray hair mingled with the black that slipped from under his hat. The old scar below his left eye turned pale in the cold weather, a white line across a rosy cheek.

Sonja leaned against his side. "Me and him, both," she said.

"Too early to be weary of winter, dear. Still five days 'til January."

"Each year, I get weary of winter earlier," she said, showing a rare smile, but it did not rise to her crystal blue eyes. Her sadness over losing Isaac weighed heavy on her heart. "Soon, I will be tired of it in September, just knowing it is coming."

Ben pushed a stray loop of blonde hair off her forehead and wedged it back under her fur hat. A few strands of silver reflected light from the low winter sun.

"We could move south, you know," he said.

Sonja huffed. "Never. Not after South Carolina." She turned toward the front porch.

"I'll start a fire in the kitchen," she said, "while you bring in the bags." She gazed at the barn in the side yard. "It's all gone. The whole bunkroom is gone from the barn."

"I told you there was a fire in there when I joined you in South Carolina in September."

"Then you told me other things that filled me with pain. I had just witnessed the hanging of our dear friend, Simon, and then you tell me Isaac is dead. That he was already in the ground for two months. My first-born son. I never–"

Ben carried the bags up the steps beside her, speaking as he passed.

"No more. Not now. It is hard for me too. Let's get in the house, and you can spend the night telling me how heartless I am."

"No. Not that, Ben," she said, but he was gone inside.

In the empty house, they spoke to each other from different rooms, noticing the echo for the first time. They had added more rooms so the whole family could visit under one roof. Now it held only the two of them. Their daughter and granddaughter lived in their own house twenty-five miles north, above the Line in Pennsylvania. Their son, Aaron, was with his growing family in the mountains of Virginia, in Fort Chiswell. Their other son, Isaac, tortured by his lost arm and experiences during the war, had left behind a widow and fatherless children in Albany.

Ben came to the doorway. "I said, 'The smokehouse is empty, but I can get some things from Mac.' I gave him all we had when I left for you. What do you want to have for supper?"

Sonja sat in a padded chair in what would have been Isaac's room, her face buried in her hands, sobbing.

He came to her and knelt beside the chair, laying his hand on her back.

"Let it out, Sonja. You can't hold it in any longer–"

She held up her hand to stop his comment. Tears streamed down her cheeks from reddened eyes.

"Some moments of grief require no words, Ben, and can only be made worse by them."

He stayed next to her in silence until her crying had softened to sniffles, then rose to retrieve a whiskey and water from the kitchen.

"Men always think whiskey will help," she said, accepting the small glass.

"The burn gives the sadness a momentary distraction," he said, "and forces the person to take in a breath. It's precious little, but sometimes it's just enough to help them think of something better. Sometimes."

"And for you, Ben? Does it ever help you?"

He sighed. "I don't bother with the water, and I use a bigger glass."

Gentle knocking sounded from the front room. Ben went to answer the door to find Delbert and Mary Freidman. Delbert was Ben's business partner, but they were also his son Aaron's father and mother-in-law during Aaron's first marriage. Delbert held a covered crockery pot. Mary held a small basket and a candle.

"You did not sit Shiva for your mourning?" Mary asked. "Your Isaac had already been buried before you heard of your loss?"

"That is true," Ben said. "We took our friend's body to his home in Canada, and couldn't visit Isaac's family in Albany until November, two months after his funeral. His widow and children were trying to move on, and we couldn't ask them to endure their grief again. Sonja and I visited Isaac's grave, then we needed to go to Virginia for the birth of our new granddaughter. She was born Christmas day."

"Blessings be on you and your family, Benjamin," Delbert said.

"You came back so soon," Mary said.

"They have a great deal of snow in those mountains. We thought it wise to come home while we could. We will visit them again in the spring."

Ben stepped back. "Please, come in."

Delbert and Mary smiled but shook their heads no.

Delbert raised the crockery pot. "This is a nice white bean stew Mary has made for Shiva. The basket holds boiled eggs to represent the cycle of life. It is a consolation meal. The stew and the eggs will nourish your bodies, and the candle will help focus your thoughts on saying goodbye to Isaac."

They handed the gifts to Ben one at a time to place on a nearby table.

"The Freidmans are Jewish, and the Pulaskis not," Mary said. "But we four were parents together for a while."

"For your Aaron and our Maggie," Delbert said.

"Our Maggie," Mary said, "who gave the four of us a grandchild as her parting gift. And their Sarah, who passed before Maggie."

"May God bless their memories," Delbert said. "You and Sonja will always be in our hearts."

Then they turned and walked down the steps. Sonja stood at the doorway of Isaac's room, out of view from the front door.

"I remember Mary telling me about Shiva

after Maggie died," Sonja said. "Bring those things into his room. We can remember him there."

Ben lit the candle as Sonja lifted the cover to the crockery pot and uncovered the boiled eggs. The bean stew was still warm, and the eggs had been shelled. Mary had slipped bowls and spoons into the basket.

"She thinks of everything," Sonja said. "I didn't realize how hungry I was."

She took some stew, gazing into the candle flame. "He was so brave when you were away in China."

Ben nodded. "I was so proud of him when he and Aaron told me what they did during the ice gorge. I left two boys to go to China, but I came back to young men."

"When the four of us moved here from Havre de Grace," she said. "Isaac built that little wharf at the edge of the canal so you would have a place to tie up your canal barges when you came home from trips to Wrightsville."

Ben smiled at the candle. "He was so happy when he was admitted to West Point. He loved being an engineer."

Sonja allowed a faint mile. "And so handsome in his uniform when he married Harriet. And then the war."

"No. Not that, Sonja. Think of happier times."

The room fell silent, and tears dropped among the beans.

Ben walked the edge of the canal in the twilight, carrying a cup of coffee steaming into the chilled air. The canal provided a water highway from the mounds of coal in Columbia, Pennsylvania, forty miles north, to the canal basin in Havre de Grace, five miles south of Lapidum. The canal basin in Havre de Grace was the gateway to the Chesapeake Bay and all the cities linked to it and Philadelphia by way of the C&D Canal.

Two of his canal barges rested nearby in the mud of the canal, drained for its winter hibernation. Looking like abandoned buildings, the deep cargo holds of the boats made them tall when sitting on the ground and the true expanse of their hulls exposed. Ben timed the last trip for two of his barges each winter, so when the canal was drained, they would settle in front of his property in Lapidum. The barges provided a hundred twenty tons of coal for the modest community and a winter home for a bargeman who had none. Barges of the Susquehanna and Tidewater Canal were Pennsylvania built, with bow and stern looking alike except for the tiller and rudder at the rear. The canal boats had deep cargo hatches fore and aft but holding a modest ten by twelve-foot cabin between them. The squat cabin roof and narrow windows in the sidewalls appeared suitable only to gnomes, sitting barely two feet above the deck. Still, the depth of the barge allowed seven feet down to the cabin floor. The snug space provided bunk beds, a small iron stove, and a narrow table. The only chore for the occupant was to watch over the barges and deliver burlap bags of coal to Ben's partner at the mercantile store a short distance away. The two barges remained tethered bow to stern, called a tandem, and the smokestack of the stern barge cabin was sending up a wisping plume of black smoke.

"Evenin' Ben." The voice came from behind.

Ben turned with a start to face the man, then smiled. "Wasn't expecting you from that direction. Evenin', Garrett. How are you today?"

Garrett Simpson was tall and slender with a horrific scar gouged in the side of his face from cannon shrapnel during the war. He never mentioned which army he fought for, and Ben never asked.

"Fair to midlin'. Just comin' from the outhouse. You?"

"Happy to be home," Ben said, "but the sadness came with us."

"Sorry to hear about your son..."

Ben motioned his cup toward the old wooden dock sitting low at the edge of the canal.

"Isaac built that. I like knowing his hands touched it and that it is still here. He was sixteen then. Almost a man. I needed to come out and look at it." Ben sighed. "That was twenty-eight years ago."

They stood without speaking a moment while crows muttered to one another in the treetops, the wind whispered among the branches, and the river gurgled among the boulders.

Garrett peered at the dock. "He did a good job for it to last that long."

Ben nodded in agreement. In his memory, Ben watched Isaac, his arms folded on his chest man-like and grinning, proudly showing what he had built for his father. He had used cypress for the posts, planks, and pegs.

"He used cypress for everything," Ben said.

Garrett cleared his throat. "I've got ledger entries ready to show you when you want. Took twenty-three bags of coal up to Delbert's so far this winter, sold five straight off the barge, and burned less than two."

"Your record-keeping is always perfect. You know, Garrett, since Delbert's son got married and moved to Baltimore, he'd love to have you help keep the books with him."

"Yeah, and I appreciate that, Ben," he said, pointing with his thumb to the barge, "but I like keeping to myself. The barge suits me, as long as it's all right with you."

"It will always be all right with me, Garrett."

Garrett lingered. "Hasn't been all that cold yet. Probably could have kept water in the canal a couple more weeks."

Ben shrugged his shoulders. "It's always a best guess. Some winters come early, and some come late. Back in fifty-two, it came early, and by January, they laid train tracks on the ice over to Perryville. Some winters, it never freezes at all."

Garrett gave his half-smile in the fading light and turned away.

"Do you have everything you need on the barge?" Ben asked to Garrett's back.

"Yep. Got a deer last week." He spoke over his shoulder. "Half is still in your smokehouse. Delbert gives me more beans and cornmeal than I can eat."

Garrett stopped on the gangplank laid between the bank and the barge, then faced Ben.

"Don't tell Delbert that. There's lots of Canvasback ducks around this year. Not so many Mallards. I like to feed'em."

"You turning them into pets, Garrett?"

Garrett chuckled. "Nope. Once in a while, I'll scoop one up for supper. I'm a terrible shot at ducks."

Garrett waved, then lifted the cover over the cabin steps and went down into the barge.

Ben released a heavy sigh and returned to his house.

Ben jerked awake in the middle of the night to a blood-curdling scream echoing within the heavy timber walls of the bedroom. The sky beyond the window was only faintly lighter than the darkened room, and the bedposts were edged by faint yellow light flickering on the walls from the parlor stove. Sonja was on her knees sobbing into her lap and pounding the cold floorboards with her fists.

"Isaac's death was my fault...for what I did in South Carolina...it was my fault," she cried.

Ben dropped next to her, trying to cradle her in his arms, but she pushed him away and grabbed her nightgown into a fist pressing it to her heart.

"What I did in South Carolina...I shot that boy in the face," she said. "God took Isaac to punish me for what I did."

"No, no. Isaac was already gone, Sonja... God didn't do that. Isaac did."

She slapped her fist against her chest.

"I killed that boy. I was in a rage when they hanged Simon just for teaching the black children. They hanged Simon, Ben, right before me. He was our friend for years. He once saved your life! The Klan wanted me to watch them hang an uppity black man!"

"It's done, Sonja. It's done. You've got to–"

She glared at Ben, her eyes wide in the meager light. She jabbed her finger in the air as if pointing at her nightmare. "That boy begged me not to, but he was with them. He wore a hood like them, and he helped them murder Simon."

"You had to stop them," Ben said, pulling her close. "The Klansmen were there to murder and terrorize that village. They had already killed poor old Celeste and would have killed more."

She drew away and held her hands out before her. "I pulled his hood off, and he was just a boy..."

Ben scoffed. "He was old enough to join in on that hanging. He deserved whatever–"

She thumped her fist against her heart. "I shot him through his face, Ben. I wanted him to see it coming. And you know it wasn't the first time I ever killed anyone. God punished me for my evil acts by taking Isaac, and I will join that wretched boy I murdered in hell."

TUESDAY, DECEMBER 28

The morning sky was steel gray tainted by a sickly yellow and crowded with ash-colored clouds tumbling from the south.

Sonja gazed at the sky. "I think even God is sad today."

"You will feel better with time."

"I will talk less of it with time, Ben. But I cannot imagine ever feeling better."

The air was wet and cold, but not as cold as usual for late December. Ben drove their buggy south on the packed earth towpath to Havre de Grace. The towpath was a narrow ribbon of ground between a sleeping muddy canal, drained for the winter, and the angry Susquehanna River charging southward to the bay. They would share the towpath with mules pulling canal barges in warm weather, but it was their open highway in winter. The towpath ran both south to Havre de Grace and north into Pennsylvania. Small blocks of ice from far upriver tumbled along the shore at the river's edge, pushed aside by the rushing current in the center.

"The river should be frozen by now," Ben said.

"The ice houses will be useless in the spring and summer if the river doesn't freeze for cutting."

"That reminds me of the first winter you were gone," Sonja said. "I was almost full term, and the river rushed over the ice then. It was frozen underneath the surface, and the river broke it into huge pieces."

"There will be no ice dam this year, dear. If so, the canal company would dynamite the ice before it got that bad. Then the water would flow over the ice and into the bay, but that is nothing to worry about this winter."

"The canal company assured us it was safe back then, but it wasn't, and the ice gorge swept away our house and our baby."

"And I was a crewman on an American ship in China, but they thought we were English, bringing in more Opium. We have visited this pain too many times, Sonja. The Chinese were trying to stop that trade when they took the ship and crew. Took us all prisoner. When they found out we were American, they didn't know what to do. They just kept us prisoners...all that time."

"I know, Ben, but..."

"I wasn't here then, and damn me for being a fool. I thought it was the only way for me to make some money for us. I never guessed I would be gone so long. But, I am here now, and with all that happened that year, the canal company will never let it happen again."

"I hope not, Ben. It took our Alisha..."

Ben smiled at her. "Who was found. Yes?"

"Yes, Benjamin, she was found, but we thought she was dead. I still have nightmares about the icy flood pulling her from my arms."

Ben peered at her from the corner of his eye.

"You agreed with me, Sonja?"

"Yes, I did."

"That always makes me uneasy, woman."

Sonja sneered and slipped her arm under his. "My feet are freezing, Ben. Let's stop at the Oyster Street Tavern for something warm to eat and an opportunity to thaw out my feet."

He glanced down. "Those are town shoes. You should have worn your boots. But better that we warm those feet now than you stick them against my back in the middle of the night."

Her eyes sparkled for only an instant, and then the light was gone again. Ben wrapped his arm around her, leaving it there until they crossed the swing bridge beside the lockhouse in Havre de Grace. The sky above town was almost blocked from the sun's faint glimmer by thick flocks of ducks in clouds of hundreds. The superintendent of the Susquehanna and Tidewater Canal, Dan Shure, stood on the front porch of the lockhouse watching the ducks come in. He waved as they passed but shook his head and frowned, pointing up.

"Blowing the wrong way, Ben," he said. "Should be coming from the north."

"Morning, Dan," Ben said. "Maybe it'll get colder later on. Plenty of ducks, though."

"Yeah. Good duck season," he said, "but if we don't have enough ice for the Menhaden run in the spring, those fish will rot before they get to market."

At the end of Oyster Street, two men were standing on the corner gazing up at the sky in a serious conversation as Ben and Sonja entered the tavern. Inside, the Pulaskis spotted long-time friend, Tobias Bond, sitting alone at a table reading a newspaper. His empty plate was set aside.

"May we join you?" Ben asked.

A smile beamed across Tobias's brown face, and he stood to offer Ben his hand. While they greeted each other, Sonja stepped forward to hug him. He smiled bashfully, glancing around the room at the other patrons. A man sitting alone at the short bar sneered and shook his head.

"I always remember the first time I met you, Tobias. You were four…"

Tobias rolled his eyes. "And my Uncle Simon brought me in to meet you. And my name then was Toby. And you wanted to adopt me, but Uncle Simon said…"

Sonja's voice went deep, mimicking her memory of Simon. "The boy needs mahogany, not oak."

As they sat down, Ben motioned for a waitress, and Tobias lowered his voice to Sonja.

"Miz Sonja, there are people who think poorly of white ladies who are too familiar with black men."

"But, you are…"

"I am a grown black man."

"I know, I know," she said. "I did not mean to embarrass you."

"It is not embarrassment–"

The waitress arrived at the table, an attractive young black woman who placed her eyes primarily on Tobias before addressing Ben. Sonja caught the meaningful exchange of glances between the woman and Tobias, settling into an intense maternal stare at his face waiting for more information, which Tobias struggled to ignore.

"What is Carl cooking today, young lady?" Ben asked.

"It is Franklin cooking today, sir," the young woman said. Her smile was warm, and her eyes flickered to Tobias as she spoke. "Mr. Franklin Curtis. He cooks every day. Old Carl sold the tavern after Nancy passed away last year, and my Daddy bought it."

"Rebecca is his daughter," Tobias said.

He glanced up at Rebecca with a quick smile, then fell into the locked gaze from Sonja, who pinioned him with a smirk.

"Does Mr. Curtis have fresh oysters?" Ben asked.

"Best of the bay," Tobias said, his eyes on Rebecca's face. "Provided daily by Tobias

Bond Enterprises."

Ben gave Tobias an impressed smile of his own. "Well done, Mr. Bond. Do you tong or dredge?"

"I have four tonger boats, six when they are not out hunting ducks. All are twenty-footers. This tavern is one of my best customers for both oysters and ducks."

"Explain tonging to me, Tobias," Sonja asked.

"Long poles with rakes at the ends. The poles are hinged together just above the rakes, and the handles are worked from the other end to open and close the rakes. It's like they are taking a bite from the oyster beds below. Then the rakes are pulled up, and the oyster dropped into the boat. Plenty of oysters are left for more bites later or in following days."

"And dredging?"

"A collection of rakes wider than a tavern table, dropped deep from a sailing boat and pulled by a chain, gouging the oyster beds below and scooping them into a chain net. Sometimes they come into the shallows and dredge the oyster beds where tong boats work. That destroys the oyster colonies."

His attention moved between Sonja and Ben. "None of my boats could pull a dredge–" He glanced around the dining room and softened his voice. "And I would find myself in serious trouble if I did, Ben. There is a lot of ill will around here over Virginia dredger boats raiding Maryland oyster beds."

Ben nodded, understanding, then glanced up at Rebecca. "I will have two dozen oysters, barely steamed." He glanced at Sonja and shrugged his shoulders. "Call it a late breakfast."

"I will have a dozen," Sonja said, "southern style. Cornmeal battered and fried."

"Mrs. Pulaski grew up in North Carolina," Tobias said.

Rebecca flashed another smile at Tobias, then skittered into the kitchen. Sonja raised her eyebrows and focused her eyes more intently on Tobias. He continued to ignore her as he spoke to Ben.

"With almost no ice in the bay, my boats are working from sunrise filling up with fresh oysters then come back to town around mid-day. The trains will buy all we offer and rush them north to big cities. If I could collect the oysters from my tonger boats when they fill, they could double our loads."

"Can you use the *Jester*?" Sonja asked. "My sloop could easily take ten to fifteen tons of oysters."

Tobias faced her at last. "I hadn't thought of that... I forgot you owned that boat." Then he sighed and surrendered to her smile and tilted head.

"What?" He asked.

Sonja's voice was almost a snicker, but a kindly one. "What, indeed, Mr. Bond? Owner of Tobias Bond Enterprises and his six twenty-foot oyster and duck boats. Tell me about you and Rebecca."

"Tell me about the *Jester*, and I will tell you about...us."

"Well," she said, "Jimmy Finley has been captain since the Navy returned the sloop to me at the end of the war."

A broad-shouldered black man, appearing carved from onyx stone, charged from the kitchen and marched to their table. He hesitated his gait on his right side, thumping the floor as he neared, signaling an artificial leg. He was nearly seven feet tall, had no neck to speak of, and upper arms the size of thighs. His apron strings had additional lengths tied to them to reach around him. As he arrived near their table, he pushed ham-fisted hands on his hips, focused his attention squarely on Ben, and addressed him in a deep and rasping voice.

"You the Pulaskis?" He asked.

Ben stood to face him, eye level with the black man's chin.

"I am Ben Pulaski, and this lady is my wife, Sonja. Are we the Pulaskis you ask about?"

The black man stuck out his hand. "I am Franklin Curtis. Owner of this tavern."

Ben accepted it. His own meaty hand appeared almost petite in the other man's grip.

"It appears," Franklin said, "that Mr. Bond there has intentions with my daughter. Since the only living people, he ever mentions that are anywhere near family are the Pulaskis, I said to myself, 'I will meet these people'."

Sonja's gaze lingered on Tobias's face, her eyes watered, and she pinched his arm. "You do think of us as family."

Franklin leaned over the table and offered his hand to Sonja, taking hers with just two fingers and his thumb. as if handling robin eggs. "Ma'am."

"Mr. Curtis," she said. "I have long thought of Toby...Tobias as family. His Uncle Simon was considered a brother by my husband and a special friend to me. He is greatly missed."

Tobias looked away.

"Yes, Ma'am," Franklin said. "Tobias told us much of his Uncle Simon. They were soldiers together. That was a large part of why I didn't break his arm the first time he tried to hold hands with my daughter."

Sonja smiled at him. "And what does her mother think of him?"

Franklin's eyes drifted toward the floor for an instant, then returned steadfastly to Sonja's. "Her mother is passed. Seven years now. I was in Petersburg. Not in Tobias and Simon's unit but not far away from them. I was among the Colored troops at Appomattox, too, but I wish I had met Simon."

"Hey, darkie," the man at the bar called out. "Get me a drink."

Franklin stepped toward the man. "Sir, I think you may have already had too many. Perhaps, you should go home."

"You just do what I tell you, boy," the man said.

Franklin moved closer to the man, but Ben

stepped between them, facing the drunk.

"Sir," Ben said, "these people are friends of ours, and he is the owner. He is also a veteran, as was my son, and is due some respect."

"I was a veteran, too, mister," the man said. His mouth was narrow with a thin mustache above it, and his eyes were pale brown. "I served under Jubal Early fighting for the South." The man pointed at Franklin. "I don't take orders from blacks or turncoat Maryland Yankees that think they're good as us white people." He raised a scarred hand with the small finger missing, pointed at Ben's face and opened his mouth to make another comment.

Franklin reached toward the man. Ben's left fist shot out from his side, driving into the man's chin, knocking him off his stool and onto the floor. The man lay unconscious but breathing. Ben turned to face the other patrons, recognizing most as friends and receiving nods of approval from them. One man stood from his table, his eyes locked with Ben's, a man who was never a friend to any Pulaski, Bartholomew Lister. He gave Ben a sneering frown and left the tavern.

Ben and Franklin picked up the man and placed him in a corner chair, laying his head on top of his arms resting on the table.

"Guess I need to get to those oysters," Franklin said.

Sonja met Ben with a cold stare when he returned to the table. "Was that necessary?"

"What will the law do if that drunk makes charges?" Ben asked, then asked another question before Sonja could answer. "What would the law do if Franklin was charged with hitting a white man?"

"He would not have hit the man, Ben," Tobias said.

"He sure looked ready to, to me."

"But he would have held himself back, Ben. He is a preacher now. He has a little church on Watson's Island, where he preaches peace and forgiveness."

Ben's face turned red before the icy glare Sonja gave him.

Tobias stood, patting Ben's shoulder. "Well...'Uncle Ben'...," he said, allowing a chuckle to carry the words. "You just made a good impression on my future in-laws. But I have work to do–"

"Oh no, you don't, Tobias Bond," Sonja said, tugging on his sleeve. "You sit back down and tell me about you and Rebecca."

Tobias sighed and took his seat, then held up a finger. "First, you tell me about the *Jester*. I thought you sailed it, but Ben owned it."

Ben smiled and focused his attention on the newspaper Tobias had been reading.

"The sloop is mine," Sonja said. "Ben and I came to the agreement that I would own and run my own shipping and mercantile company, *Jester* Enterprises. He has Pulaski Shipping."

"And she has a partner in that," Ben said without looking up, his tone flat. "Robert Turner."

Sonja flashed her eyes at Ben and sighed, her neck flaring the color of plum.

"Robert is not a partner. He is an associate. Never anything else. His business acquires mercantile goods for me, and occasionally the *Jester* carries cargo ordered through his company..." She gazed at Ben. "For which I charge a shipping fee."

Tobias leaned back, showing a half-smile, glancing between Ben and Sonja in silence.

Ben cleared his throat and patted Sonja's hand as he smiled at Tobias. "It really isn't that bad," he said, showing a smirk. "I shouldn't aggravate Sonja about Robert as I do..."

Sonja pulled her hand away from Ben's. "No, you should not."

Ben returned his attention to the newspaper. "The *Aegis* says Georgia has approved the fifteenth amendment. That will ratify negro suffrage into law. Negros have the right to vote."

Sonja nodded toward the unconscious man sitting in the far corner. "Do you think that will matter to people like him?"

"Ah, looking at him reminds me," Ben said. "The market in guano is rising. I want to discuss that with Delbert."

Tobias displayed a wry smile and shook his head. "I must leave you two. I have work to attend."

Sonja held up her hand. "No. You need to tell me about you and Rebecca."

Tobias waved his hand over his shoulder but did not look back as he left the tavern.

"But..." Sonja muttered at Tobias's back, then frowned at Ben.

"You and your guano. Only a man who owns canal barges and a schooner can get excited about hauling tons of fertilizer."

"Seagull and bat droppings," he said, pointing a fingertip to the side of his nose. "That's excellent fertilizer. Since we are not selling much mercantile out of our northbound barges, we can use some of them to carry guano. The farmers love to get it."

"You want to fill our barges with fertilizer?"

"Some," he said. "Most are going up empty as it is. Edward can bring several barges worth of guano in a single *Osprey* cargo, and we can fill the barges directly from our ship. We can spare a couple barges from that trade to carry mercantile."

"Yes. And it stinks. And so, will your boats that

carry it. Whatever merchandise my boat brings for the canal, don't put it in the barges that carry guano."

"Mmm," Ben peered at the man at the table who was raising his head and wiping blood from his nose, then returned his attention to Sonja's cold glare.

After the meal, Ben and Sonja walked up Washington Street to meet with George Milton, Esq., the man who had served as their lawyer for twenty years. On their way, they passed a man and woman in quiet conversations, glancing up at the sky. Above the flights of ducks, the gray clouds continued their march north.

"The color just ain't right," the man said to his companion, "and it's going the wrong way."

Stepping beyond the couple, Ben spoke in a muted voice to Sonja, "People worry too much about the weather."

Ben and Sonja mounted the outside steps to George's office above the old wooden National Bank building sitting at the end of Washington Street. The steps were well worn in the center, and the siding was beginning to show its age. As they settled into padded leather chairs before George's desk, the lawyer withdrew several sheets of paper from a drawer. He had lost his crown hair over the years but retained a thick set of mutton chop side whiskers that flared out from plump cheeks like bird wings. The buttons on his stylish vest under his open day coat struggled against the pull to free his belly. His smile was still boyish, and his brown eyes large and friendly. He gave the false impression of someone easily manipulated, but he had the legal cunning of a hungry wolf that Ben admired.

"There is no longer any law that prevents Tobias from owning his lot or that barn, Ben. The fifteenth amendment has an impact on state laws. Still, there is a lot of resistance at the county level. Nothing official, mind you, but some are happy to delay allowing him official owner recognition."

"They can go to hell," Ben said.

"Perhaps so, Ben, but things will work smoother for me to appease the few who resist."

"Yes, Ben," Sonja said, taking his hand gently and drawing his attention to her, quenching his spark of fire with long practice.

Ben sighed. "Of course."

George smiled. "Give it time, Ben. Tobias will be the owner. There is no question of that. He has many friends in Havre de Grace, many white friends. Some of whom have significant influence and go to him for their duck hunting. Most of those friends never owned slaves. Even though there are still some in positions of power who did and still resent losing them, give it time."

"Seems to me, George," Ben said, "We've already 'given it' since 1776. We declared 'all men equal' then."

"It should have said 'all men and women are equal'," Sonja said.

George glanced at Sonja and blew out his breath, then returned his attention to Ben. "In the meantime, you must remain the official owner and sign these papers, for which there are fees and taxes."

Ben frowned. "How much? I mean, of course, I will gladly pay them, but you know I have always been keen with numbers."

George chuckled, handing the pen to Ben. "Tobias has already provided the money. You just need to sign the papers."

As Ben signed the papers, Sonja spoke with George.

"Are tax records up to date for the *Jester*, George?"

"Yes, ma'am. Jimmy Finley is always timely with fees for the *Jester*. He seems to be an efficient captain."

"Good. I intend to have him take the *Jester* to support Tobias's oystering."

"That's an excellent idea. Oyster demand is tremendous in large cities, and the train can take them straight away. I see he is tying up at the end of St. Clair Street, now that the railroad steamer no longer uses it."

Coming back from George's office, Ben and Sonja noticed Constable John Hopkins coming their way. He recognized them and waved them toward him.

Sonja smiled at John, muttering under her breath to Ben, "Now what?"

"Nothing to worry about," Ben said, then smiled at Hopkins as he approached.

The deputy touched the brim of his hat to Sonja but spoke to Ben. "I was on my way to Judge Atkin's office about you. It appears that Harris Bolton has a broken nose and lost two teeth."

"Who is Harris Bolton?" Ben asked.

"The man you struck at the tavern earlier today. Lost a finger in the war. He's pressing charges against you for assault as witnessed by Bartholomew Lister, one of our town's undertakers."

Sonja glared at Ben and opened her mouth to speak. Ben raised his palm between them.

"Don't."

Hopkins continued. "Apparently, Lister has acquired a record book of a former town deputy who also served as a provost marshal during the war. Lister says it provides several reports of your violent behavior over the years."

Ben frowned. "That was Brandon Alexander. He was–"

"A known liar and opium addict. Yeah, I know. But the charges by Bolton appear valid, and the deputy's notes support it. This will have to go before Judge Jessup."

"Are you going to put Ben in jail?" Sonja asked.

Hopkins kept his attention on Ben's face. "You gonna run off?"

"No."

"Didn't expect you would, Ben. I'll let you know the court date when Jessup informs me. In the meantime, stay away from both Bolton and Lister. Bolton has been before Jessup before, and the judge doesn't like him. So, this will probably blow over unless you stir it up. You hear me?"

Ben nodded in agreement. "Are we finished?"

Hopkins smiled and nodded to Sonja. "Have a good day, ma'am."

Sonja tugged on Ben's arm. "I want to talk to Jimmy Finley. Let's go to the St. Clair Street wharf if you can keep from punching someone before we get there."

At the dock, Sonja and Ben found Jimmy in

conversation with Robert Turner, standing before the *Jester*, which appeared to be in pristine condition. Ben glanced at Robert, then put his attention to the sloop.

"The old *Jester* still looks good, Sonja."

Hearing Ben's voice, Jimmy looked up from his conversation and released a beaming smile to Sonja. Stepping toward her, the sling holding his right arm came fully into view.

"Mrs. Pulaski. It's so good to see you again." Then he nodded to Ben. "Mr. Pulaski." His eyes returned to Sonja. "I was so sorry to hear about Isaac...and Simon."

"As are we both," Robert said, taking a half step back when he received Ben's glare, then peered at Sonja. "Delbert is better than either the *Whig* or the *Aegis* in getting news around town.

"Jimmy," Sonja said, "What has happened to your arm?"

"I'm afraid he strained it moving one of my stoves," Robert said.

"Let him tell it," Ben said to Robert.

Jimmy glanced between Ben and Robert then faced Sonja. "It isn't bad. Mrs. Pulaski. We were unloading a new stove over in Charlestown, and it slipped. When I caught it, it wrenched my shoulder. Old Doc Harper says it'll be all right in a few weeks."

"I didn't know he still practiced," Ben said.

Jimmy smiled. His smiles were infectious, and people around him were rarely dour.

"He was fishing over on the North East River and was on the dock there visiting some friends."

"Jimmy," Sonja interrupted, "I wanted to talk to you about hauling oysters from tonging boats that belong to Tobias Bond,"

Jimmy grinned. "I know Tobias. Good man. Glad to help."

"But," Sonja said, " it doesn't look like you'll be able to do that. Do you have a crewman?"

"Had two, but one was hired on to a schooner hauling cargo down to Norfolk and Hampton Roads for a while. Just me and Willard for a while. Where would the *Jester* need to go?"

"I think Tobias mentioned tonging near the mouth of the Gunpowder and Bush Rivers," Sonja said.

"It takes a while to get there against that contrary wind, but we would get back here fast, that is, if I had a full crew."

"I think I can help," Ben said. "My bargeman Garrett would probably do it. It would get him out of that little cabin for a while. I'll talk to him when we get back to Lapidum."

"Great," Jimmy said. "I know Garrett, too. Me and him'll get along fine."

Sonja gave Ben's arm a quick touch. "Thank you, Ben." Then to Jimmy, "I'll let Tobias know, and he can discuss his plans with you."

"Sure thing, Mrs. Pulaski. I'll be right here."

She smiled at Jimmy and Robert as she turned away. Ben turned without acknowledging Robert. Sonja placed her hand on Ben's arm.

"Ben, why don't you take the buggy home to speak with Garrett. I want to talk to Tobias so he can meet with Jimmy. Then I would like to do some shopping at McCombs' store. I read in the Havre Republican that the store has a new shipment of ladies' dresses. It will be boring for you."

Ben grumbled. "Perhaps Robert can help you

pick out a dress."

"Benjamin, that is enough. You tell me, and you told Tobias, you only bring that up to tease me. What you just said is mean."

"I don't like him," Ben said.

"Damn it, Benjamin Pulaski, there has never been anything between Robert Turner and me, except business."

"And that kiss at Mamie Stewart's boarding house."

Sonja halted and faced him with fire in her eyes, and her face flushed red.

"Good Lord, Ben. That was sixteen years ago. And I slapped him onto a table for it. And you slipped away from a family Christmas dinner to settle it with him."

"All right. All right, Sonja."

"That's all you have to say to me?"

'Would you like me to come back for you later?"

"You are infuriating. No, do not come back for me. It's only five miles. A brisk walk."

"But you might have some bundles to carry."

"If I do, then Mr. McCombs will be happy to send one of his clerks to bring me home. Ben...I need some 'woman' time."

Robert and Jimmy watched Ben and Sonja in the distance, not hearing the words but the tones of voice and seeing them walk away from each other in different directions.

Robert spoke softly to Jimmy. "Ben can be a very cold man."

Jimmy frowned. "They've always been like an aunt and uncle to me. Why do you say such a thing,

Mr. Turner?"

"One Christmas Eve, Benjamin Pulaski pointed a pistol in my face and warned me to stay away from his wife."

Jimmy blinked several times. "Oh, why did he do that?"

Robert turned away without answering. Jimmy simply shrugged his shoulders.

Alone, Sonja strolled along the streets of Havre de Grace and came to a stop before the Methodist church. The door was open, so she entered. The air was chilled inside, and no heat arose from the little iron stove she passed near the doors. At the front pulpit, below a large white wooden cross, a woman arranged flowers on side tables. The woman spoke over her shoulder as she worked.

"The funeral isn't for another hour. I haven't lit the stove yet. No sense wasting coal. The mourners are still with the family at their home."

"I'm not here for a funeral," Sonja said.

The woman spun around to face Sonja. The displeasure emanated from her oddly narrow face that always seemed to be in a perpetual frown, more so at that moment.

"Mrs. Pulaski," the woman said. It was neither recognition nor greeting, more of an accusation.

Sonja halted. "Nadja," she said.

"Are you a friend of the family?" Nadja Lister asked.

"No."

"Well, I know you are certainly no member of this church or of any that I know of."

Sonja stood in silence.

"What do you want in here?" Nadja asked.

The woman's beady dark eyes seemed closer together than usual, near to merging in her sneer.

"A minister, perhaps," Sonja said.

"He is with the family," she said and returned to her flowers.

Sonja remained where she stood, gritting her teeth several seconds, then left the church.

Moments later, Sonja found herself before the Catholic Church on Warren Street. She stood near the doors a long moment, hesitating, biting her lip, rubbing her fingers against her thumbs.

"The doors are unlocked, madam," the priest said as he passed and mounted the steps before her.

He was elderly, bald with a broad red face and sparkling pale blue eyes. His smile was warm, and his belly round inside his black robe. He opened the door then turned to welcome her inside.

"Just coming back from a walk. Please, come inside, madam."

Sonja fidgeted with her hands. "How..." she started, but her mouth was dry and her words muffled.

He tilted his head and peered into her eyes. "How, what, my child?"

"How...how does one...confess...in there?"

His eyes softened. "Are you troubled, child?"

"Yes...I am...by many things."

"When was your last confession?" he asked.

"I am not Catholic," she said. "I was baptized a Lutheran."

His smile went out to her. "Our God loves Lutherans as well, child. I cannot hear your confession because I could not give you absolution, but I am here to talk with you if you like."

She searched in his eyes, then tears slipped

from hers, and she turned to walk away.

"I am here if you need me," the priest said to her back.

Sonja picked up her pace, rounded the corner onto Union Street near the Harford Hotel, and made her way past the public school and Town Hall down to Tobias's property. By the time she walked the city blocks getting there, she had regained her composure.

In Lapidum, Ben was in excited conversation with Delbert about selling guano when Deputy Hopkins entered Delbert's Mercantile Store. The exchange halted as Ben turned to face Hopkins, whose gaze was focused on Ben.

"You look like you've come to see me, John."

"I thought I'd ride down here to tell you."

"And..."

"Old Judge Jessup wants you in court before him tomorrow. He looked at the complaint and says to bring George Milton with you. Harris Bolton is hell-bent on charging you with battery. The Judge already saw Deputy Alexander's old notes Bart Lister found."

"That shouldn't count against me, John. Alexander was provost marshal then and swilling laudanum."

"That isn't the time covered in the notes. This was when he was still a deputy."

"What do those pages say?"

"Damn, Ben. Do you have to be reminded of a time you cowhided a Harford County deputy?"

Ben frowned. "Oh...yeah...that. It was only a frail buggy whip, and it happened over in Cecil County. Alexander was rude to my wife."

Hopkins sighed and wagged his finger at Ben. "Ben, most of that journal was about you. You had that man hating you, and he wrote everything down."

"But they hanged Alexander. He was a criminal himself."

"Not then, he wasn't, Ben. Not when you horsewhipped him. The Army hanged him for crimes committed as a provost marshall during the war. Before that, he was a reputable county sheriff's deputy. This looks really bad for you. You best get together with Milton so he can read what Alexander wrote. You could wind up in state prison for all this."

Hopkins handed Ben the subpoena to appear in court and left the store.

Ben glared at the document and pointed it at Delbert. "So help me, God, Delbert. If I could dig up Brandon Alexander right now, I'd cowhide him again. Even from the damned grave, that man causes me trouble."

Delbert sat on his stool in silence behind the counter, examining his fingernails.

"What?" Ben asked.

"I said nothing, Benjamin."

"Well, sometimes a man can only take so much before he has to do something to correct things."

Delbert kept his eyes on his fingers. "And how much correction did you achieve with your cowhiding?"

"I had to put that man in his place, Delbert."

"What lies in our power to do, it also lies in our power not to do."

"One of your Hebrew prophets?"

"No, Ben. A Greek philosopher. Aristotle. But if you wish something from the Ketuvim, there is this: 'Like a city whose walls are broken through is a person who lacks self-control.'"

Ben turned to snatch open the door, then spoke over his shoulder as he left.

"I have plenty of self-control," he said as he slammed the door.

Mary came through the back door, bringing Delbert his lunch. "What was that?"

"Just Benjamin," he said.

"Ah," was her only comment.

When Ben returned to his house, he found Mickey O'Grady sitting on the front porch with a wide grin on his face.

"Where the hell have you been, Benjamin," Mickey said. "No one to greet me or offer me coffee, and me stranded on this porch by myself."

"Doctor Micheal Patrick O'Grady, what a pleasure to see an old friend on this troublesome day."

Mickey stood. "How can you call this a troublesome day. The sun hides behind gray clouds, the wind is wet and chilled, and the snow in the yard is filthy. It all looks like a lovely Irish spring day to me."

"Liar," Ben said. He bounded up the steps and onto the porch to greet his friend in a bear hug, glancing through the window to inside the house. "Did Alisha and Cathy come with you? What brings you here?"

"No. No. And following a bad dream."

"Well, if it's bad dreams you're after, we have plenty to spare. Poor Sonja has been plagued by them."

Mickey's cheerful smile faded, pushed away by a frown. "You know I consider you folks the only family I have..."

"Of course, Mickey. We've always thought of you as family. What is it?"

"I've been having worries, Ben."

"About who and what, Mickey?"

"It's more a feeling, but it nags at me of late. Like two feeling I've had before that came to sad endings."

Ben pulled him by his sleeve. "Come in, and I'll start us a fire and get down some whiskey. What two feelings did you have that came to poor endings?"

Ben stepped ahead of him, going to the kitchen to fetch a bottle and glasses.

Mickey took a seat near the front stove and spoke to the ceiling so Ben would hear him. "I had more than two in my life, and I've grown to pay them serious attention."

Ben returned to the parlor, setting the glassware on the table near Mickey, then flipped open the iron stove and snatched a poker.

"Probably have a few embers among the coals," Ben said, jabbing the poker into the cinders.

He grabbed a few pieces from the coal bucket to toss them in and followed that with some split wood. Then he plopped into the chair on the other side of the end table from Mickey and poured them each a drink.

"So. Tell me about your two feelings."

Mickey turned in his chair to face Ben, all expression faded away. "Both were about Isaac. On the day before I had to take off his arm, and the second was at the beginning of the week when I heard he had taken his life."

Ben held the glass untouched before his lips,

then set it down, making eye contact with Mickey.

"What do your feelings tell you now?"

"I have an image in my mind that won't leave me."

"What image, Mickey. Who?"

Mickey took a sip from his glass and sighed. "It is all blackness and deathly cold, Ben."

Ben glared at him. "Who?"

Mickey peered into Ben's eyes.

"Who, Mickey?"

"...Sonja."

Ben picked up his glass and drained it.

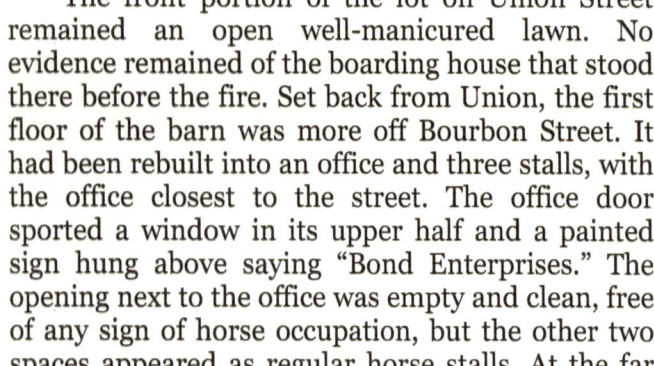

The front portion of the lot on Union Street remained an open well-manicured lawn. No evidence remained of the boarding house that stood there before the fire. Set back from Union, the first floor of the barn was more off Bourbon Street. It had been rebuilt into an office and three stalls, with the office closest to the street. The office door sported a window in its upper half and a painted sign hung above saying "Bond Enterprises." The opening next to the office was empty and clean, free of any sign of horse occupation, but the other two spaces appeared as regular horse stalls. At the far corner of the barn, the outside stairs went up to the second story. A sign jutting from above the stairs read "Rooms for Rent."

Sonja stood before the office door and knocked.

Tobias was smiling when he answered the door.

"Mrs. Pulaski, you sure are determined to hear

about me and Rebecca."

They both laughed as he motioned for her to step inside, although he left the door open.

"You can sit in this chair, Mrs. Pulaski. It's close to the stove."

"You're leaving the door open?"

"It's better for both of us. My neighbors on this block, I own half of it, keep to themselves mostly but are always friendly to me and my borders. But the folks across Union Street don't care for all the colored folk coming in and out of here. They don't hesitate to send for Deputy Hopkins if they think something wrong is happening. Although it never is."

"I'm sure it isn't. So, what are your plans with Miss Curtis?"

Tobias chuckled. "After I finish getting our house built, I intend to marry her."

"Oh? I mean, I am not surprised you intend to marry that pretty woman, but I had no idea you were building a house. Where?".

"Not far from the AME church."

"Your...Enterprise must be doing well."

"It is, but my profit margin is quite thin. Too thin to cover the cost of the lot and house."

"So how–that is none of my business."

He smiled. "That's true, but since Rebecca and Mr. Curtis see you as my aunt, I am happy to share privileged information with you. I have agreed to sell this lot when the house and new business location are completed. In return, the future buyer is helping me secure the necessary money."

"And can you tell me who this benefactor is?"

"Someone who has long wanted this lot. Mr. A.P. McCombs. He is willing to wait a few years, as long as it remains promised to him. Mr. Milton is taking care of the documents. I don't think Mrs. Stewart was aware of how valuable this property was when she gave it to me."

Sonja patted his hand. "Oh, I am sure Mamie knew exactly what it was worth and what it would become worth. I am so happy for you."

He released a long sigh. "So, let me show you around and tell you what your...nephew has accomplished."

Outside, he pointed to areas of the old barn, which had been refurbished considerably.

"The barn is thirty feet front to back and forty-five feet wide. I have my office there, where we were, but it is only ten by eight, and my apartment is behind it, through the little door behind my desk, and that gives me ten by twenty-two feet for my quarters. Next is the compartment for the cabriolet and my driver has a ten-by-ten apartment in the rear as part of his salary. We split the carry fees evenly, and he keeps all tips. The next stall is for the cabriolet horse, and beyond that is a double stall rented for horses of my tenants."

"How many tenants do you have?" She asked.

"I put a five-foot-wide hallway down the center upstairs and created eight apartments..."

"Eight?"

"Yes. Two are used by duck guides, as part of their salary, and the rest are rented out, either seasonal or for weekend duck hunters."

"I am impressed, Mr. Bond. Simon would be so proud of you."

He glanced away for a brief moment, then turned to face her. "I wish I could have shown this to him."

In the long silence of the moment, Sonja took in a deep breath and forced a smile.

"I remember when Mamie had this barn built," she said. "I rarely came out this way after that, but I thought it was farther back from Bourbon Street. Your office is barely off it."

"That is actually convenient for customers and inquiries. Also, the space on the other side gives me room for a garden."

Sonja paled. "Oh...I thought all of the old garden was under the building now."

"Mrs. Stewart thought so as well when I drove her cabriolet. But plants began to come up that had been placed there before. The ground is very fertile there."

Sonja followed him as he stepped beyond the corner stairs and motioned to the garden space.

"We have a good garden here, and it is still far enough away from the outhouse that...well, it is far enough away."

Sonja's attention was fixed on the healthy plants.

"Potatoes and radishes still living, Mrs. Pulaski. The mild winter lets them live."

A shudder swept over Sonja. She glanced back at the position of the water pump and then back at the remaining garden, fixing her memory of the garden and the previous barn.

Her voice was little more than a mutter. "She is uncovered."

"Excuse me, ma'am. I did not hear what you said...are you unwell, ma'am? You look sickly of a sudden."

Sonja's eyes were fixed on a spot in the garden. Her breath was shallow, and her lip trembled.

"Ma'am, would you care to go back to the office so you can sit down?"

Sonja spoke through gritted teeth. "Yes," she said, still glaring at the spot in the garden.

Back inside the office, Sonja calmed herself with several deep breaths, then forced a smile.

"So, I have some good news for you. Jimmy Finely will gladly support your oystering boats. He has a strained shoulder in a sling, but if you can provide him a crewman to assist Garrett sailing my sloop, they will be devoted to your oystering for the season. I will provide Jimmy's salary for the first few weeks until you two work out an arrangement. After that, I leave it to you and Jimmy to work out sharing of the profits."

"That's very generous, Mrs. Pulaski."

She hesitated. "Tobias..."

"Yes, ma'am?"

"I have questions about Mr. Curtis. His church. What denomination is he?"

"None, I don't think. Christian?"

"How...does he...minister to his...flock?"

"Ma'am, I don't know if I could answer such a question fairly. I think you need to ask him."

She reached forward and placed her hand on his arm. "Yes, of course. Tobias, you have done so well here. I am so proud of you and happy for Miss Curtis."

Sonja spoke briefly, then left the office, crossing the front lawn onto Union Street, glancing back toward the garden, remembering that terrible night when fatal blood was spilled, and what was buried there.

Minutes later, Sonja stepped inside the Oyster

Street Tavern and took a seat at a small table in the corner. Rebecca came to her smiling.

"Want some more fried oysters, Mrs. Pulaski?"

"Rebecca...I would like to speak with your father...about his church."

Rebecca glanced back at the kitchen then gave Sonja a worried expression.

"I...I'm not sure he would want to talk about that here."

"Oh, I didn't think that would be...oh, I, I shouldn't have come for that..."

Rebecca had already left the table for the kitchen. Sonja studied her hands, unsure what to do at the moment. Franklin charged from the kitchen, and his tall form loomed over her.

Sonja peered up at him and stuttered. "I...I..."

Rebecca joined them and looped her arm under her father's.

"Papa," she said with a chuckle. "You always come out like a charging bull."

"I was just eager to speak with Mrs. Pulaski about my church, daughter."

Rebecca smiled at Sonja, then poked Franklin's arm with her fingertip, speaking to him in a whisper so other customers would not hear.

"Your eagerness is what other soldiers refer to as a bayonet charge."

He chuckled and gave her a sheepish grin.

"Now, sit Papa, I will go watch over the stove. You can trust me with the cooking for a few seconds."

Franklin did not sit nor look into Sonja's face as he spoke in little more than a whisper.

"You are troubled?"

"Does it show, Mr. Curtis?"

"I have a church," he said. "A chapel, really, allowed me through the kindness of a businessman, Mr. O'Brien, who owns property on Watson's Island. He feels its presence will have a good effect on the fishermen who house there full-time during the menhaden season. He is concerned that since the island sits in the middle of the river, it is without the proper 'civilizing influence' as he calls it."

Sonja did not speak.

Franklin cleared his throat. "Perhaps you could come there with your husband on Sunday. You could come after the service if that suits you, ma'am."

She frowned. "Not with my husband."

"Then Rebecca? She could meet you near the canal basin. She rows a couple worshippers from the Harford County side of the river. Tobias brings a few from the Cecil County side."

"Yes, thank you, Mr. Curtis. I could do that."

"I hope I can help, Mrs. Pulaski."

"I don't know, Mr. Curtis, but I fear my demons are getting stronger. Today is only Monday. Could we not meet before Sunday?"

"Well, I meet with a small group of veterans Wednesday evenings. I close the tavern at six and meet them at seven."

"Does Rebecca go with you then?"

He peered into Sonja's face. Her eyes were reddened.

"Yes, she does. She holds the lantern while I row."

Sonja met his eyes. "May I join you and Rebecca on Wednesday?"

The afternoon sky looked much like the one seen that morning as Sonja wandered along the towpath toward Lapidum. There were no shadows among the bushes or trees created by the dismal sky, just a morbid vacancy of light that matched her emptiness. She halted at open views of the river, gazing at the undulations where the water dove over the boulders into the frothing eddies behind them. The passing trance gave her respite, and she lingered in the thoughtless moments it gave her.

Garrett's greeting startled her. "Afternoon, Mrs. Pulaski."

She peered at him a long moment, then shook her head to clear her thoughts.

He stood on the deck of the barge he called home for the winter.

"G-good afternoon, Mr. Simpson."

She glanced beyond the barge, up the gentle slope from the canal to her front porch framed by the towering oaks.

"I am home already," she said to herself.

A familiar figure stood waving at her. Her throat tightened, and pain stressed her voice as she said his name.

"Mickey," she said in a whisper that only she could hear. "We need to talk, old friend. I cannot bear it any longer."

Supper was little more than cold salted meat and stale bread from the day before, washed down by apple juice not far from fermenting. It was poor fare, far less than usually graced the dining room table at the Pulaski House. They had been away for months, and the home larder not yet replenished. Sonja muttered her apologies to Mickey for the poor fare. The mild burn from the early applejack relieved the tension in Sonja's throat.

Ben was not always sensitive to Sonja's moods but knew when she needed time with old friends that did not include him and found evening work to do in the barn. Mickey and Sonja wrapped themselves in winter coats and settled onto the old front porch chairs Ben still found useful. The house had grown over the years since the two-bedroom cabin it was when Ben first rented it. Their shipping business allowed them to purchase and later renovate the house, keeping up with changing times. But the worn ladder-back chairs still sat on the front porch overlooking the front slope and the river beyond. Mickey sat downwind so he could enjoy his cigar despite Sonja's odd aversion to soothing tobacco smoke. The sky above the river was filled with cloudy turmoil of a darker gray as the only admission of a setting sun trapped somewhere behind them.

"I have been worried about you," Mickey said.

She reached over to pat his arm.

"You always know when I need you. When I was in my worst pain over losing Alisha..."

Mickey lit his cigar, blowing the smoke out into the yard.

"We were both in pain in those days, Sonja. You had lost a daughter, and I had lost my wife and child—all of them taken by the river out there. At least later, you discovered your daughter alive. Kept by that woman on Shad Island."

The heron returned to survey the canal in front of the property and flew away complaining.

Her voice trembled. "The pain was unbearable..."

"And if you had allowed the river to consume you, Sonja, Alisha would have found herself an orphan when she discovered who she was."

"My loss was assumed, but yours was tragically real. How could you..."

"Save the life of a distraught woman who flung herself into that river? How could I not?"

Sonja examined her hands, glancing in the direction where the heron had gone.

She faced him. "How could you even care for anything after losing your own wife and child to that same river? The one you called 'the Bitch.'"

Mickey sighed. "Pulling you from the river pulled us both back into life."

"You cursed yourself at that moment, Mickey. You became a piece of my soul and share too much of its burden."

"Months later, I met Benjamin. Only then did I learn who you were...Did you ever tell him?"

She peered up at the darkening sky. "No."

"Even after I pulled myself from drunkenness to work on his barges?"

"Never. That is my act to explain to God. That and others. You were with me in South Carolina. You know that sin, but there is another you don't."

"That night in South Carolina was filled with violence, Sonja. If you still have other secrets for me to carry, consider them carefully before you let them out."

They sat quietly listening to the ringing of hammer on anvil echoing from the barn. The wind stirred the bare oak limbs above them, whispering among the branches, and the unseen heron in the sky repeated its complaint. "What in the world is that man doing?" Sonja asked.

Mickey chuckled. "Bending iron nails."

She peered at Mickey in the lamplight shining from the parlor window.

"Why would he do that?"

"He has done that for years, Sonja. Are you telling me you really don't know?"

He turned his face toward hers. Tears filled her eyes and cheeks, and her voice was soft as a child's and pleading.

"I don't want to go to Hell, Mickey. I want to see Isaac when I die."

"Sonja..."

"I have done such awful, grievous...murderous things. How can I ever atone for that?"

"No..."

"You were there. You were with me in South Carolina, Mickey. You watched me shoot that boy in the face. God took Isaac from me for that."

Mickey spat out his words. "That 'boy' was a

young man terrorizing freed slaves, helping to hang Simon, our friend, while the boy's father beat to death an old woman who talked back to him. And you were not the only person with a rifle in your hands that night."

"We killed them all, Mickey. Even the ones who surrendered. We buried their bodies in the marsh."

"We did what had to be done."

She released a ragged breath, watched an eagle grab something small from the river. "Did we?"

"They had to disappear, Sonja. It was the only way to keep it from getting worse."

The silence between them became heavy, punctuated by the ringing from the barn and a dog barking somewhere in the village. Sonja drew her coat tighter around her neck against the fingers of the wind tugging her collar to get inside.

"Why does he bend nails?" she asked.

Mickey chuckled. "So, he can straighten them."

She gazed open-mouthed at Mickey a moment. "Surely not."

Mickey smiled as if speaking with a child. "Our beloved Benjamin has a contentious relationship with this world, Sonja. And when it becomes horrific, when the devil himself rages among us, there is no one better to stand by you, to stand with you, to stand between you and the devil."

"Maybe. And in the peace, Mickey?"

"He bends nails."

She sighed. "I have too many crooked nails, Mickey, and he cannot straighten them for me."

"I know," he said. "Something dark is coming."

He paused to peer at her in the lamplight, heavy silence coming over him for a long moment.

"What is coming, Mickey?"

"I don't know, Sonja, but it hovers over you like a black specter, and my Irish gift of foreboding gives me nothing to fight it."

He took her hand, and together they listened to the rhythmic ringing of hammer on anvil, sounding a steady dirge.

Tobias readied for the night as darkness finally settled over Havre de Grace. The cabriolet was backed into its compartment, the horse was in her stall, brushed and fed. The driver had gone down the lane to visit the cook who hid his evening meal in her room. Samuel rarely spent the night in the small apartment Tobias provided for him. And the owners of the mansion who employed the cook were unaware of the missing food or their cook's bed warmer.

Tobias locked the office door and slipped back into his own apartment, carrying a small shovel of bright red coals for his little stove. After putting a piece of split wood on the emerging flames and lighting the wall lamp, he settled into the padded rocker beside the stove with a new weekly in his hand. On Monday nights, Rebecca visited with her aging Aunt Cleo, reading to her from books and magazines, so Tobias did not intrude. One of the passengers in the cabriolet that day had left behind the December twenty-fifth edition of Harper's Weekly, and since Samuel did not read, he gave it to his employer.

Tobias only scanned the front-page drawing under the headline "Home for the Holidays." He glanced at the article about President Grant's opinions on Cuba when his thoughts drifted to the little polished walnut box set against the wall. He reached down and brought the box onto his lap where he could view inside it from the lamplight above. The box was a fine piece of work, edged and latched with brass, once holding jewelry, but discovered empty in the basement of the burned boarding house. Inside were a wide curved bone or maybe part of an old bowl, most of a human jawbone, the head of a human thigh bone, and an intricately carved ivory dress button. Figuring out the origin of the bones had become a guessing game for Tobias and Miss Rebecca Curtis.

"Your mystery grows, old woman," he said to the bones.

"I thought you were an old slave. Maybe buried in an unmarked grave long before this land was cut up with roads and lanes. Maybe the button wasn't yours, but it was in the same dirt as your bones."

Tobias picked up the jawbone.

"Your teeth were still strong when you died. I saw many bodies and parts of bodies at Petersburg. Black and white all look the same once the skin is ripped away, but most blacks had teeth wore down. You have white people's teeth."

He returned the jawbone to the box and lifted the thigh bone.

"And your hip bone wasn't worn down from harsh labor. You had a healthy life and food easy to chew."

He returned the bone fragment, fingered the curved bone, saying, "I'm still not sure about you," then picked up the button.

"Once, I thought you might have been a favorite until your master turned on you. Pretty slaves were cursed with that kind of attention. But, now I think you are something else, someone else. You scared the hell out of Sonja Pulaski. That woman can be hard as nails if need be. How could you scare her?"

Tobias held the button higher in the lamplight.

"Sonja knew you. 'She is uncovered,' she said in the garden. She knew you and knew where you were. You are uncovered. Uncovered from what?"

He returned the button, closed the box, then set it down in its usual spot, and reached for the poker to stir the coals. Yellow light from the wood fire painted his face, making it appear almost bronze, then he peered back at the box.

"You were supposed to be under the barn."

Tobias rose and went to his writing desk and withdrew the papers delivered by George Milton. He turned to put the lamplight over his shoulder and flipped through the pages.

"There you are. There is your address Mrs. Mamie Stewart."

He sat down, opened the ink well, and dipped his pen.

Dear Mrs. Stewart,

I wish to tell you yet again what a grand and wonderful thing you did in my life when you left me this property. I am happy to tell you that your gift has allowed me to ask a wonderful woman to marry me. I am building a house for our future in another part of town and being helped nobly by the man who long wished to purchase this property. I will send a formal invitation when we decide on a date.

In the meantime, I must trouble you with a mystery regarding your property.

Do you know who was buried in the garden?

I would be grateful to learn the story behind his or her burial if you know it.

Sincerely,
Tobias Bond
c/o Bond Enterprises, Bourbon Street
Havre de Grace, Maryland

Sonja walked alone in the darkness. The pebbles beneath her bare feet were painful. She could not see where she stepped, but she hurried on, knowing something was coming after her. She went into a clearing bathed in light and turned to face her pursuer. Three figures emerged from the darkness. Two were holding up a third between them. A man in the middle was emaciated and blindfolded, wheezing and rasping with each breath. On his left stood a shorter figure gripping the man's arm. The left figure grimaced, his teeth outlined in blood, and his face above the mouth was gone except for tattered strips of bloody flesh. On the man's left was the gray rotting figure of Lydia Binterfield, gripping the man's arm with one hand

and holding an ax with the other. Lydia spun to face the man as the small figure held out the man's arm.

Lydia chopped off the man's arm.

The man in the middle screamed. It was Isaac. He screamed again. "Ma! Ma! Don't let them."

The deformed figure had a pistol now, and he pointed it toward Isaac's face and smiled at Sonja. It was the boy she had killed. Gunfire exploded into Isaac's face, and the clearing rained bloody rotting tissue.

Sonja screamed and screamed and screamed.

"Sonja," Ben called to her, shaking her shoulders. "Sonja!"

She screamed again, opening her eyes and seeing Ben's face.

"Stop them," she begged.

Ben pulled her to him. They were on their knees in the middle of the parlor, where Ben had found her. She glanced around, confused, her face wild with terror. Mickey stood in the doorway to the dining room.

"It was a dream," Ben said, stroking her back, keeping her close to his chest.

Sonja peered over his shoulder to the doorway. "I'm sorry, Mickey. Sorry to wake you."

She whispered to Ben, "They did not build the barn over her."

"It doesn't matter, Sonja. There is nothing there. You saw me break the bones. There is nothing there."

⚬ᴖᴖᴖᴖᴖ⚬

Sonja, Ben, and Mickey sat together in the parlor. The world outside the lamplit room was still in slumbered darkness, and Sonja could not face the demons of her dreams again so soon. She had made coffee and asked them to join her, but the three sat together in uncomfortable silence. The clock on the mantel ticked while Sonja drew coffee circles on her side table with her fingertip. The men waited for her to speak. She would glance up with her mouth opening, ready to begin, then her eyes would drop back toward the coffee rings as she lost her will. Ben waited for Sonja to say more, surprised that she wanted to tell Mickey about Lydia as well. Ben knew some of it from over the years. Sonja had released snippets when the burden of the story became too great for her to hold in, but they had been mere flashes of images, thinly described and soon halted.

Sonja released a long heavy sigh and raised her chin, her eyes gone cold. "I have kept this inside me for too long. I thought I needed to confess to a priest or a preacher, and maybe I still should. But I need to tell you what I did, all of it. Even before I shot that boy in South Carolina, I had already committed a murder."

Mickey's eyes went wide.

"Yes, Mickey. This is my other secret that I must burden you with. You both should know it, and I cannot bear to tell it twice."

Ben dropped his gaze to the floor.

"I killed Lydia Binterfield."

Mickey and Ben were motionless, their eyes fixed on her face. The clock ticked dozens of times before Sonja spoke again.

"There were five of us who hated Lydia as the very devil. Junie, Sissy, Jason, Mamie and me. We were all there with her at dinner. Lydia Williamson Binterfield was a monster. She took pleasure in making others suffer, especially her half-brother Jason and her slaves, Junie and Sissy. Especially them. And she hated Mamie and me because we were not afraid of her, only loathed her."

The men's eyes were intent and unwavering.

"Sissy was Junie's daughter," she said. "Both were brought up to Havre de Grace with Lydia from southern Maryland when she married Herbert."

Sonja took in a deep breath and balled her fists.

"Junie was also Lydia's aunt."

Mickey and Ben exchanged wide-eyed glances.

Sonja gazed at the yellow firelight seeping around the edges of the parlor stove. "Lydia grew up on a plantation in southern Maryland. Lydia's father raised her as white because she was light enough to pass, but her mother was one of her father's slaves. The father sent that slave to South Carolina after Lydia was born. Lydia's slave Junie was actually her mother's sister. Her aunt."

Mickey stood from his padded chair and stepped into the dining room. He returned with a full whiskey decanter, pouring some into his coffee cup, then offered it to Ben, who accepted a pour into his cup as well. Mickey offered the decanter to Sonja, but she waved it away.

"Lydia had offered Sissy her freedom," Sonja continued. "But, it was a ploy to convince Junie to voluntarily follow Lydia down to a family plantation in South Carolina, Palmetto Haven."

Sonja's eyes peered above their heads, seeing the past.

"Going farther south terrified Junie, but she did it for her daughter's freedom. Then for sport Lydia told Sissy of her mother's agreement. She convinced Sissy to sign an indenture in return for keeping her mother in Maryland. Lydia never intended to free either of them. Lydia joined a dinner with all of us to play her evil prank. When Lydia announced Sissy's agreement in front of Junie, Junie struck Lydia."

Mickey sipped his whiskey. "So, who killed Lydia?"

"I already told you," Sonja said. "I did."

Sonja stood, pulling her shawl higher on her shoulders, stepping to the window. She gazed at her own reflection in the glass as the two men seated behind her waited for the whole horrible truth.

"There were others who joined the killing," Ben said to Mickey. "She's told me that much."

"Hatred accumulated around Lydia," Sonja said. "She exuded it and relished it."

Sonja turned to face them. "All of us in that dining room hated her, and she incited it with glee. We were her audience. She relished her moment. She intended to take the boarding house from Mamie, and this house from us–"

Ben stood. "What? I never knew–"

"She inherited Herbert's bank. She held the

mortgages. It was like an orchestration, Ben. She was in her greatest moment. She had something mean-spirited for each of us that night."

Sonja released a single wracking sob. Ben went to her, placing his hands on her shoulders.

"No more for now. Tell us the rest later."

She pushed his hands away. "No! I have to tell it all now."

Mickey stood as well. "Maybe you should rest, Sonja–"

"No, Mickey. You think you know my worst moment? When I wanted to die in the river?"

Ben glanced at Mickey.

She laughed, but her voice was empty. "You must hear who I really am." She peered at Ben. "You both must know."

She pointed to their chairs. "Sit," she said, placing her hands on her hips, owning the moment, opinions be damned.

"When Junie struck her, Lydia gave a look of glorious satisfaction, opening the door to tortures for Junie not yet invented. Junie screamed at Lydia. She said, 'How can you treat people like you do? I'm the same color as your momma!' Lydia's face flared scarlet. 'Don't you dare,' she yelled. But Junie pointed her finger at Lydia's face. 'Your momma was my sister. My Sissy is your first cousin.'"

"Lydia jumped to her feet and slapped Junie's face, threatening to have her whipped to death in front of her daughter.

"Junie smiled at Lydia and swept her arm around the room. 'No hiding it here, Lydia,' she said. 'Everybody in this room knows your secret. You don't got no Spanish royal blood in you.' Junie rubbed her own arm. 'You got nigger blood in you, woman. And your own uncle sired your daughter. Every slave on both plantations know that.'

'I will have you hanged,' Lydia hissed through clenched teeth.

'Junie grabbed a candlestick from a side table and struck Lydia. Blood poured down her face.'

Sonja balled her fists before them. "It had to be done. And I joined them. We each participated; Sissy after Junie, then Jason, who had suffered humiliation under her for years, then Mamie, to save her boarding house...and then me. One of them handed me a brass-handled walking stick. I struck at her with all my strength. I think I landed the fatal blow. After my strike, Lydia lay on the floor in a pool of blood in the dining room."

Mickey stood near her. "So, you buried her in the garden behind Mamie's house?"

Sonja gazed at him with empty eyes. "In twelve pieces, so there would not be a body to be found. Then we burned our bloody clothes and made a pact amongst the five of us."

"Lydia did not go to Spain, did she?" Ben asked. "Even her earlier trips you told me about? Before you told me about the bones."

"She never left the garden, Ben. Mamie duplicated Lydia's handwriting and used a friend living in Spain to receive and forward letters. Over the last nineteen years, every letter from Lydia actually came from Mamie, written in her boarding house in Havre de Grace."

"All the instructions to her lawyer?" Ben asked, "...All the...your inheritance of the plantations, all of that from Mamie? Tobias getting the land under the boarding house after the fire?"

"Mamie," Sonja said. "And all the plantation

changes directed to her lawyer. Most with my help, until after the fire. Then it was only Mamie. I was truly shocked to inherit those plantations. I never wanted anything like that."

"And the other three of the five?" Mickey asked.

"Junie and Sissy escaped north," Sonja said. "Poor Jason killed himself over the love of another slave who had his child but left Havre de Grace without him. I took them away from him in the *Jester*."

Mickey dropped down onto his seat. Ben glared at Sonja in disbelief.

"None of Lydia's change was real," Ben said.

"All of it was real, Ben," Sonja said. "Just none of it was from Lydia. It was all Mamie."

Sonja snatched up her coffee cup and stepped to the front door, where she pulled it open and threw her coffee out into the night. Then she took up the whiskey decanter near Mickey, filled her cup, swallowed a deep drink, and returned to her chair.

Mickey gazed at Sonja with wide eyes and his mouth open, then composed himself and turned to Ben.

"Earlier, you told Sonja that you had broken up her bones. I assume the bones you spoke of were Lydia's. And yet, what Sonja just told us was a surprise to you as well."

Ben rubbed his mouth with his hand and shrugged his shoulders. "I only knew that Lydia had been killed and buried in the garden behind Mamie's boarding house. And that was not until a year after the killing–"

"Murder," Sonja said. "Call it what it was."

"When a dog dug up some of her bones," Ben said, "and Sonja had to tell me about the body parts. I dug them up, mixed them with oyster shells, broke them into pieces, and re-buried them."

"Why oyster shells?"

"People around here mix crushed oyster shells for the calcium to help garden soil produce. Smashed-up bones look like crushed oyster shells."

Mickey nodded understanding, standing before Sonja. "Mad dogs have to be put down. Just like what we had to do in South Carolina, Sonja. Just like what soldiers have to do in a war. Afterward, we have to go on. We have to put it behind us."

Sonja emptied her cup and forced down the last mouthful of whiskey. "Not everything can be put behind us, Mickey. Not Isaac. Not that boy. Maybe not even Lydia, as evil as she was."

Mickey stood, "That boy was evil whether he realized it or not. The damnation falls to his father." He stepped onto the front porch, closing the door behind him.

"Sonja," Ben said. "You can't link that to a murdering Klansman—"

Sonja punched her finger at Ben. "That boy!"

"That murdering Klansman," Ben said. "You cannot link him to the death of our son. The death of our son by his own hand."

She balled her fists. "No! Don't say that."

"By his own hand, Sonja. Not by the hand of God."

"No. You weren't there. You weren't with him."

"And neither were you, Sonja Pulaski, but true is true. Isaac shot himself to end his nightmares."

"Well, by God...Maybe I can end mine!" Sonja

said as she dashed into the bedroom.

Ben lunged after her, catching her at the chest of drawers beside the bed, where she kept her pistol. She had it in her hands. He grabbed her, pulling her elbows, breaking her grip on the handle, then yanked it from her, tossing it onto the floor. Sonja rained slaps against his face. He grabbed her around her waist, lifting her off her feet. She twisted within his arms to get away, kicking him with her heels, reaching over her head, pulling at his hair.

"Let me go. Let me go, Goddammit, Ben! Let me go."

"No."

She grabbed at his hair in a frenzy, filling her fingernails with his skin and blood.

"Sonja! Stop it! Stop it, now!"

He flung her onto the bed, and as she bounced, she grabbed at him, scratching and kicking, screaming sounds that were not words.

"Let me go!"

Ben fell onto the bed with her, encircling her legs within his, wrapping his arms around her, grabbing her wrists, pulling her back against his chest. She jerked her head back, smashing into his nose. He tucked his head behind a pillow and tightened his grip.

"No," she said, her demand becoming a whimpering plea. "Let me go, Ben."

"Not until you are you again. I don't know who that was I just wrestled, but it wasn't my wife."

They lay with heaving rasping breaths, her face on her pillow and his buried in her hair.

"I should have been with him," she said, crying softly then. "Maybe I could have stopped him."

She sobbed, then whimpered, and the tension of her body melted away as she folded within Ben's arms, and his tears slipped from his cheek onto the strands of her hair.

When quiet returned to the inside of the Pulaski house, Mickey left his lit cigar balanced at the edge of the porch and slipped back into the parlor. He gently closed the door to Ben and Sonja's bedroom, lifted the whiskey decanter from its perch, and carried it with him back onto the porch, gingerly closing the front door. He sat on the steps and drew on his cigar to rekindle the red glow and drank from the decanter until it was empty. Mickey then set the decanter aside and leaned back with his elbows resting on the floorboards, peering up into the black sky.

"Lord, forgive me my blasphemy, one more time. But if you're up there after all, and with the war we just had, I can't believe you pay us as much attention as we need. But... but, if you are up there and you can hear me, then you best get your ass down here and help these poor people."

He took a last draw from his cigar and flipped it out into the yard, watching the tail of sparks follow it down. Then he raised his eyes to the sky again. "Amen."

WEDNESDAY, DECEMBER 29

Sunrise over Lapidum was merely a lighter shade of gray. Sonja lay curled on her side in exhausted sleep as Ben dressed for his trip into Havre de Grace. He slipped her revolver into his pocket, then donned his vest and coat and stood next to her, studying her face in the growing light from the window.

Her voice was strained from the long night of crying, followed by too little sleep, her words forced through the dryness. "Are you going to court?"

"Yes. Will you still be here when I return?"

They both knew what the question really meant.

She opened her eyes. The bright blue was more the color of new steel but rimmed in red and bagged with dark circles underneath. "Yes."

He sat beside her, resting his hand on her hip.

"No more attempts to join Isaac?"

"I didn't mean that, Ben. I just needed to feel something more than grief."

"You scared the hell out of me, Sonja. Promise you will never do that again."

She laid her hand on his. "I promise."

"Mickey will be here while I am gone."

"My jailer?"

Ben scoffed. "Such duty would require far more than just Doctor O'Grady."

Mickey chuckled from the open doorway, the aroma of fresh coffee drifting into the bedroom from his cup.

"I have Sergeant Major Laudanum as my reserve," he said, "and I strongly suggest the prisoner take another teaspoon of it to help her get some rest."

Ben arched his eyebrows in question to her, and she gave him a resigned nod, then he reached for the small vial and teaspoon sitting on her nightstand. She raised enough to take the liquid, twisted her lips in a sour comment, and lay her head back onto her pillow. He kissed her forehead then left the room, patting Mickey on the shoulder as he went.

Garrett was waiting in the buggy to ride to Havre de Grace to work on the *Jester* with Jimmy and Tobias. After simple one-word greetings, Ben took the wagon onto the towpath. The mare seemed eager and was soon into a jaunty trot of her own choosing. She had spent too much time in barns while he and Sonja were away, well cared for by friends in Lapidum, but with little exercise. Even in the chilled air with her breath puffing vapor clouds over her shoulders and back as she went, her head was high and her rhythm energetic. He let her keep her pace as long as the horse enjoyed it, and the mare enjoyed it all the way to the southern edge of the Havre de Grace canal basin. She slowed, entering the last section of towpath where the trees and canal banks shrank away, leaving just two lanes of open pathway. The thin ribbon of dirt divided canal water from river water for the last quarter mile to the barns, creating the twelve-acre canal basin. Even in the canal's winter slumber, the basin held enough water to float several barges.

Judge Andrew Jessup lived in Havre de Grace, but the county courtroom was in Bel Air, the county seat, fifteen miles away. He was nearing ninety years old then and no longer sitting on the circuit court bench but had long served the county as a judicial consultant to the sheriff. So, when matters came before Jessup, he frequently held judicial interviews in his home office on Adams Street.

As Ben neared Adams Street, he turned the buggy down the service lane that ran parallel between Adams and Stokes Streets. He let the mare have a leisurely walk among the back gardens and outhouses that edged the path. He brought the buggy to a halt behind the home of Dr. Wallace Harper, who had been the family physician for many years. The perfectly tended lawn edged in colorful flowers and the modest little shanty where Sonja had taken refuge during Ben's years in China were all gone, replaced by a large garden. A black man hacked away in the garden, taking down the last drying stalks of previous growth, laying it by for future planting in the spring. The man noticed Ben and gave a short wave. Ben smiled and returned the wave but lingered a moment longer. The black man saw him still there gazing at the property and came near the lane, resting his arm on the handle of his hoe.

"Can I help you, suh?"

"I remember the little building that Doc Harper used to have back here. It was his office when he first came to Havre de Grace."

The man nodded, understanding. "It's long gone from here, just like the good doctor."

"Oh, he moved away?"

"No suh, he passed on last winter. The missus had already passed couple years before that."

"Mmm. Do you own it now?"

The man released a hearty laugh. "I only wish. No, suh. It was bought by Mistah Turner. He and his wife moved in last year."

"Robert Turner?"

"Yes, suh. He's my employer. We have a real fine garden here."

"Well, I'm sorry to know the Harpers are gone from here but thank you for speaking with me."

The man turned away, and Ben raised the reins to flip them on the mare, but then stopped.

"Excuse me, but do you happen to know about the freedwoman that worked for Doc Harper."

"She works for Mr. Turner, now."

Ben smiled and said, "Well, I need to head on to Judge Jessup's house."

The man rolled his eyes, "Uh-oh. I hope it goes well."

The back yard to Judge Jessup's house was entirely enclosed by a picket fence, except the narrow front to his carriage house, leaving no place to tie his horse. Ben drove the buggy around to Adams Street and tethered the reins to one of the three iron horse head hitching posts erected at the front edge of the yard.

Ben mounted the steps of the wide front porch to find George Milton standing with Robert Turner. Ben shook hands with George, stepping on the opposite side from Turner.

"Morning, George. Are we having this hearing

on the porch?"

"Deputy Hopkins, and Attorney Watkins for the plaintiff, are already inside speaking with Jessup." George motioned toward Turner. "Mr. Turner is here as a character witness."

"For Bolton?" Ben asked.

"For you," Turner said. "You consistently act the rogue toward me personally, but otherwise, your reputation for stern fairness is well known in this town."

"You do this for my wife," Ben said. The tone was more a statement than a question.

"Your wife is my friend, Pulaski. I do it for her and my own wife."

"I just learned you had a wife. Bought the Harper house, did you?"

"Yes. And you should know that even there, I am not free to sully your name. Our cook had a much better opinion of you than I. Actually, I am likely here more on her behalf than either Sonja's or even my Elizabeth's."

George stepped back from between them. "This morning keeps getting colder."

The men faced each other.

"Congratulations on your...purchase," Ben said.

Turner slipped his hands into his pockets. "Thank you, Pulaski."

"Is your wife from around here?" Ben asked. "Local woman?"

"Not at all." The comment was curt. He hesitated, then continued. "We married in London during my visit last year, had been acquainted since childhood. She was Elizabeth Cuttingham, of the Kensington High Street Cuttinghams."

Ben moved his hand forward, pulled it back,

then extended it fully, offering it to Turner. "Congratulations on your marriage, Mr. Turner."

Turner pulled his hand from his pocket, paused. then sighed, accepting Ben's hand. "Thank you, Mr. Pulaski. Call me Robert."

"And call me Ben."

George had his hands behind his back, rocking on his heels and smiling, making eye contact with each man, his belly nearly filling the space behind their handshake. "Must have been like this when Grant and Lee met at Appomattox."

The three were smiling when Lester Watkins walked out. He paused before Ben.

"Kindly inform your wife that there are still papers to sign regarding the estate left to her by Mrs. Binterfield. She will need to stop by my office."

He went down the steps without speaking to the others. Deputy Hopkins followed him out onto the porch and talked to the trio.

"Bolton got drunk last night and started a fight in the United States Hotel. I have him locked up at my office."

Ben smiled and drew in a deep breath.

"Judge Jessup said he was tempted to throw out the charges entirely," Hopkins said, "except for Alexander's notes as a deputy, concerning you, Ben. He wants to see us all tomorrow at noon. Anyone not inside his office before the twelfth strike of his hall clock will spend a week in jail, if not the entire month of January."

Hopkins chuckled. "And that includes me." Then he walked off the porch.

Ben, George, and Robert remained on the porch chatting a moment until Judge Jessup's white-gloved butler opened the front door, clearing his throat.

"Beg pardon, gentlemen, but the judge's exact words were, 'Get off my damned porch.'"

He smiled, bobbed his head, and gently closed the door.

George tipped his hat to the other two men and made his way toward the south end of town. Ben and Robert rode together in the Pulaski buggy to Robert's office.

"I've ordered several fine English fowling pieces," Robert said. "They came in on a schooner from Philadelphia yesterday."

"American shotguns are not fancy enough for ducks?"

"The duck shooters that come down from farther north have developed a taste for English long guns, nobility and all. Mr. McCombs has already asked that all I receive go to his store. Still, I would like you to see one of them. One that I am keeping for my own. I can finally afford one. They are magnificent pieces."

The explosive sound of a large-bore gun reverberated among the buildings, filling the sky with startled ducks scattering from the water in all directions. The sound was far greater than that of a typical shotgun going off during a busy duck season.

"Damned punt guns," Ben said. "Just a small boat-mounted cannon crudely designed to resemble a rifle that only a giant could actually fire."

"Exactly, Ben. They slaughter hundreds in a single shot for the restaurants and litter the bay's surface with bloody feathers. One could not possibly consider that sport."

"No, just mass killings. It drives the prices

down for Havre de Grace ducks, and the firing pushes the ducks away to other inlets. Short-term profit that forces them to kill even more ducks to make their daily money. Our Mr. Bolton is notorious among the punt shooters."

"And the dredgers are doing much the same for the oysters," Robert said. "I understand your friend Tobias will be working with Jimmy to take on extra loads of tonged oysters from down at the Bush River."

"Yes."

"Kindly let him know that Washington restaurants have ordered tons of ice from Maine and Massachusetts to come down Saturday."

"I don't understand the connection, Robert."

"The shipping clerks for those trains are also grabbing up promises of oyster deliveries for New Year's Eve and Day in Washington City. That city will gorge itself on oysters which is driving up the oyster prices. They want ducks too. The clerks are signing commitments to buy. Tobias needs to trot down to the train station and get all the commitments he can. If his men can fill the *Jester* and meet that train, he will make a small fortune in a single day."

Inside Robert's office, he unlocked a cabinet at the back wall, withdrew a double barrel percussion shotgun in new pristine condition, and handed it to Ben.

"It is a Purdy, of London, of course. Forty caliber, muzzle-loaded, but with rifled barrels. Double rifled at that."

"Beautiful scrolling in the steel," Ben said as he held it to the light at the front window.

Robert pointed to a spot of metal below the

hammers. "That's a platinum disk with the tiniest hole in it to allow a bit more air for most efficient combustion."

Ben gazed closely at the spot, then rotated the gun in his hands. "Beautiful workmanship."

Robert flashed a boyish grin. "You may not like me, Ben, but you must admit this is a beautiful gun."

Ben returned the rifle. "I do not dislike you, Robert. I did. But that was to my own embarrassment and a selfish failure in the trust of my wife. Thank you for showing me this. I have seen far more than a finely crafted gun today.

Robert gave a bow at the waist. "One day soon, perhaps you and your wife can join my wife and me for dinner."

NOTICE TO OYSTERMEN.

STATE OF MARYLAND,
STATE OYSTER POLICE FORCE,
Baltimore, Feb. 15, 1869.

I HEREBY give notice that after the 28th day of this month Dredging for Oysters in any River in the State of Maryland must cease.

This notice is given in consequence of the Attorney General of the State having published an opinion on the 13th instant, "contrary to his first impressions" regarding the construction of section 16 of the Oyster Law, and also of the decision of Judge Joseph A. Wicks, in the case of pungy "Ray," of Baltimore, Captain John Jones, which was seized by the State Oyster Police Force, agreeably to instructions from the Commissioners of the State Oyster Police Force," and tried at Chestertown, Kent county, as a test case, on the 13th instant.

The reviewed opinion of the Attorney General and the decision of Judge Wicks being that Dredging for Oysters in any River in the State is unlawful, I shall be governed accordingly in the discharge of my duty.

The time is allowed until the 1st proximo in order that this notice may be known to all interested.   HUNTER DAVIDSON,
Commander State Oyster Police Force.
Feb 26, 1869—2t

Port Tobacco Times, (Port Tobacco, Md.), 05 March 1869. *Chronicling America: Historic American Newspapers.* Lib. of Congress.

The morning work planned for the crew of the *Jester* was lost. After several tacks across a hateful wind trying to push them back to Havre de Grace, the *Jester* finally made it to the mouth of the Bush River near noon, twenty nautical miles from Havre de Grace. On Jimmy Finley's maiden voyage into the Bush River, he steered the sloop too near the point at low tide and without familiarity, running her aground. The tong boats of Tobias Bond Enterprises, already in the mouth working the oyster beds, lost precious daylight hours helping the *Jester* kedge off the shoal into the river's main channel.

Jimmy admitted he had never been up the Bush before.

Tobias pointed to his tonger boats with more than a bit of agitation straining his voice.

"Every one of them knows where the shoals are. Lawrence was in the lead boat out there waving at you to swing wide of the point, so you wouldn't run aground."

Jimmy mumbled, looking away. "Didn't see him."

The *Jester* finally settled between her anchors in the middle of the river's mouth as tong boats moved back and forth over the oyster beds like swimming beetles. The chop in the water remained throughout the day, constantly slapped by the wind, preventing the tong boats from carrying full loads due to fears of swamping. Still, having the sloop close gave them frequent opportunities to transfer the oysters before their weight endangered the boats. The volume in the sloop's hold wasn't near the double load Tobias hoped for. Yet, it already represented more than the single loads the boats usually brought home in the afternoons.

In the afternoon, another ship entered the river from the bay, similar in rigging and length to the *Jester* but cutting closer to the shore than *Jester* dared.

Jimmy pointed to the newcomer. "Log canoe, and it's pulling a damned dredge. They'll ruin the oyster beds in here."

Garrett peered out at the vessel. "What's a log canoe? That don't look like any canoe I've ever seen."

"More than a real canoe, but still called that because its hull is carved from five logs together as if they were one."

Garret and Tobias screwed their faces trying to understand the description.

"Made from logs. Adze-cut into a single hull. Looks like board-built but has more hull weight, so it has a shallower draft and carries more sail. It can run full speed in three feet of water while this old sloop would need five or six and still not catch her."

"Well, he ain't slowing down," Garrett said.

"Heading right in the middle of my boats," said Tobias. "Hey!" he yelled and waved his arms at the ship.

"Garrett, pull up the anchor," Jimmy said. "Tobias, hoist the jib, so it'll pull us around. Then help me with the mainsail."

As the log canoe sailed past the *Jester*, into the middle of the tong boats, the *Jester's* bow tracked her as she came about. The log canoe was named the *Virginia Owl*, painted on her low-set transom.

"They're not supposed to the dredging in Maryland waters," Jimmy said. "They're Virginians. Hell, they ain't supposed to be dredging up here at all. This is tonging waters."

The *Owl* slid between the tong boats, dragging her dredge going precariously close to one. The man in that boat dived into the cold water. Another tonger jumped to his oars, getting to the aid of the man in the water. The *Owl* loosened her sails to come about while her crew hauled in the dredge and dumped the oysters on her deck. Then she tightened her sails to cross the wind again for another run through the boats. The *Jester* gained momentum and moved toward the outer rim around the tong boats, putting her bow to where the *Owl* would come out next.

"That bastard," Jimmy said.

The *Owl* changed course as she crossed the oyster bed, aiming for water that would soon be behind the *Jester*. The *Owl* was much handier and quicker in the wind than the old *Jester*, and she slipped behind the *Jester*. The *Owl*'s crew gave bawdy laughter as they hauled in the second basket of oysters, running among the boats, bumping the unmanned one. The boat's load shifted off-center and canted near to sinking. The man in the water was pulled into another boat.

"Steer starboard," Jimmy called out to Garrett, pointing to the right as he ran for the stern cabin.

When Jimmy emerged from the cabin, the *Owl* was beginning another turn to run through the oyster beds again. The *Owl*'s crew dropped the dredge as it filled its sails, crossing the wind again.

Jimmy made an exaggerated motion showing his revolver and yelling to the *Owl*, "Stand off, or I will shoot."

The *Owl* did not veer away. Jimmy fired into the air. Still, she did not alter course. *Jester* completed her turn. The *Owl* passed, placing the ships facing stern to stern for the instant.

"Stand off, damn you," Jimmy yelled.

The Owl's captain laughed and made a crude gesture with his hand on his crotch.

Garrett dashed to Jimmy's side, yanking the pistol from his grip, then placed one hand against his hip in a marksman's stance and tracked the *Owl*'s captain with his front sight. He fired. The *Owl*'s captain screamed, raising his bloody hand as more blood spread across his trousers at his crotch. The crewman at the *Owl*'s tiller yanked it to swerve the bow between the ships and block Garrett's view. Another man on the *Owl* ran to the bow with a rifle, firing at the *Jester*, but the bullet passed through the *Jester's* rigging without damage. Garrett fired again, raising splinters on the boom rest near the man's head with the rifle, who crouched behind the oyster pile.

The *Owl* headed upriver on that pass but would have to pass the *Jester* again to get back out into the bay. A crewman slipped one of the chains to the dredge, releasing its load and allowed the *Owl* to come about swiftly, picking up speed, swinging wide of the *Jester*. The rest of the *Owl's* crew laid low behind cover except the tillerman, who raised an empty hand while steering with his other, taking their ship through shallow water back into the bay. Garrett kept his aim on the tillerman until the *Owl* was beyond range. The oysters shifted again in the abandoned tong boat, allowing water inside, sinking the boat.

Tobias gripped his hands into fists as one of his boats sank. Jimmy regarded Garrett with awe.

Garrett handed the revolver back to Jimmy.

"Sorry to yank it from your hands as I did, Jimmy."

Tobias scanned the other boats for the man who went in the water, cupping his hands to call out to him. "Are you all right, Lawrence?"

"Just wet, cold, and mad," Lawrence said.

"Excellent shooting, Garrett," Jimmy said.

"Ain't nothing to shooting a hog, Jimmy. They just stand there and let you do it. And don't tell Ben I'm a good shot."

"Why not?"

"I told him I'm a poor shot at ducks, but I just like to feed'em."

Jimmy gave him a half smile, not clear about Garrett's comment but eager to help with the overturned boat.

The three men worked together to rig the *Jester's* mainsail boom to raise the sunken boat.

Late in the afternoon of another sunless day, the sloop *Jester* nearly flew into the Havre de Grace docks riding before the wind under full sails, wing, and wing, with the jib full-bellied on the left, the mainsail bulging on the right and the tonger men working as crew. The boats were towed behind the *Jester* like ducklings in a row. Only one full load each was taken from the tong boats due to their late start and conflict with the Virginians, though hopes were high for the next day. Jimmy recovered some of his sailor's reputation by waiting until the perfect moment to order the sails dropped, letting the sloop slide up to the dockside like a landing bird. The hull gently touched up against the wooden wharf as soft as a lover's kiss.

Sonja's plan to meet secretly with Franklin Curtis and his daughter Rebecca vanished the moment it was spoken. She could not come up with a ruse that would not cause Ben to be suspicious. He insisted that he accompany her to Watson's Island even though he promised to not interfere with any private conversation she wished to have. She struggled to convince him to not go, but he was adamant. Rather than cancel her planned conversation with Franklin, she yielded to Ben's insistence, especially after hearing about his meeting with Robert.

"I dearly hope Robert's memory of your visit to his office today was as cordial as you tell it," she had said. "I recall the first time you admitted to me your previous visit to his office...When you failed to mention the pistol."

Ben had shrugged his shoulders and looked away.

Darkness had settled when Ben and Sonja met Franklin and Rebecca north of the canal basin. The rowboat was waiting on the riverside of the towpath, just across from the southern tip of Watson's Island, where Franklin's church sat high on the far side of the bank. Near the church, there was a lumber mill on the island, supervised by a man who knew the Pulaskis. He and his wife both attended Franklin's services on Sundays, and the man, who had served in the United States Colored Troops, joined in with the other veterans on Wednesday nights. Two other wives came with their men but met together in the sawmill office, so the men could have both their comradeship and privacy. Sonja and Rebecca joined them while Ben preferred to wait at the boat and smoke his pipe. Light from the church and the sawmill filtered down to the shore of the island.

Ben had just lit his pipe when Tobias ambled down from the church to join him.

"Is the service over already?" Ben asked.

"They're just getting started, Mr. Pulaski. And it's not a service, just discussions about things that still trouble them."

"Tobias, I have known you since you were four years old..."

"Aw, please, don't you start that too."

Ben chuckled. "No. No. No. I just wanted to tell you to call me Ben. I would prefer that."

"Yes. Yes, sir. I can certainly do that."

"So, then. You have nothing that troubles you?"

"Oh, some, I guess. Most men usually do. But to be honest, my reason for being here on Wednesday nights is to spend more time with Rebecca."

Ben smiled and blew a thin stream of smoke into the air. "Your Rebecca is a pretty lady, with a nice smile and eyes that will keep a man home at night. I'm glad for you. Sonja tells me you're building a house for you two over near the AME Church."

"Yes, we are. But it's nothing against Mr. Curtis's church. It's just that there are several other black families living close by the AME, and we'll feel comfortable there. Makes no difference whether always free or just freed, most black people can relax better around their own kind."

"I think most folks want a home like that."

Seagulls called to each other, flying in the darkness above them

"Mr. Pul...Ben, I heard from Mickey that Aunt Lettie didn't want to see you when you took Uncle Simon home to Canada...It broke my heart when I heard that they hanged him down in South Carolina. It made me want to kill rebs again, but seems to me that Aunt Lettie would want you to stay for his funeral. She shouldn't have been alone."

"She had people around her. Friends she had made during her years in Canada. And she carries a lot of hurt, Tobias. No one can understand how bad that is except her. She did NOT want him to go to South Carolina to teach freed children after risking his life fighting for the Union. He had helped free his people, her people, and she wanted him back home in Canada. It was hard enough on her for him to leave her in the safety of Canada and come down here to fight for the Union. Being hanged by the Klan for teaching children was more than she could bear."

"But you called him your brother. Didn't she know that?"

"All she knew was the pain of losing him. Just like Sonja's pain of losing Isaac."

Ben puffed on his pipe, then tapped Tobias's shoulder.

"What was the name of the little girl you brought to Havre de Grace when you were working with the Underground Railroad? The one with the bad fever who died."

"Jeezie."

"You talked about her a long time. Have you forgotten her? Is her death not as important to you now?"

He faced Ben, the yellow light from the sawmill office outlining his features and showing a frown.

"Of course not."

"The other night, I was telling Sonja that she'd find a way to help the pain of losing Isaac to fade, that it would get easier. But, she told me, 'I will talk less of it with time. But I cannot imagine ever feeling better.' Maybe that's what Lettie was trying to do. Push away the pain by not speaking about it with us."

They continued to talk, broken by long periods of quiet reflection. Tobias also told Ben of the confrontation with the Virginia dredger at the Bush River.

"I hated the war, Tobias, and I was glad that it was over, but it wasn't over for Isaac, and now men are willing to die for oysters."

"It's not oysters, Ben. It's the money they bring. That's what Uncle Simon taught me. It's always about money. Oysters are money. Ducks are money. Slavery was all about money. If a man could own another man, he wouldn't have to pay him wages. Even if the owner had to buy the slave, the cost of the slave over the ten years it took the owner to work him to death was far less than he would pay in wages. And the slave worked longer hours. That war was about money."

"I am not so sure about that, Tobias. The war kept the country together."

"And did so by creating taxes on income. Even in destitution, the southern citizens contribute to the federal budget."

"That is far too complicated for me, Tobias. You certainly have your uncle's understanding, which is far beyond mine. Simon would be so proud of you."

Ben made several suggestions for actions to take against dredgers, some of which included him joining them with a gun the following day. Still, Tobias assured him that he, Jimmy, and Garrett could do whatever needed to be done. He pointed out that Ben should not be involved, especially since he was under the watchful eye of Judge Jessup.

"You know about that?" Ben had asked.

"Most of the town does," Tobias answered.

There was a short period of loud voices coming from the church that did not sound like either a peaceful meeting or harmony. Then the meeting abruptly ended, and voices trailed off in different directions.

"Sounds like some of my boat passengers are ready to go back to Cecil County," Tobias said, then made his way up the slope to the church.

Ben smoked another bowl of tobacco before Franklin and Sonja came down to the boat.

Sonja sounded relaxed in her voice. Ben was relieved and curious to hear her mind.

"We appear to have more boats than we need, Ben," Franklin said. "Tobias is not needed to take anyone back to Cecil County, and we still have two boats to take back to the Harford County shore. I think Tobias should row Rebecca and Sonja back in one, and then you and I can take the other one."

Ben stiffened and eyed Sonja with a scowl.

She stepped close and whispered to him. "Please, Ben. Do it for me."

Soon Franklin was rowing Ben across the river. The lights from the lanterns at the canal basin provided more than enough guidance for Franklin's rowing.

"Is Sonja all right?" Ben asked. "Did she...find what she needed...from you?"

Franklin's smile showed in the light from the lantern Ben held.

"Maybe. It will take time. I think most of what she was looking for was already hers, but she is not ready to speak of her darkest worries. Sometimes the shortest path is the hardest. She will see that in time."

"What do you mean, Franklin?"

"I am sure she will be happy to discuss all that with you at home. I thought maybe we could talk a little. Sonja has some concerns regarding you."

"About what?"

Franklin chuckled. "About you."

"About me? She spoke to you about me."

"About you, Ben and...God."

Ben was silent a long moment. "We don't speak much."

"You and Sonja? You two don't speak about God."

"Oh, she does, from time to time, but I thought you were asking about God and me."

"I was."

"Well, then you got your answer. Why'd you bring Sonja into it? I'm only speaking with you because she asked it of me."

Franklin sighed and pulled on the oars. "Is that your decision or his?"

Ben sat in silence.

"I said–"

"I heard, Franklin."

"And?"

"I'm not deaf. If he ever spoke, I'd hear him."

Franklin stopped rowing, and the boat rocked in rippling water, drifting neither north nor south. "Maybe he's speaking, and you don't hear him."

"Maybe he isn't there, and I'm wasting my time considering it, and so are you."

"You suspect he isn't there?"

Ben shifted in his seat, finding a lantern pole, then set it into its hole in the gunnel and hung the lantern.

"So, Ben, do you suspect God isn't there?"

"I've seen too much evidence that he isn't, and none that he is. You were in the last war. I was in two before that—one against the British and one against the Seminole. Then me and Sonja sailed our schooner with rotting wounded from the war down in Mexico. The Brits deserved it. The Seminole, probably not. I've never figured out the one with Mexico, but Isaac survived it without injury. If God's handwork is around us, it is blood and pain and agony."

"But God sent his son—"

"To be butchered. Just like mine."

Franklin began to row again. The current swung the boat akilter, and the lantern rocked out over the water, reflecting yellow light flashing from the waves.

Ben gazed at the yellow flashes beyond the boat.

"Do you read the Bible, Ben? Growing up, did you read the Bible?"

"Couldn't read. Knew my sums, though. Never let anyone cheat me. Sonja used to read the Bible to me. Then to the boys and me."

"Did she teach you to read?"

Ben peered into the lantern light. "No. No, she would have, but I wouldn't let her. Pride."

"But you read now?"

Ben kept his attention on the lantern flame swinging at the end of the pole.

"Simon. A runaway slave. He taught me to

read. He had been taught by his owner in southern Maryland. We were in China together. Prisoners. The Chinese thought we were British. The Klansmen hanged him in South Carolina. Hanged him in front of Sonja for teaching children."

Yellow tears slipped down Ben's cheek, glistening in the lantern light.

"Now, there's a fine example of your God, preacher," Ben said. "Lets a man who risked his life to free your brothers and sisters and teach them how to read and write too. Had a wife and son in Canada. Left them behind to come back to do that. And your God let him get hanged by men filled with hatred for your kind, preacher."

Ben spat into the churning water.

Franklin pulled on the oars to move the boat toward shore.

"I understand that your son was not killed in battle."

"He was mortally wounded, but it did not show. Only his lost arm. His battles raged long after the surrender. The guns of his battles never went silent, never stopped firing, never stopped killing him. God killed my son by never letting him find peace."

"That is a harsh feeling to carry, Ben."

Ben spat again into the rippling water. "Harsh, yes. Why not. If he has a problem with my harshness, what about his? He can kiss my ass."

Franklin let the oar's tip glide through the water. The rippling settled, and the incoming tide pushed the boat against the river current, taking it upriver.

Franklin began rowing again, fighting the tide. "Sometimes, Ben, in our pain, we say harsh words that we do not really mean."

"I say harsh words because this is a harsh world, preacher. I expect no more of it. It is the way of things."

"And when things go well, does that not stand against the harshness?"

The boat moved farther upstream with the tide.

"Not at all," Ben said. "Even a broken clock is on time twice a day."

"So, happiness is simply the rare absence of harshness? The natural condition is harsh? Maybe there is room among your harshness to consider other possibilities."

"I have said many harsh things over the years. Some worse than others."

"And others less harsh?"

Ben chuckled, but there was no mirth in his laughter.

"Yes, I have said many harsh things in my life, Preacher, but don't misunderstand me. I meant every damned word and take none of it back."

The river current strengthened and pushed them against the tide toward the canal basin.

Ben limped as he stepped up onto his front porch where Mickey sat outlined by the parlor lamplight, smoking his cigar.

"Are you saved yet, Ben?"

Ben dropped onto the chair beside him, rubbing his knee. "I didn't drown. Damned odd tide coming in, though. Pushed the rowboat against the river current."

"That's a lot of push. Your knee aching?"

"Sometimes, my joints take turns complaining." He tilted his head toward the window. "She still up?"

Mickey held up his fresh cigar. "She told me goodnight right before I lit this one, and the bedroom light just went out, but I still hear noises in there."

"She told me you saw a darkness over her. Is it still there?"

"Over you both. It grows stronger."

Ben stood, releasing a sigh, then shook his head. "I think I'm starting to feel it, too. G'night Mick," he said, then went inside.

The darkened bedroom was touched by flickering yellow from the parlor stove flitting in through the open door. There was no stove in the bedroom. The parlor stove served that purpose for both front bedrooms on either side, as had the cabin's central fireplace before that. Before the place became a larger house and other rooms were added. He walked around the bed, where she lay on her side with her back toward him.

"You have a nice talk with Franklin, Ben?"

Ben smiled, hearing her voice, and sat on the edge of the bed, placing his hand on her hip. "Yeah, I think I managed to convince him to go back to drinking and carousing."

She drew her hand from under the quilts and slapped his arm. "You did no such thing. Did you have a serious talk with him? Tell me."

"You first. That's why we went there."

She rolled onto her back then sat up, pulling her covered knees within her arms. "I don't know yet. There are things I must learn to tell myself before I can tell another person."

Ben sighed. "Is that all you have to say?"

"You do not judge me. And these are not things to talk about now to someone new in my life. I just need to think about them a while and decide what needs to be said, what should be said."

"Did you tell him about Lydia?"

"No."

"The boy in South Carolina?"

"No."

"Isaac?"

"Yes. I told him about Isaac."

"Simon?" He asked.

She glanced away and sighed. "Yes. That, too, but not the boy."

"That was a lot to tell, but was it enough?"

She returned her gaze to his face. "Almost too

much. It was too much, Ben. For now, it makes the hurt worse. The pain of knowing it hurts. For now, that's all I can discuss with him. I need to know him better."

"Until you can trust him not to judge you?"

"Until...yes. Maybe then."

They drifted into silence, listening to the sound of Mickey coming inside and watching him go through the parlor. Ben removed his boots and stood to slip out of his shirt and trousers, then stepped around to his side of the bed and slid under the covers next to her.

Sonja rolled over to face him. "What about your talk with Franklin? Did it help?"

"I didn't need any help."

"Benjamin Pulaski, you are as stubborn as a mule and half as talkative."

"As is my wife who just admitted as much."

They turned on their sides facing away from each other, neither slipping into the easy breathing of sleep.

Moments later, Ben spoke. "What do you expect me to say?"

"Only what you feel and believe. That is what I tried to share with Franklin."

"You only told him about Isaac and Simon, but not the boy."

"My heart is breaking because my Isaac is dead. And somehow losing him is connected to me killing that boy...and helping to kill Lydia years ago. That is why I could kill the boy. I had done it before."

"And what magic words will he be able to tell you from the Bible?"

"Not what you think, Ben. Not magic or

chanting. Simple words to help the pain...to be less. Didn't talking with him help you at all?"

"It makes matters worse to pick at a scab, Sonja. It makes the wound putrid. It's better to wait until the scab falls off on its own. That's when the skin is healed. You should not..."

"I should not do what?"

He turned to face her, smelling her hair and the scent of her body.

"You should not begrudge yourself for staying alive, Sonja. The world is full of vicious animals and people who are just as vicious that want to kill you for reasons only they know. You should not begrudge yourself for killing a poisonous snake or an attacking wolf. That's what Lydia was. That's what those Klansmen were. Don't waste your worry on one rabid wolf because he wasn't fully grown."

She sat up on the side of the bed, facing only the greater darkness in the corner.

"And Lydia, Ben? How do you describe her?"

"I already have. A poisonous snake. Her poison would have killed you or killed your life with her evil."

"Hasn't it already? It is always so simple for you, isn't it?"

Ben sat up, throwing off the bed covers, and then stood.

"Staying alive is difficult, Sonja, but making the decision is simple. You either live, or you don't. Our son couldn't face his life, so he gave it up."

She stood facing him across the bed, his silhouette outlined by the dying firelight from the parlor stove. "Benjamin Lenz Pulaski, you are full of shit, and you know it. You cried when you remembered Isaac during our Shiva."

"Of course, I cried, but it doesn't change what happened. He is dead, and we are not. I am sorry for his pain and know now how great it was, more than I suspected. But he left his pain behind for his wife and children to shoulder. And you. And me."

She dropped into her rocker in the corner of the room, sobbing. "You are a cruel son of a bitch."

Ben's shoulders sagged. He left the bedroom, crossing the parlor and entering the other front bedroom, closing the door behind him. He laid on the bed with his hands behind his head, then stood facing the closed door, clenching his fists. He muttered to the door in the darkness, speaking to Sonja.

"I did not kill our son. He killed himself, and your God was not there to stop him."

He dropped onto the side of the bed, sitting in the darkness, listening to her cry in the other bedroom.

"Damn you," he said to himself. "Damn you for hurting her again. Damn you."

THURSDAY, DECEMBER 30

It was sleeting when Sonja came from the bedroom wrapped in her wool robe and went to the kitchen. A fire was burning in the kitchen stove, a pot of coffee sat off to the edge of the top, keeping the coffee warm, and Mickey sat at the table.

"Morning, Sonja."

"Morning is almost over, Mickey. I took the laudanum again last night after Ben came home. I guess you overheard our words last night?"

"Kinda' hard not to."

She poured herself a cup of coffee and sat

across from Mickey. "Well, we always told you that you were family. I guess you might as well hear us at our worst."

"Grief is no one's worst, Sonja. And that spat was nothing compared to the anguish the three of us have shared in the past."

She reached over to pat his hand. "And like the best of family, you know what to say to make us feel better."

She pointed her cup toward the dining room and the parlor beyond. "Is he up?"

"Since a while ago. Ben took Garrett with him," Mickey said. "He has to see Judge Jessup again today."

"I thought he went yesterday."

Mickey shook his head. "You folks don't talk enough."

Her unspoken question blossomed across her face.

Mickey set down his coffee cup. "The man who charged Ben for hitting him did not show up yesterday, so the judge ordered everyone to see him today or go to jail. Ben said he was going to stop by Robert Turner's house and pick him up on the way."

"All right. Wait. What? Robert Turner is riding with Ben? Ben is picking him up?"

"Yes. They might go duck hunting together after they see the judge."

Sonja's mouth opened and closed several times without uttering a word, then her face filled with a frown. "Ben and Robert? Hunting together? With guns? Loaded guns?"

"That's what Ben told me."

Sonja's mouth was still open when Mickey left

the kitchen.

In Havre de Grace, Ben stood again on the front porch to Judge Jessup's house. The prosecution and defense had taken positions on either side of the front door, each eyeing the other with suspicion.

The judge's butler opened the front door. "The Judge will see you now," he said, then stood aside to let the visitors enter, pointing them toward the study. Jessup was sitting behind his desk, holding a worn leather-bound journal. His hands were heavily wrinkled and dotted with liver spots. His appearance always brought to Ben's mind a vulture wearing spectacles. Jessup had a hawk beak nose, narrow umber-shaded face, and skinny neck protruding from a wide rumpled white collar. His thick glasses showed his rheumy eyes much larger than they were.

Jessup spoke to Deputy Hopkins. "Everyone here?"

"Yes, Your Honor."

Jessup glanced among the expectant faces. "Who are you, and what are you doing here?"

Lister spoke up. "You told us to be here, Judge. Pulaski hit Bolton for no reason."

Jessup rolled his eyes then scowled at Lister. "This is an informal inquiry, but everyone in this mob needs to identify themselves, so I can keep you and your complaints straight."

Lister opened his mouth to say more.

"Not you," Jessup said, then pointed at Watkins.

"Lester Watkins, Esquire, Your Honor, representing the plaintiff, Mr. Harris Bolton, and material witness Mr. Bartholomew Lister. Both of whom are present."

"George Milton, Esquire, Your Honor, representing the accused, Mr. Benjamin Pulaski, and character witness, Mr. Robert Turner. Both of whom are present."

"Coffee?" Jessup asked.

Watkins and Milton exchanged glances.

"Here 'tis," the butler said as he set the covered cup and saucer on the judge's desk.

Jessup peered at the butler. "Cream and sugar?"

The butler smiled. "One measured ounce of cream and two rounded teaspoons of sugar, sir," he said, then stood beside the judge.

Jessup uncovered the cup, sipped the coffee, and then flicked his hand at the butler, dismissing him. The butler glanced at Robert, rolled his eyes, and left the room.

Robert leaned close to Ben and whispered. "Jessup's butler is my housekeeper's husband."

"Make it plain and simple, Watkins," Jessup said.

"Mr. Bolton ordered service at the Oyster Street Tavern, but the negro there refused to serve him."

"What negro?"

"Franklin Curtis, Your Honor," Watkins said.

"The tavern owner," Milton said.

Jessup sipped his coffee then wagged his finger at Milton. "You'll get your turn."

Watkins continued. "The negro became sullen, and when Mr. Bolton chastised him, Benjamin Pulaski attacked Mr. Bolton."

Watkins motioned to Lister, who stepped

closer to the desk and opened his mouth.

Jessup waved his fingers at Lister. "You already said your piece. Shut up." Then he focused his frown on Milton. "Your turn," Jessup said, shifting his frown to Ben.

"Mr. Bolton was drunk and abusive of the tavern owner," Milton said. "Ben Pulaski interceded on Mr. Curtis's behalf."

Jessup showed a toothy grin eyeing Ben. "And now we address the crux of the issue, Mr. Pulaski. You are well known to be a violent man." He waved the old leather journal. "Your violence was documented by an officer of the law on multiple occasions. Did you once horsewhip Deputy Alexander?"

Milton pulled on Ben's arm before he could speak and stepped forward. "Deputy Alexander was a known liar, Judge."

"He once attacked my wife when I was out of town," Ben said. "I did not know it until later. Otherwise, I would have killed him."

Jessup's face flared plum red. Milton hissed at his client. "Shut up, Ben. Say nothing more."

Jessup sipped from his coffee, allowing a moment for the color to return to his face. He placed his elbows on his desk and rested his chin in the palm of his left hand. "On the contrary, counselor. I want to hear Mr. Pulaski's thoughts."

"Brandon Alexander was an evil man, Judge," Ben said. "Evil doesn't just blossom of a sudden. It grows and becomes worse over time. He was evil while he was a deputy, too. His actions worsened as his power grew when he was appointed provost marshal during the war. That journal is filled with his lies."

Jessup released a heavy sigh and straightened himself within his high-backed chair, holding up the journal. "There is a good deal of verifiable truth in these pages."

"The worse lies are wrapped in the truth," Milton said, but Jessup ignored him, keeping his eyes on Ben.

"Was there a witness to Alexander's attack on your wife, Pulaski?"

"A neighbor. He came to her assistance right after it happened while my wife was bruised and bloodied. Alexander was still in our house."

"What did Alexander say to this man?"

"Alexander had no comments," Ben said. "My wife had hit him in the head with a piece of firewood. He was unconscious at that time."

Lister stepped forward. "Alexander told me about that. The woman had invited him in. My wife knows all about Sonja Pulaski. She is a trollop."

The distance between Ben and Lister was over two yards. Ben's feet were still off the floor when his blow landed against Lister's jaw. The sound of breaking bone echoed in the office. Lister collapsed unconscious into the arms of Watkins and Bolton. Hopkins grabbed Ben's arms, holding him from behind.

"What are your orders, Judge?" Hopkins asked.

In the silent moment that filled the room, all conscious eyes focused on Judge Jessup, whose head was bent over the opened journal in his hands. He raised his face without expression and locked eyes with Ben.

"I was studying the journal brought by Mr. Lister. What happened?"

Hopkins stuttered. All the others stood in

shocked silence.

"I believe Mr. Lister fainted," Robert said. "He seems to have struck his face on the floor when he fell."

Jessup kept his eyes on Ben's but spoke to Bolton. "Mr. Bolton, do you wish to spend time in court regarding Mr. Pulaski's actions toward you."

"I, I wasn't going to do this much, but Bartholomew said I should."

"So, without a plaintiff, Mr. Watkins, do you wish to pursue the matter of the misunderstanding at the tavern?"

"No, sir."

"Everyone out of this office except Mr. Pulaski," Jessup said, then closed the journal and laid it on his desk until only he and Ben remained.

Ben stood in silence, waiting for Jessup to speak while the judge tapped his fingertips on his desk. Finally, the judge motioned to a padded chair across the room, where Ben settled with bated breath. Ben opened his mouth to speak, but the judge waved his finger to silence him.

"My wife and I," Jessup said, "we're good friends of Mamie Stewart and her good friend Sonja Pulaski. I well know of your wife's fine reputation in this town and of the sullied one attributed to Nadja Lister."

He paused a long uncomfortable moment, sipping the last of his coffee.

"I should have you locked up for months for what you just did in my presence. You damned fool."

Ben placed his hands on his knees, wiping the sweat from his palms.

"But..." Jessup said, "my wife would rise from

her grave if I failed to acknowledge the noble reason that drove you to your act just now. You are a brash man, Benjamin Pulaski, and you have not improved with age. I have known you as such for over thirty years, and I will tell you this: If Bartholomew Lister had said that name in referring to my wife, I would have killed him on the spot."

The judge glanced toward a portrait of a smiling young woman above the fireplace, drew in a deep breath, and slowly released it. "In honor of my wife's memory, I am sending you home to yours."

"Thank you, Your Honor."

Jessup motioned to the portrait. "You should thank Matilda Gatton Jessup. We once owned nine beagles because she could not tolerate the thought of taking one away from his brothers and sisters. It is well that I am a judge and not a hog farmer, Pulaski. Else we would have been penniless and surrounded by thousands of pigs...each with a name of its own."

Jessup stood and offered Alexander's journal to Ben. As Ben accepted it, the judge spoke again. "Now, get out of my damned office."

The sleet had stopped, but the clouds remained dark and sullen without even an area of lighter gray to mark the location of the sun. The furled sails were spotted with mildew and heavy with dampness from several days without sunshine. Tobias had resigned himself to be the third crew member of the *Jester*. Although Jimmy had greater ship experience and Garrett the nerve of an experienced soldier, Tobias had mastered the ever-changing world of commerce on the Chesapeake Bay. He knew ducks, he knew oysters, and he had honed that knowledge into a successfully growing company, one he desired to develop further. He dared not leave it to others as he prepared to become married.

Tobias's tonger boats shuttled from the rich oyster beds inside the Bush River to the deeper water at the mouth where the *Jester* was anchored. The water was cold but free of ice, and the oysters were going to be perfect. It was only minutes into the afternoon, and four of his boats had already come alongside almost top-heavy with their first loads of oysters, while the other two headed toward him with their second. The *Jester's* cargo hold was nearly half full, and there remained sufficient time to draw third loads from each boat. Then they could rush before the wind back to Havre de Grace in time to meet the six o'clock train to Philadelphia. He was going to make a small fortune that day. His grin as the boats neared was boy-like in its evident joy.

Jimmy nudged his arm and pointed farther out in the bay. "Another ship is coming."

"Is it that log canoe again?"

"Nah," Garrett spoke nearby. "Bow looks like this'n. She's sitin' deep in the water."

Jimmy frowned. "I don't like the looks of it. She's carrying every sail aloft the mast and rigging will take. She's in a hurry to get to us."

Tobias watched the oncoming sloop a moment. "Jimmy, could you bring your revolver up on deck?"

Garrett squinted as he peered at the sloop. She's got five, maybe six men on her deck and flying a Calvert flag. That's a Maryland government boat. Customs maybe? Oyster Police?"

"Well, we're not doing anything illegal," Tobias said.

Waiting was short as the other sloop came toward them with full sails drawing all the wind power they could hold and only spilled the wind and lowered sails at the last moment. She kissed up alongside the *Jester* with precision.

Jimmy smiled. "Damn. They're good."

A man with a gold-colored strip across his cap's bill stood near the bow. He had an insignia of sorts near his hat's peak and a badge of the same symbol on his coat.

"What ship is this, and what state are you?" He called out.

"*Jester*, out of Havre de Grace," Jimmy said.

"I am Lieutenant Stringer of the sloop *Delilah,*

for the Maryland State Oyster Police. Are you dredging? You must have a license to dredge and may not dredge in any Maryland river."

"We are not dredging, sir."

"Then you must be a buy boat. I will see your license for that at once."

"This boat is not a buy boat," Tobias said. "She is in legal cooperation with those tonger boats on the river and will carry their cargo to port to be sold there to the evening train."

The Lieutenant glanced along the *Jester*'s deck and commented to one of his crew, a black sailor who dashed to the stern.

"I know this boat and its captain," the Lieutenant said, speaking to Tobias, "but I do not know you. What kind of cooperation is that, mister?" Stringer asked.

"I own the tonger boats," Tobias said, pointing into the mouth of the river, "And the men working them are my employees. The owner of this sloop, Sonja Pulaski, has agreed to let the ship be used for this purpose to capture more productive time for my boats over the oyster beds, for which I will pay her crew for their time."

Stringer eyed Jimmy. "That true Cap'n?"

Jimmy nodded yes.

"I'm coming aboard," Lieutenant. Stringer said and hopped over the gunnele onto the *Jester*'s deck, approaching Tobias. "Then you have licenses for your boats?"

"Yes, sir," Tobias said, reaching into his coat to withdraw a waterproof canvas pouch and showing the papers to Stringer.

The man examined the papers. "You Tobias Bond?"

"I am."

The black sailor stayed on the police boat deck but stepped near to Stringer. "No dredger chain, sir, or any boom in the stern that could haul one up."

Stringer faced Jimmy. "There's a Virginia dredger been seen in these waters of late. Shallow draft. You see her?"

"A log canoe named the *Virginia Owl*," Tobias said. "She came in here and almost sank one of my boats yesterday. The man working it had to jump in the water to save himself."

Stringer spoke directly to Tobias. "We'll take the *Owl* if we come across her. I have the authority to impound any out-of-state vessel raiding our oyster beds."

"Don't think he'll be back anytime soon," Tobias said, nodding toward Garrett. "That man shot the *Owl's* captain in his hand."

Stringer scoffed. "Oystering is big business. He'll just wrap his hand and come back for more of our oysters."

"I think not, Lieutenant," Garrett said. "He were groping his nuts to us when I shot his hand."

The crew of the *Delilah* chuckled, and Stringer shared a smile, speaking to Garrett. "What did you use?"

Garrett pointed a crooked finger at Jimmy. "That revolver Captain Finley has."

Stringer kept his smile. "What was the distance?"

"Thirty yards, give or take. He were on the move opposite us."

Stringer folded his arms in front of this chest. "If you ever want to join us, you go to Annapolis harbor and ask for Commander Hunter Davidson.

He's my superior."

Garrett smiled and nodded his head. "I knowd him. We served together on the *Virginia* at Hampton Roads. He's as fine a gunner as either navy had."

Stringer glanced between Jimmy and Tobias, then returned the canvas pouch to Tobias and nodded to him. "Mr. Bond." Then he saluted Jimmy. "Captain Finley," then turned back to Garrett, pointing his finger, "Ask for Commander Hunter Davidson."

Once back on board the *Delilah*, Stringer removed his hat in salute, primarily at Garrett, as did all of his crew. They chuckled as they raised their sails for the arduous tacking ahead of them to make distance southward against the wind for the twenty-five nautical miles back to Annapolis. It would be dark before they reached home.

Tobias turned toward Garrett. "Are you going to join the Oyster Police?"

"Nah," he said. "I ain't gonna get shot at over oysters. Soon as winter's over, I'm going back to the canal."

By late afternoon the *Jester's* hold was full of oysters, and three of the tongers were rowing to their camp on the western shore of the Bush River. They would begin gathering more oysters at first light the next day. Two came aboard the ship to help transfer the oysters to barrels when they reached Havre de Grace. The *Jester's* sails filled out with a boom, and she leaned with the wind, dashing north up the bay as if her holds were empty.

Once back in town, Tobias drafted his cab driver and ducking guides to assist the others. The men, including Tobias and Garrett, worked feverously to pack the oysters into barrels for the train and deliver them to the railroad station just as the train arrived. The railroad clerk was almost giddy over the quality and quantity of the oysters, offering only the slightest haggling in his attempt to reduce the earlier offer. With the railroad draft in his pocket, Tobias bought supper and the first two beers for his crew, except one. Garrett preferred to walk back to his barge in Lapidum for a quiet dinner by himself.

In Lapidum, Ben and Mickey stood on the steamer dock that jutted into the Susquehanna River as the dreary sky dimmed to a darker gray. The angry ripples of the river were higher each day, slapping the dock posts, splashing water onto the planks. Seagulls were perched atop the pilings at the far end of the dock from the men, tucking their heads low to keep warm.

Ben glared at the water, his hands stuffed in his coat pockets. "I've never seen the river this high in the winter."

"I thought if I came here, Ben, I'd get a sense of something I needed to do, but the foreboding sticks in my mind and no idea of what to do about it comes to me."

"Don't be in a hurry to leave, Mickey. We're glad to have you here."

"I hoped I could do something to help, but I'm nothing more than the Raven Mr. Poe wrote about. I've only brought you and Sonja worry."

Ben turned to face him. "So, your premonition didn't go away after Sonja spoke to the preacher?"

"Nothing changed," Mickey said. "The feeling remains, nagging at me. It's like there is something

I'm supposed to do; to protect you two, but I don't know what that something is."

"Well, at least Sonja seems to be a little more at peace. Maybe your being here helped that to happen."

One of the seagulls screeched, jumping into the air trying to fly away, but the Bald Eagle swooped down and grabbed him in his claws, carrying him high into the trees on the opposite shore.

"Didn't know eagles ate other birds," Mickey said.

"They eat everything," Ben said. "Especially in the winter. Not as many fish and even eagles can't see them below churning water. Still, I believe seagulls are on the bottom of their supper menu."

Mickey watched the eagle climb higher in the air with its prey.

"I punched out Bartholomew Lister today. Think I broke his jaw."

Mickey spun around, gawking at Ben. "Does that judge know about that?"

"Yes. Did it in front of him."

"Where? Why?"

"In Judge Jessup's house, because he—"

"In front of the judge?"

"Lister called Sonja by a crude name."

Mickey looked away, then back into Ben's eyes, his own wide in amazement. He held his hands out in question.

"You are insane, Benjamin. How are you not in jail at this very moment?"

"The judge pretended he didn't see it happen. Sent the others out. Told me I was a damned fool."

"A damned lucky fool."

"Mickey, I didn't even realize I had done it

until I saw Lister fall back into his lawyer's arms."

"His lawyer was there, too? Good God, Ben! Do you want to go to prison...again?"

Ben gazed out at the water rushing by, swirling over boulders now hidden below the undulating surface.

"Sonja's reputation saved me from prison," Ben said. "The judge's wife had known Sonja and Mamie, and he let me go because Sonja's name was sullied by an insult even he would begrudge."

"Does Sonja know?"

"Oh, hell no, Mickey. That's why we're talking out here."

Mickey continued to stare wide-eyed and open-mouthed at Ben.

Ben shrugged his shoulders and hung his head. "I know. I know."

Mickey's face drew into a frown. "Maybe it's you I need to protect Sonja from. Maybe you are her darkness."

Ben gazed out at the river again. "Maybe you're right, Mickey."

"I shouldn't have said that, Ben."

"You rode twenty-five miles in the cold because you were worried about us. And I don't doubt that I have brought some darkness into Sonja's life through my thoughtless acts. But if you are still sensing a darkness over both of us, there is something else. Please stay with us a while longer and help us see it.

Mickey turned to walk away, heading for the bridge arching over the empty canal, huddled within his heavy coat.

Ben remained on the dock, his eyes fixed on the troubled water. In his mind, he saw her from the departing ship as she stood on the pier waving bravely, standing with their two sons. She was pregnant then, but neither knew it when Ben sailed away. The voyage to China was planned for nine months, but it was three years before he returned to find her destitute, indebted, and living in a shack in the back yard of another man. Yes. He was her darkness.

FRIDAY, DECEMBER 31

Harris Bolton lay low in his skiff, its sides barely eight inches above the water. The barrel of his punt gun was aimed just a few inches above the waterline, resting on a mount at the bow of the boat. The punt gun was far more than he could raise and hold, but it had a half-pound of black powder and a full pound of number six shot with the loaded barrel. That would give him over three thousand lead balls $1/10^{th}$ of an inch, each spread over his muzzle fire. A single shot would net him a hundred to a hundred fifty ducks with a single firing.

He waited for the out-of-towners to make the first shot. They usually shot too soon and stirred up the ducks. Then he would wipe the horizon clean with his punt gun. The upper bay was filled with resting ducks at sunrise. The surface was black with them, even as the morning light filtered through the gray clouds that plagued them these past few weeks, one could see the massive swarm of ducks coating the bay.

Two ducks rose into the sky, disturbed by the cough of an amateur hunter, then followed by the wasted volleys from his boat. That blast released a mass of rising ducks blackening the gray sky until it was full of targets. A punt gun could not miss. The explosion of Bolton's gun was unimportant to the cacophony of Canvasbacks reaching for the sky. They were caught in their frenzy to fly by the blast of pellets from the punt gun, dropping them from the sky in a torrent of falling feathered bodies, splashing onto the surface of the water. Bolton ignored the hisses, boos, and insults yelled from duck hunter boats as he paddled among the horde of dead ducks scooping up their bodies for restaurant sales and butcher shops in town.

"Go to hell," Bolton responded to the duck hunters, who called out to him in anger. "You are only here for sport, in your fancy shooting clothes. I'm making a living."

Bolton rowed along the shoreline off Water Street. Seeking the dock near one of his buyers. He would have to visit several taverns to sell all his ducks. He glanced up the hill beyond Water Street toward the backs of buildings that faced Oyster Street above. He focused on the back of the Oyster Street Tavern.

"Franklin Curtis, you uppity bastard. You could buy my whole take just for your customers today and tomorrow, and I'd be done. Maybe even go out for a second load. Uppity bastard, you won't buy from me."

Rebecca Curtis balanced the covered urn within her right arm as she tapped on the office door to Lister Funeral Services. The business occupied half of the Lister house with a separate entrance. Nadja Lister answered the door with a scowl that quickly softened, almost but not quite coming to a smile.

"Miss Curtis, may I help you?"

Rebecca shifted the urn among her hands. "Papa asked me to bring this oyster stew. He heard about Mr. Lister's injury and sends his condolences. He thought this would not only ease his pain but maybe lift some of your added burden of caring for him and the business."

"Yes. Well, no one realizes the amount of work we shoulder to care for the dead and their family. Come in. Follow me through the parlor and dining room to the kitchen, though I am not sure how much Bartholomew will be able to take. He cannot open his mouth."

The kitchen was spartanly supplied with dishes and utensils, each spaced precisely the same distance apart, aligned in perfect order, although the two items at each end appeared unwashed. Nadja pointed to the kitchen table.

"Oh, Papa sent a new bamboo straw that your husband can sip the broth through. He says–"

"Just set it here," Nadja said. "Tell your father that Mr. and Mrs. Lister appreciate the thought."

Dust motes rose from the table surface as Rebecca set down the urn. Nadja motioned Rebecca toward the rear door from the kitchen. Off from the kitchen, Bartholomew Lister stepped from his tiny office with his nose held high in the air. A bandage wrapped around his head, pulling his jaw up and inward. He struggled to speak through gritted teeth. "That smellss wwonderful."

Rebecca gave him a bright smile, "Oyster Stew with goat's milk."

"Mmmm. Franklinn makess the besst," He said.

Bartholomew held a bone in his hand, and as he stepped into the kitchen toward the urn, he leaned forward to place the bone on the table.

Nadja spoke in a harsh tone. "Not on my kitchen table."

"It's clean," he said, sounding as he had said that many times before.

He waved the small bone toward Rebecca. "My hobby. I study ancient relics, ancient bones. When graves are dug, I investigate the soil before those newly passed are interred."

Rebecca peered at the bone in his hand, and he brought it closer to her, so she could examine it."

"Oh, really, Bartholomew," Nadja said. "Take that rotten bone from my kitchen."

"It's not rotten, Nadja. It is ancient. And it is clean. Just dark from being in the ground so long."

"I want nothing from the ground," she said.

"You eat potatoes, dearest. The bones lie with them."

A scowl settled on her face, and she opened her mouth to speak, but a knock rapped at the front door.

"That should be Mrs. Metzer," Nadja said. "Her two daughters passed from fever last night. She will be wanting a double funeral."

Nadja nearly ran toward the office.

Bartholomew peered after Nadja then smiled at Rebecca, pointing at the urn. "If you will ladle some into a mug from next to the sink there, I can sip it in my office while we talk about bones."

Rebecca glanced back toward the route back to the office, where voices mumbled in sadness.

Bartholomew turned back into his office. "She will be busy trying to sell Mrs. Metzer the Taj

Mahal. We have plenty of time to talk about bones. Come look."

Like a boychild showing his treehouse, Bartholomew told Rebecca of his early studies in Anthropology and his childhood experience touching a dinosaur bone. His excitement of discussing his favored interests allowed him to ignore the pain in his jaw for the moment.

He held the mug gingerly to his lips, spilling a few drops of the stew on his chin bandage. Rebecca grabbed the bamboo straw from the kitchen table and handed it to him. He peered at it closely. "A flute?"

"No, sir. It is a straw for taking liquids. Papa says Army hospitals had them to help soldiers with jaw wounds."

Bart put his lips to the straw and drew some liquid, but much dripped from his mouth.

"You need to put the straw inside your lips," Rebecca said.

Bart hesitated.

"It is clean," Rebecca said. "None of us have used it."

Bart shrugged his shoulders and wrapped his lips around the straw, then filled his mouth. He gulped his mouthful, then gave her a wide smile under sparkling eyes, still speaking through gritted teeth.

"How amazing. I have been starving, taking only a drop of this or that. You have saved me, young lady." He swallowed another mouthful. "Now about these bones."

Rebecca leaned forward to observe.

"So, this bone, it is a rib bone, from high in the chest. Quite likely from an ancient native Indian who lived on this very ground where this town stands today."

"From here in town?" she asked.

He chuckled. "There was no town here, not as you think of it. Maybe a village of a few people living in huts made of branches and animal hides."

"My good friend discovered some bones in his garden," she said. "Would you like to look at them to see if they are ancient Indian?"

"Oh, I would love to do that. I have found no one in this town interested in such things except old Doctor Harper, who passed away a few years ago. Yes. Yes. Bring them to me anytime."

"I will be back after lunch," she said.

"Wonderful. Bring me more old bones to examine."

Rebecca refilled his mug before leaving through the rear kitchen door and returning to her father's tavern, eager to speak with Tobias. After the lunchtime rush, Rebecca took a walk to Bourbon Street to visit Tobias at his office. Samuel, the cabriolet driver, spotted her coming down the road and slowed his cab near her.

"Beggin yer pardon, missy, but if yer lookin for Mr. Bond, he's out on the water all day collecting oysters down bay."

She smiled and thanked him, then after hesitating a moment, she continued to Tobias's office. Rebecca's handwriting was excellent, and she wrote most of Tobias's contracts, so she had a key to his office. Tobias had once shown her the bones during a rare Sunday after church when they found themselves briefly together in his quarters. Tobias had appeared genuinely interested in the story of the bones dug from his garden.

"He will want to know," she said, stooping to pick up the box, "He will be so excited to learn what Mr. Lister has to say about these bones. I can't wait to tell him."

Bartholomew had just settled back into his chair at his desk when Rebecca tapped on the kitchen door. Nadja had gone upstairs for an afternoon nap in preparations for evening services at the Metzers.

"Ah, Miss Curtis," Bartholomew said as he opened the door, spotting the wooden box. "You have brought me a treasure, have you?" "

Rebecca hesitated. "Um, sir, you had mentioned earlier that you might be interested in looking at some old bones my friend found in his garden."

"Come in child."

Accepting the box from her hands, his eyes widened. "Oh, yes. And what a lovely box. Surely that was not in the ground holding the bones."

"No, sir. After my friend found the bones, he cleaned them off and placed them in this box. He thought they were human."

"Well, young lady, bring them into my office, and let's have a look at them."

She set the box on his desk, and he ran his fingers over the lid.

"A very sturdy box, it is. No one does such excellent work anymore. Casket work, I think. How appropriate for something to hold old bones." He pulled the lid open. "It's sealed quite well."

Lister lit a second lamp over his desk, pulled out a large magnifying glass, and excitedly settled into his chair to examine the bones, turning them over and over, studying them.

He glanced up from the glass at Rebecca. "And you say the ivory button was buried with the bones."

"Yes, sir. That's what Toby, that is Mr. Bond told me."

His eyes lingered on her face a moment longer. "Toby? Bond? Tobias Bond? This was found on his property? At the back of...of what was the Stewart property, Mamie Stewart's?"

"Yes, sir."

"Mmm. No cemetery ever near there."

He refocused his attention through the magnifying glass, speaking to himself and the bones more so than to Rebecca. "Definitely human. Piece of skull here, jaw bone with a few teeth remaining, and the head of the humerus. Definitely human. And I think the same human. Most likely female. Now for age."

He brought the lamp closer, then laid the skull fragment on a dish and dropped a liquid from a vial. He rubbed the piece with a spotted cloth.

"Not been in the ground as long as the other Indians I have found. Don't think she was Indian or slave. Teeth are in too good a condition for that."

He sat up straight in his chair and patted Rebecca's hand.

"I'm afraid the pain in my jaw is getting the best of me now. I would like to study this some more tomorrow. May I keep it overnight?"

"Um. All right. Yes, sir."

Watkins meandered through his mansion in town, once the Binterfield Mansion, sipping his morning coffee after a pleasant breakfast, visiting the many rooms so eloquently furnished and arranged. He would have never attained the wealth on his own to live in such lavish surroundings. Before Lydia moved to Spain, he had a simple apartment off a service lane in town and a modest office, barely acquiring sufficient fees to pay for both. Lydia gave him permission to set up his office within a corner of her mansion when she moved to Spain. Then Lydia supported him with generous retainers until she died there. She became his sole client. Recruiting new ones was proving a challenge.

Now, his bank balance, created by those retainers, was draining away. In the spring, he may be forced to let his servants go. The thought of cooking his own food, and worse, the idea of emptying his own nightjar, was repugnant. He had hoped the lawsuit against Pulaski could remedy his financial worries, but Bolton's withdrawal dashed those hopes. Pulaski presented himself as a rustic ruffian, with his better-than-thou rejection to showing his affluence. The man owned a seagoing schooner, ten canal barges, and the sloop his wife claimed to run. And rather than building on Union Avenue in Havre de Grace, he shunned the town, staying in the village of Lapidum.

He has plenty of money, Lester thought.

Still, after the well-witnessed attack of Bartholomew Lister by Ben Pulaski in the presence of Judge Andrew Jessup, that suit should be an easy win. Especially if taken away from Judge Jessup and litigated in Bel Air, where Pulaski was no favored son.

I need to visit Bart Lister to ensure his well-being after his horrible attack by Pulaski...and to ensure his intent to sue.

Lester ambled into his office to sort through his mail received yesterday and days before but not yet opened. One ignored letter from weeks before was an invitation to attend a Bon Voyage party in Philadelphia with a law school classmate. His schoolmate had been appointed to the U.S. State Department by President Grant as acting third undersecretary for the Consulate in Madrid.

Spain, he thought. *Did Lydia leave more property there? An estate, perhaps? It could be sitting there waiting to be claimed. And I already have written authority from her to settle her estate.*

He smiled and withdrew a paper from his desk drawer, dipped his pen in the ink well to write the wording for a telegram. He hesitated, flipping open the out-of-date invitation, mumbling to himself. "What is his name? Ah, yes. Harold."

Dear Harold, he began.

After mailing the letter, Watkins tapped on the side door to the Lister residence. The house was modest of unpainted wood, offering a well-worn door to the private dwelling of Bartholomew and Nadja. The highly polished walnut door that faced the street provided the public entrance to the funeral business. He heard the shrill voice of Nadja ring inside the house calling to Bartholomew, but no one opened the door. Watkins waited another moment then began to turn away when Bart opened the door, his head bandaged around his jaw and a liquid stain in the fabric under his chin. Bart carried a napkin in his hand as he opened the door, speaking through clenched teeth.

"Mr. Watkins," he said in greeting, motioning

for the lawyer to come in.

They sat together on unpadded wooden chairs in the sparse parlor, Bart dabbing at his lips with the napkin. The Listers rarely entertained non-paying guests, hence there were no wall hangings or doilies to be found in the parlor. The side table, standing perfectly centered between the two chairs, sported several nicks and scratches surrounding a chipped oil lantern. Only the ancient, scrolled iron stove holding a meager fire facing the chairs confirmed the room as a parlor.

"Having oyster stew broth through a bamboo straw," Bart said, "spilt some dashing to answer the door."

"Sorry to cause you to rush, Bart. Just came by to check on you and bring you some papers to sign."

"That is kind of you, sir. More witness papers?"

"No, not these. Bolton took the coward's way out while you absorbed Pulaski's rage. No, this is to sue Pulaski for all he's worth."

"Good. Son-of-a-bitch. Do you think Jessup will do anything?"

Watkins opened his valise and withdrew several documents. "These papers will initiate the suit against Pulaski and plead for a writ to have the case heard in Bel Air."

"What will we get?"

"With his ships, barges, cargoes, and farm, he is worth well over one hundred thousand dollars, probably more."

"Let's go into my office where I have pen and ink."

Passing through the kitchen, Watkins inhaled the aroma of the oyster stew. "That smells wonderful, Bart. Your wife's recipe?"

Lister shuddered his shoulders and shook his head no. "She is more at home with receipts than recipes. No, that lovely stew is from Franklin Curtis. He sent it by his daughter out of kindness."

"Ah," Watkins said. "He makes his with goat's milk," glancing into the empty urn. "I will have to stop by there before I ride to Bel Air."

Along the waterfront, Harris Bolton had sold the last of his ducks, walking away with only half the money he expected. The United States Hotel refused to purchase any because of his recent experience with another patron, and the Nixon Hotel complained of the condition many of the ducks were in and would not pay market rates.

"I know damned well they will charge full price for the meals, though."

He bought a bottle of cheap whiskey at a mercantile store on Market Street, then ambled to DuBois' coal wharf, sitting on an empty crate near the edge. In the distance, a sloop made its way toward Havre de Grace, running before the wind with bulging sails. Bolton stood to watch it come in.

"Damned if it ain't one of the Pulaski boats. Heard they're hauling oysters."

He finished the bottle as the sloop angled toward the wharf, but not where they usually tied up. Right there in front of him.

"Got special permission to tie up closer to the train station," he said.

He threw the empty bottle into the water before the bow of the sloop, then leaned against a post peeing off the dock as the ship came close. Someone on deck yelled at him, but he made a crude gesture toward them then turned to walk away.

"Think I'll have some oyster stew," he said.

Moments later, he stumbled through the door to the Oyster Street Tavern. He made his way to the short bar where he liked to perch while watching the pretty negress waiting tables there. He was not quite to his usual chair when Franklin Curtis marched out from the kitchen to confront him.

"Not tonight, Bolton. I don't want you in here causing trouble."

"I won't cause–"

"No, you won't because you won't be in here."

"I'm a white man, and I can go anywhere–"

Another man grabbed Bolton by his collar from behind and turned him around.

"Evenin, Dep-ty," Bolton said.

"Bolton, you go home and sleep it off," Hopkins said. "You can come back tomorrow."

Hopkins escorted Bolton outside and placed him on a bench facing the abandoned bank across the street.

"Now you stay out here a while, then go home," Hopkins said, then returned inside the tavern to join his wife for oyster stew. He smiled to himself knowing they would enjoy second helpings, and it would be free that night for getting rid of Bolton.

<hr>

In the silver twilight that might have been golden had the sun shown, Ben and Sonja met with Robert and Elizabeth Turner at the Oyster Street Tavern. A man sat snoozing on the bench at the edge of the street.

Robert spoke as Rebecca escorted them to their table. "Ben and I thought it would be more enjoyable to meet here without either spouse having to bother with dinners." Robert and Ben hung the ladies' coats together.

Elizabeth whispered to Sonja as the men hung the coats, "Are they both in trouble at home?"

Sonja grinned at the conspiratorial tone. "Ben must feel that way," she said. "He has donned a neckcloth and his best coat without me requiring it. He thinks a neckcloth and a hanging are similar choices."

Elizabeth snickered. "And Robert gave the housekeeper the evening off before telling me of our engagement. A peremptory strike, I believe they call it in the military."

The reputation of Franklin's oyster stew had flown around town, and the tavern was busy with hungry customers. Franklin produced unending pots of stew while Rebecca and two cousins hurried from table to table, delivering the liquid gold. Several women among the customers begged for the recipe; some even offered cash. But Franklin turned them down with humility admitting the recipe had been his wife's, and he could not let it go.

Even during Franklin's busy evening, he had managed to make earnest eye contact with Ben on several occasions. Robert was quick to notice Franklin's motion. After his third helping, he begged leave to return home to loosen his trousers, to Elizabeth's embarrassment. Elizabeth presented a pleasant mixture of English formality but tempered with a personal nature that Sonja found appealing.

As they parted for the evening, Elizabeth gave Sonja a friendly hug saying. "We should get together for tea, so we can complain about our husbands. It is an English sport, you know." She followed that with a wink.

Franklin and Rebecca were inside collecting the last dirty dishes from the tables and putting out lamps. The cousins had already left for home. Ben and Sonja re-entered the tavern, where Franklin asked Ben into the kitchen and suggested perhaps Rebecca could escort Sonja home. The ladies rebelled and decided to spend some time together chatting in a corner of the tavern where it was still warm.

Sonja patted Rebecca's hand as she spoke. "Since Tobias has finally admitted to your father that he sees me as an aunt, then soon you will be my niece."

There began a conversation that drifted into its own universe, long known to women and frequently ignored by men, to their loss.

In the kitchen, Franklin addressed Ben in great sincerity.

"Promise to hear me out, Ben. Please. And give me answers from your heart, not from your ass."

Ben smiled. "You're a one-of-a-kind preacher, Franklin Curtis. I admire your directness, even as I disagree–"

"You're disagreeing, and I haven't even spoken."

"We've already talked about this, preacher. You and I."

"Can a man only speak of it once?"

"What you are going to say has been said thousands of times, Franklin. And thousands of times it made no difference, except to those who believe in fantasies, and even then, only for brief moments."

Ben's voice rose, echoing into the customer area. Sonja shook her head, saying, "That sounds like Ben's 'talking-to-a-traveling-preacher' voice."

Rebecca smiled. "Papa can get persistent when he has the spirit. Your Ben has a fight on his hands."

Franklin stood with his arms folded over his chest. "You evade my questions, Ben. You promised to answer fully and completely. Are you going back on your word?"

"You received my word through trickery. You approached me as a friend but turned into a preacher on me."

"Can I not be both?"

"Only if I agree to that arrangement, but you asked me as a friend."

"Ben, we had part of this conversation before."

"Then ask me point-blank. What is it you really

want to know?"

"I've been asking you, Ben. Do you believe there is a God?"

"And I've answered that the best I can."

"Answer me again, Ben."

"I've seen no evidence of an almighty God, Preacher, and I've seen decades of evidence where there was no such thing, no hint of such a thing. If he exists, he gives not a whit for this world nor the people in it. He allows far too many of them to suffer and die with his back turned on them, even those who foolishly pray to him as they are butchered like farm animals."

Ben's words echoed throughout the tavern. Sonja brought her hand to her mouth, sharing a sad expression with Rebecca, who cast her eyes down. They turned away to watch beyond the windows to the lamplighter going from lamp to lamp along Oyster Street. As the lamplighter walked beyond the last lamp, another form leaned against the lamppost across the street from the tavern. A man's face brightened from his match as he lit his cigar.

Franklin's baritone voice matched Ben's, "God sent his only son to earth to help us believe, Benjamin. Jesus performed miracles to prove God's love."

Ben's voice roared. "If he was God's son, then his father sent him here to be butchered. Just like I sent my son to be butchered on the battlefield, and my son's torment drove him to leave his family, to take his own life! To blow his brains out alone in the wilderness, begging for your God to help him. What kind of God can do such a thing to his son? What kind of father can do that!"

Ben grabbed pots and pans nearby and

smashed them across the room.

Sonja walked toward the kitchen, tears streaming down her cheeks. Rebecca stayed in her seat, mumbling quiet prayers for her father and Ben.

"I am sure God forgave him," Franklin said.

"Bull shit! Franklin. Suicide does not earn forgiveness, isn't that what the Bible says?"

"Not in those words, Ben. But that is the belief of Catholics."

"Then damn God as a trickster, speaking out of both sides of his mouth!"

Ben slammed his fist on a counter, kicking a pot that had fallen to the floor.

"You cannot mean such a thing, Ben. Try to calm yourself."

"I am giving you your goddamned straight answer. Free of evasion and to the goddamned point, Franklin!"

"Are you not fearful of going to hell for such words, Benjamin?"

Ben laughed. "I have no fear of going to Hell if there is even such a place, which I suspect not."

"But what if there is, Ben. What then?"

Ben took in a deep breath then slowly released it to calm himself. "If there is a Hell, then there is a Heaven. And if there is a Heaven, I am not afraid of Hell."

"How can you be so confident of such a thing?"

Ben took in another deep breath, then wiped his eyes with his shirt sleeve and pointed at Franklin.

"I know this without a doubt. I am loved by Sonja Pulaski. Why she does, I don't know, but she loves me despite myself. And I know that woman is going to heaven...and I will follow behind her like a wet stray dog following an angel. And God, if there is one, will just shake his head and smile at her, letting me follow her in."

Franklin smiled at Ben and sighed.

"And I will tell you this, Franklin Curtis, I do not care to go anywhere that Sonja will not be. Now or later."

Ben leaned against the counter, spent from his comments, staring at the floor.

Franklin spoke with a dry voice. "I have nothing to say to you now, Ben, but I do believe you just spoke to God himself."

Sonja came into the kitchen, stepping next to Ben, and placed the palm of her hand against his cheek as tears continued to stream down her own.

"Benjamin Pulaski," she said, lifting his chin to face her, "you old ornery rascal, there are times when you terrify me, when you drive me insane or make me furious at you. But of all the things I ever heard you say, what you just told Franklin has laid my heart in your hands until the end of time." she took his hand in hers.

"Well," Ben said, standing straight, meeting her eyes, and with the slightest quiver in his voice, "that'll do just fine."

"Let's go home," she said.

Ben directed the buggy's horse toward the canal basin with Sonja close to his side. She spread the heavy wool blanket over their laps. Lanterns on the barges, the mule barn, and the Lockhouse would give the Pulaskis enough light to get across the swing bridge and onto the towpath, where Ben would need to light the buggy lantern. There were no stars in the cloud-filled sky. Points of light in the darkness coming across the river from Perryville winked out momentarily as a boat far from shore passed before them going upriver, pushed against the river current by the rising tide.

Ben stopped to light the lantern across the swing bridge and then let the mare continue her own pace on the pathway she had traveled day or night uncounted times over the five years they had owned her. The horse's leisurely gait rhythm and the buggy springs' mild rocking relaxed Ben and Sonja into a shared silence comfortable within long marriages. Silence, except for the horse's steps and the river slapping the outer sides of the towpath, coupled with the warmth within the blanket, offered peace from the emotional turmoil they had in the tavern.

On the far end of the basin, just before the towpath curved to enter the canal proper, the horse abruptly stopped, snorting, startled by something she heard or saw. Ben leaned forward, peering into the faint lantern light lying on the towpath. A light far brighter than a noon sun swept across the towpath. Instantly the horse's head and shoulders were a bloody mass in the explosion that ripped through the air, pushing Ben down off the buggy and pulling Sonja down with him wrapped in the same blanket. The blast had come from the river. Ben pulled Sonja with him down into the muddy canal, where they lay against the bank.

He asked in a forced whisper, "Are you hurt?", as he felt along her body.

"No," she said.

He put his hand over her mouth. She pulled it away and spoke in a whisper. "It was like a train rushing by right before my face. What was it?"

"A punt gun."

They lay against the bank a minute listening but heard nothing except the ringing in their ears from the explosion. Moments later, when precious night vision began returning, Ben took her by the hand and whispered close to her ear.

"We need to stay in the canal until we can be sure the shooter has gone. But we need to move beyond here and into the trees in case he comes ashore with a different gun."

Ben led her within the muddy canal, staying close to the towpath side and grateful for the cold evening that had stiffened the mud. After traveling a quarter-mile, they stopped to listen again for a long moment, then hearing nothing worrisome, they climbed onto the towpath.

They had walked less than another mile when they met Mickey coming toward them. He carried a lantern and Ben's revolver stuck in his waistband.

"So glad you two are all right. Was that an explosion I heard?'

"A punt gun," Ben said. "Killed our mare, but she stopped short of putting us in the center of the shot."

"Mickey," Sonja said, "How did you get down here so fast?"

"I was already on the towpath when I heard the explosion."

She hugged him, and Ben patted his back.

Well after dark, the *Jester* unloaded her oysters and crated them to the railroad station. The six o'clock train had already passed through, but the eight o'clock train was just as eager for oysters as was the earlier one. The price per barrel was not as high, but still higher than the usual price, even for winter. New Year's Day for 1870 was a monumental celebration in the north, five years after the end of the devastating war and the first full year of prosperity under President Grant, the victor of that war. Even as southern veterans of that war lingered by the train stations for handouts and brief opportunities for work paid in pennies or biscuits, or perhaps shoes. Befriending Garrett was having a profound impact on Tobias's thoughts regarding old enemies.

Weary from the long day of physical toil in cold, wet weather, Tobias made his way to his quarters on Bourbon Street. A deafening gunshot echoed in the night, reverberating among the trees and houses. He halted to listen for more, but all remained quiet. He unlocked the door to his office, almost stumbling through the front room, not bothering to light the little coal stove there or seeing the note from Rebecca, but on to his bed in the back room. There to strip off damp cold wool socks from cold toes and rush into flannel long johns, and then to snuggle gratefully under thick quilts and heavy wool blankets for a night of warm sleep well-earned.

Lester Watkins stopped by Bartholomew and Nadja Lister's home on his return to Havre de Grace from Bel Air. Nadja opened the door holding a lamp and peering out with a frown, but that was her natural countenance, so Lester took no offense by it.

"I have good news for your husband," Lester said. "His lawsuit against Benjamin Pulaski will be heard by the circuit court in Bel Air."

Her smile was toothy, more like a hunting dog being fed fresh meat. She escorted Lester to Bartholomew's office, where her husband typically lingered in the evenings until long after Nadja had fallen asleep. She leaned against the doorframe while Bartholomew barely followed the words spouted by Lester regarding the lawsuit until Lester had spent his words and allowed his host to speak.

"The Curtis girl brought me some bones," he said, the excitement filling his comment but not shared by Lester.

At the mention of bones, Nadja withdrew to find her padded chair in the parlor, hissing the word to herself, "Bones."

Bartholomew set the walnut box on his desk and affectionately tapped its top. "Bones were discovered on the old Stewart Property, now under the usage of Tobias Bond."

Lester feigned interest, glancing at the clock above the desk, showing the lateness of the evening and reminding him of the hours since he last ate.

"Three bones were unearthed in the garden there, a piece of skull, a portion of jawbone, and the head of a humorous. Adjacent to the bone fragments, in the same dirt, was an intricately carved ivory dress button, an expensive button."

"A slave caught stealing? An Indian from a time before that?" Lester asked, ignoring the rumble in his stomach.

"No," Bartholomew said. "You recall my early education in osteology before I delved into morphology."

Lester nodded his head that he remembered, but he did not.

"There are newer sciences, now, Mr. Watkins. Paleontology and anthropology, all aided by the study of bones."

Lester stifled a yawn. "And so, Bartholomew, what exciting detail have you identified."

"In a nutshell, these bones quite likely are of a white woman buried in the past thirty to fifty years in what was once the garden of Mamie Stewart's boarding house. And...she was murdered."

Lester sat up straight, giving him his full attention.

Bartholomew explained his theory of the bone staining by the earth, the condition of the teeth, and the head of the humorous. He finalized on magnified attention to the skull fragment.

"Her skull was punctured by a sharp object when blood still flowed along the bone and stained the edges of the small hole. Which means she was alive at the moment of trauma and obviously not so afterward. The other damage to the skull bone occurred post-mortem."

"Perhaps," Lester began, "we should ask the state coroner to examine the bones and then appeal to the county sheriff to proclaim the property a murder site."

Bartholomew shrugged his shoulders. "I don't see how the coroner could know more about bones than me."

Lester smiled. "Then listen to more. You will love to learn this, Bartholomew. Do you know who legally owns the lot where the bones were discovered?"

"I believe it is Tobias Bond," Bartholomew said.

Lester sniffed. "It actually was bequeathed by Mamie Stewart to Benjamin Pulaski until such time that Bond can fully own it and pay its taxes."

"What does this mean to our lawsuit against Pulaski?" Bartholomew asked.

"Probably nothing," Lester said, "but it will raise hell with him trying to settle the property with Bond if there is a murder investigation going on."

They both smiled. Lister withdrew a little bottle of brandy from a shelf above his desk and filled small glasses for him and Lester. "As long as it causes problems for Pulaski, let's do it," Bartholomew said through clenched teeth, held tighter.

As they toasted, Lester reminded Bartholomew, "You must let me take your lovely box of bones. I will see that it is returned."

SATURDAY MORNING, JANUARY 1

In the Watkins-Binterfield Mansion, Lester sipped his morning coffee, reading the *Aegis Intelligencer* from Bel Air. On the table just beyond his finished breakfast plate sat the walnut box. His cook came to collect his plate and silverware.

"Would you care for more coffee, Mr. Watkins?" His housekeeper asked.

"Yes, bring some fresh cream. This is growing warm."

She nodded her understanding and turned as someone wrapped hard at the front door.

"See who that is," he said.

The housekeeper returned, still carrying his empty coffee cup, as well as a small envelope that she handed to him on her way to the kitchen.

"What is this?" he asked, but she was gone from the room. Inside the envelope, he found a telegram from his friend in Spain. "Already?" he said as he scanned the brief note, then reread it three times.

```
Les,
Such information already collected
and sent last year. Requested by
Parker Lexington, Esq.
No Emigration, marriage, or burial
records in Spain re: American Lydia
Binterfield. Assumed Lexington request
per your orders. Come visit. Spain
marvelous.
Teddy
```

Lester slammed his hand down on the table.

"I'm coming," the housekeeper called out from

the kitchen.

He spoke to the letter. "Lexington?" That damned farm manager I hired to run Lydia's southern Maryland plantation. Then I turned it over to Sonja Pulaski per Lydia's will. What was he doing pretending to be a lawyer and looking into Lydia's estate in Spain?"

He leaned forward with his elbows on the table, rereading the telegram when the housekeeper rushed into the room. "Your coffee and fresh cream, sir."

He dismissed her with the flip of his hand, "Yes. Yes. Find something else to do."

He sipped his coffee, then added sugar and some fresh cream, then more cream, gazing up at the chandelier over the table as he swallowed.

He muttered to himself. "What were you doing?... Doing what I was going to do?"

He paused a long moment, then smiled, "You sneak. You were looking for a way to get to her Spanish estate. You were going to take over the plantation and whatever else you could grab."

He sipped his coffee, holding the telegram in the fingers of his other hand.

"You got nothing from Spain. There was nothing there."

He stood and walked around the room, flipping the telegram paper before his nose. He froze in mid-step, staring at an old painting of Lydia she kept because her husband hated it.

"There was nothing in Spain. No record she was ever there, unless without knowledge of the American Consulate? Nonsense, Lydia would have insisted they kissed her ass. They would celebrate her death...but knew nothing of it or her."

He rushed to his office and withdrew her will. It had befuddled his mind that Lydia Binterfield, who hated the Pulaskis with a passion, would leave her entire estate to Sonja Pulaski.

"Oh...oh my God...those letters from you when you changed. After you went to Spain..."

He rummaged through his other drawers until he found the deed to Mamie Stewart's property after the boarding house had burned down and the written instructions from Mamie. He leaned over his desk, pressed flat the instructions from Mamie, not the paper she signed in his presence before she left town, but the list of actions she brought with her. He flattened out the single sheet of paper next to her signed instruction.

"The list is much neater," he said, "such properly formed letters of one gifted in calligraphy."

He yanked open his file of instructions received from Lydia during her absence in Spain, pulling up the last one she sent him. He laid it next to the list from Mamie Stewart, then fell into his chair, gawking at the papers.

"Oh my God," he mumbled, and mumbled the words again. Then he yelled at them, "Oh my God!"

The housekeeper met him in the foyer between the office and the rest of the main floor.

"How may I help you, sir?" but he waved her away, saying, "Not you."

He dashed into the dining room, closing the door and stepping next to the table. He slid the walnut box close to him, slowly opening the top and peering down at the bone fragments. A broad smile spread across his face, and his eyes sparkled.

"Hello, Lydia. How was Spain?"

The buzzards, seagulls, and eagles were already contesting ownership of the body and gorging themselves on horseflesh by the time Ben and Mickey returned under pewter morning skies. The gelding they brought from the Pulaski barn snorted at the sight and smell of the dead horse, trying to back away. Mickey took him back up the towpath a hundred yards while Ben unfastened the harness and traces to the staves. Two canallers arrived from barges in the basin carrying pushing poles to help Ben slip the carcass into the river. One of the men worked for Ben, Claude Haney, was spending the winter in a barge cabin. The two had investigated the abandoned horse and buggy earlier and had gone back for the poles.

Claude, a tall black man who had his wife and baby with him in his barge, introduced the other, a short canal company man who hoped to pick up a few coins getting rid of the horse. They pushed the carcass as far into the river current as the poles would reach.

"The water's not freezing," Claude said, "but it's sure cold enough, so the horse flesh won't fester in it."

"Least there's no tide coming up against the river," the company man said. "That old mare will be well below Spesutie Island before the next one. What shot her?"

"A punt gun," Ben said.

The canallers exchanged a quick glance. "Told ya it was a punt gun," the company man said.

"The shooter had to be real close to tear up that horse like that," Claude said. "Punt gun pellets are the size of a woman's pinky nail. He couldn't have been more than three good paces away."

"I was in the buggy when he shot," Ben said, "if my horse hadn't balked when she sensed him, my wife and I would be dead."

"Who would do such a thing, Mr. Pulaski?"

Ben waved for Mickey to bring the gelding to the buggy, then answered the canaller. "I know exactly who it was, and I know where the son of a bitch lives."

Ben thanked the men for their help and gave them each two silver dollars. Ben addressed the company man. "Come see me in the spring if you don't have a boat assignment then."

The canaller smiled and walked away with the other, stuffing the coins into his pocket. Three days' pay for fifteen minutes of work.

Ben heard the company man speaking as they walked away. "I know some folks who could make good use of that horseflesh."

"I should have thought of that," Ben said to himself.

After rinsing the blood off the staves, Ben and Mickey strapped the fresh horse into the buggy's harness and single tree. Ben stepped up to the driver's seat while Mickey hesitated on the other side footrest, examining the surrey post on that side.

Ben watched him. "What did you find?"

"Pellets on the outside of the post."

"Point to where they are."

When Mickey did that, Ben's face flared crimson. "That would have hit Sonja in the head."

Ben pulled out his revolver and double-checked that the cylinder was full, then returned it to its holster.

"Ben..."

Ben slapped the reins on the haunch of the gelding, spurring the horse into a trot.

"Ben...Ben, we need to go to the deputy sheriff's office and report this, along with your suspicions."

Ben spoke through gritted teeth. "I know damned well who did it."

"You told me yourself on our walk down here that you saw nothing but the flash and your horse tattered to pieces."

Mickey snatched the reins from Ben's hands, pulling back on them and bringing the buggy to a halt. "Stop, Ben. Do not go after Bolton."

Ben's eyes were fired with anger. "The hell I won't. He could have killed Sonja."

"And you will leave her a widow, of a murderer. Stop the darkness, Benjamin. Stop it now. Don't give her anymore."

Ben gripped his fists, spewing angry half-spoken profanities. After a moment, he released his fists, blew out his breath, and lifted his hat, running his fingers through his hair, looking toward the muddy water still in the basin. Then Ben yanked the revolver from its holster, nodding an answer to a question only he knew, and handed the gun to Mickey. He folded his arms, leaned back on the seat, and gazed straight ahead.

"You have the damned reins, so drive the damned buggy to the damned Sheriff's office."

Soon Ben paced within the cramped space of the deputy sheriff's office on Washington Street. After the civil war, the old provost marshal office had been broken up into separate spaces. The office's footprint returned to its original meager area. There was a small front office with barely sufficient room for the desk, filing cabinet, deputy's chair, and a visitor's chair. Beyond the office was single door access to a solitary jail cell, afforded after moving the visitor's chair out of the way. Ben had pushed the cell door open to allow himself the full twenty feet from the front door to the cell's barred window at the back.

"Settle down, Ben," Hopkins said. "I'm writing all this down, and I'm going to have you sign it. And Doctor O'Grady here will sign as a material witness, at least to the damage to the horse and your buggy. Then I will interview the two gentlemen who helped you dispose of the dead horse, who you say will confirm the sound of a punt gun around midnight. I already heard from some other folks in town who say they heard what sounded like a punt gun about that same time. Then I will interview every licensed punt gunner who works nearby, and that will include Mr. Harris Bolton."

"And don't forget," Ben said. "My wife said she and Franklin Curtis's daughter, Rebecca, saw a man that could have been Harris Bolton leaning against the lamp post across the street from the Oyster Street Tavern just before we left."

"I won't forget, Ben. I will take statements from everyone necessary to get to the bottom of this." Hopkins twisted his wrist and shook his hand to loosen his muscles, then set the pencil down. "I need to rest my hand a bit. I'm starting to cramp from all this writing."

Hopkins opened the courier pouch from Bel Air to review wanted handbills and other notices from the county seat. He chuckled, holding a sealed envelope. "This one's for you, Ben. I suspect it matches the message I just got from circuit court."

Ben opened the envelope, read the notice inside, and looked at Mickey, saying, "Hells Bells. Lister is taking me to court in Bel Air. "

Mickey sighed and shook his head. "When?"

Hopkins answered. "Next Tuesday. January 4th. Ten a.m." Then he wagged his finger at Ben. "Try not to punch anyone in front of the judge this time. Now leave me alone so I can write up all this you've told me. Come back later to sign it, or you can sign it when I come out to Lapidum to interview Mrs. Pulaski. But for now, just go away."

Outside, Ben stretched in the chilled air as they walked down Washington Street toward the center of town.

"You've been up all night, Ben," Mickey said. "Let's head back to Lapidum."

"You've been up too," Ben said.

"Yes, but I had a nap in the afternoon."

As they crossed St. Clair Street, Tobias and another man ran across in front of them, heading toward the docks.

"Tobias," Ben called out to him.

"Can't stop," Tobias answered, running on. "Overslept."

Ben watched him trot down to the *Jester,* speaking at his back. "Yeah, I could use some sleep. But, probably not get any of that after Sonja hears about me going to court in Bel Air. Can't put it off, Mickey. Let's go home."

⋯⦾⋯

The wind from the south was more robust than on Friday, and there was still no break in the cloud cover. The salty smell of the ocean clung to the air, a scent of the birthmother hundreds of miles away beyond Hampton Roads, spewed up by waves prowling the Atlantic.

Laborious sailing and near-constant tacking to claw across the wind getting to the Bush River were tedious and muscle-wrenching work each morning. But the flight before the wind dashing back to Havre de Grace in time to meet the evening trains was exhilarating. Tobias was eager to fill the *Jester's* holds again. At the same time, both Jimmy and Garrett were pleased with their promised percentage of the profits. Tobias was keen to make as much money as possible while the train clerks were eager for oysters. Still, he also had the image of his Uncle Simon, driving him to generous fairness with those who also worked toward the profit. Simon had instilled bold pride and honor in his adopted nephew. The tonger camp on the western shore of the Bush River kept all five men and boats at the ready each morning before the *Jester* arrived. After being told of an extra bonus for keeping the *Jester* filled and prepared to depart in the late afternoon, the men were energized. That bonus was in addition to the nightly visits from certain ladies from the peninsula village a mile inland bringing locally distilled whiskeys. The tongers met the *Jester* each morning where she anchored. Their longboats filled to overflowing with the bivalved delicacies. They continued the back-breaking pace of three boatloads each per day. No army or navy could have been more satisfied with their efficiency.

Tobias rubbed his hands together as the tightly woven cargo net came up from the boats hauled by the boom with hundreds of oysters to be quickly released into the hold. The cargo hold was covered with fresh seaweed each day to give the oysters soft landings and help keep them moist. Bucket loads of cold brackish water were also hauled up after each boatload and tossed on top of the oysters. The water and the weather would keep them nearly ice-cold for delivery.

"It's almost like loading money," Jimmy said.

Garrett swung the boom back out to lower the net down to the next boat.

"I never much cared for oysters, myself," he said, "but I'm happy to help ship them up north. Those folks got more dollars than sense, anyway."

Tobias and Jimmy laughed at the joke. Garrett was coming out of his shell since he began helping on the sloop. The three were becoming friends in that easy association of hard work and frequent conversation where bits of secrets were shared without drama and taken in without judgment.

Garrett straightened his back to ease his muscles. "But, I would have eaten a bushel of raw oysters pulled out of the saltwater if they'd been offered at Petersburg."

The explosion at the crater during the battle of Petersburg flashed through Tobias's mind, and the bloody image of Uncle Simon's wound that nearly killed him. Tobias and Garrett glanced at each other at the moment, locking eyes only briefly but seeing it in each other.

"You lose someone close there?" Garrett asked.

"Almost did. My Uncle, but he made it that time."

Garrett nodded as he pulled on the boom rope. "Glad he made it."

"You?" Tobias asked.

"Two cousins and my sister's husband."

Tobias swallowed. "I'm sorry, Garrett." he said.

Garrett nodded, turning his attention out on the river. "I managed to walk on to Appomattox, knowing it was coming to an end, knowing Lee couldn't ask any more of us, knowing he wouldn't. Three days without food, 'til Lee surrendered. Grant stopped the slaughter and sent us food, and then sent us home."

"We were amazed you fellas could still walk," Tobias said.

Garrett and Tobias pulled on the boom rope, shoulder to shoulder, raising the next load of oysters. Garrett smiled. "Sometimes God watches over the stupid as well as the brave."

They released the oysters into the hold as Jimmy poured more cold water.

"And sometimes God turns away from our murder and cries for us," Jimmy said.

Tobias and Garrett regarded him in surprise.

"I never knew," Tobias said. "I thought you stayed..."

"Took a ball in the gut early on," Jimmy said.

"Antietam. Wounded my first time on the field and then mustered home. The Navy had taken the *Jester* then, but I couldn't do much anyway."

The three halted for just an instant, sharing the moment and the recognition, then put the memories back in the dark to speak no more of it, and went on with the work at hand, the oysters.

After emptying the first loads of the day, Tobias called the tongers up on the ship for a meeting. "I know you agreed to be out here three days, but I learned that the demand for oysters will be high for Sunday as well. Can you stay one additional night? Then when you are finished tomorrow, we will bring you onboard, tow your boats back to Havre de Grace and pay you on the docks as soon as the oysters are delivered to the train."

The men discussed it among themselves and agreed. "Long as the bonus goes along for that additional day," one said, to the murmured agreement of the others.

"It will," Tobias said, then turned away, glancing up at the sky.

The clouds were darker, and the wind blowing north was stronger. Even within the confines of the Bush River, bad weather getting worse would be risky for the men and the boats.

In Havre de Grace, Ben and Robert placed their guns and lunch into Robert's rowboat at the water's edge near the basin's outlet lock. Robert set a bulky canvas bag near his feet. Vast flocks of Canvasbacks were unrestrained by the overcast sky, milling about on the Susquehanna Flats. Ducks dove for the grasses growing on the bottom or argued with one another, while the single males harassed the females. Flocks of ducks that flew in together rose or settled en masse, their great fluttering providing bass drums to the cacophony of spirited quacking and officious murmuring filling the air. The occasional shotgun barks disturbed small batches that rose into the air like small tornados, leaving lost members floating on the surface. The fallen were quickly scooped up by shooters, and the surviving ducks soon settled again, not far away.

Ben took up the oars and rowed out toward the closest ducks, the bow of the boat bucking slightly as it ran into one-foot waves pushed by the wind. Robert took the time to examine Ben's shotgun.

"Why, you have an English gun, Benjamin. I would have expected you to have a Colt or Remington."

"It was a Christmas gift, Robert, from my younger...well, from my son. It is a break-open breech. Lancaster. I have more brass cartridges in my coat pocket."

"Ten or twelve gauge?"

"Twelve," Ben said. "You may try it on one of your ducks if you like."

"Thank you, sir, but I am content with my Purdy."

As their boat approached the closest flock, Robert suggested an area away from the ducks and other shooters. I have learned a method to draw the ducks to us and allow us to stay away from the noise of the other boats. Robert Pointed farther out on the Flats. Ben shrugged his shoulders and pulled the oars. Robert opened his canvas bag to withdraw several delicately carved wooden and painted decoys.

"Those are fine carvings," Ben said.

Robert held one of the decoys up for Ben to examine. "These beauties will bring a flock to us."

"Where did you get those, Robert?"

"The man who built this boat, John Holly, sold them to me. His son, James, carved them. Looks like a real Canvasback, doesn't it?"

"Almost a shame to set those out in the water," Ben said.

"See, they are weighted at the bottom to keep their heads up, and the wave action will give them motion. We'll have both hens and drakes around us in short order."

"I know John Holly," Ben said, "but I didn't know any of his sons were old enough to do that kind of work."

"James is only a boy, but he is a wonder with wood."

Robert set out the decoys, tied loosely to keep them nearby as a group. In just a few minutes, the ducks began to land near the decoy flock. As Robert stood, the ducks started to chatter and rise into the air. Robert took two from the air before they had gained more than a few yards overhead.

"Good shooting, Robert," Ben said as he pulled to the fallen birds.

"Now for you, Ben. Pass me the oars for the locks near me, and I will row for your shots."

Ben took one duck from the next two shots, reloaded with cartridges, and then took down a pair skimming the water at thirty yards.

"Three is just enough for me and Sonja and Mickey," Ben said.

"Then I'll try again," Robert said but struggled unsuccessfully in the rocking boat, trying to ram powder, and shot down the barrels for his next shots. "Drat. I did want to bring home a second pair for my housekeeper and her son."

Ben extended his hand to Robert, handing him two more cartridges. "Robert. Use my gun."

"But...my Purdy..."

"Hell, Robert. Mine is English-made, too. Surely your pride can accept using it, instead of your old muzzleloader."

Robert peered at Ben. "You are becoming philosophical, Benjamin."

Ben raised his eyebrows. "I am brash but not unobservant."

Robert halted in mid-motion, then turned entirely in his seat to view Ben.

Ben blushed. "I have been reading stories, fiction, in the Harper's magazine. Sonja tells me it will improve my vo...vocabulary."

"That it has done, sir."

Ben's attention was drawn across the flats toward the Cecil County shore. "Let's cross over to the other side. The ducks seem more settled here."

Ben leaned back with a strong pull on the oars, increasing the pace as they crossed the Flats, glancing over his shoulder to correct his direction. Robert followed Ben's attention until he recognized Ben's destination.

"Imagine that, Ben. Our friend Harris Bolton is moving into that little cove ahead of us."

"Yes, imagine that," Ben said as he pulled harder on the oars, sending the boat ahead.

Robert scanned the nearby shore. "Em, Ben. Are you sure this is where you want to go?"

Ben laid the oars inside the boat, letting it drift ahead on its course. "Hand me my gun, will you, Robert?"

Ahead of their boat, Bolton was moving into the bottom of his punt boat, snuggling up behind the stock of the big gun, lying prone with only his head above the sight. The little cove was dotted with a couple hundred ducks sitting close together in front of his boat. As Robert handed Ben his shotgun, Robert discharged one of the barrels into the air. Many of the ducks in front of the punt boat rose into the air. Ben frowned at Robert, snatching the gun from his grip. Bolton glanced back over his shoulder with his face screwed into a grimace, but the ducks circled close by and settled again downrange of the punt gun. Ben opened the breech and removed the spent shell, then shoved it into his coat pocket. He withdrew a fresh cartridge, slipped it into the breech and closed the gun with a snap. As their boat drifted closer to the punt boat, moving within the calmer water of the cove, Robert faced away while he reloaded his own gun in the cumbersome process necessary for muzzleloaders.

The rowboat drifted closer to the rear of the punt, several yards away but still coming. Ben raised his shotgun, aiming at the ducks sitting on the water just in front of the punt boat.

"Ben, Benjamin, what are you about?"

Robert frantically worked his wooden ramrod down his gun barrels. As the distance between the boats narrowed to less than a few yards. The barrel of Ben's gun lowered.

"Ben," Robert called in a strained whisper. "Ben, you cannot. Not like this."

Ben pulled back on the hammers, letting the aim fall lower and lower, then brought his fingertip to the edge of the trigger, aiming down the groove between the barrels. The boats drifted closer, the bow of Ben's boat nearly touching the stern of the other, bringing the top of Bolton's hat into the pattern area that could come from the shotgun. Ben placed his fingertip on the first trigger. His heart pounded in his chest and in his ears. His vision blurred at its edges, red replacing the gray waters in his periphery and the red drawing in closer to the end of the barrels and the back of Bolton's head.

Robert rammed the packet of shot down the barrel, punching it against the powder bag. He stood behind Ben.

"Ben. I cannot allow you to do this."

Ben thought of Bolton, muttered the words, the sound of them lost amid the pounding of his heart, fogging the steel of the breach with his breath. "You could have killed Sonja, you bastard."

Ben leaned over Bolton, took in a deep breath, then let out half, the perfect preparation for a steady shot.

Robert brought up the barrels of his shotgun, pointing them at Ben's back.

"Stop, Ben. Stop."

Ben muttered the word again. "Bastard. Damn you, Bolton." Then he yelled it, "Bastard!"

Bolton raised his head and turned his face upward toward Ben, looking up along the same twin barrels pointed down at him, with Ben's angry eyes hovering above them.

Robert held his gun barrels against Ben's back. "No, Ben!"

"Bastard," Ben yelled, his head filled with rage, the pounding from his heart and the blackness folding around his tunneling view of Bolton.

Bolton froze. His face paled. A wet stain spread across his trousers.

A shrill scream pierced Ben's ears then all sound was lost to him. An overwhelming silence encased him, filled his mind except for the sound of Sonja's breathing, lying next to him, and she whispered his name. Ben yanked the gun barrels toward the sky and fired both cartridges. Ducks launched into the sky at the sound of the double explosion. The rowboat drifted beside the punt boat as Ben punched Bolton's shoulders with the hot ends of his barrels.

Robert dropped onto his bench, his hands shaking. "Jesus, Joseph, and Mary."

Ben snarled at Bolton. "If you ever come close to anyone in my family, any of my friends, hell anyone I just take a liking to, I will kill you, Harris Bolton."

Bolton grabbed at the barrel of his punt gun, pulling it up from its braces.

"You're empty, Pulaski," Bolton said.

Robert grabbed the side of the punt boat and placed his barrels against Bolton's cheek. "My gun is loaded."

Bolton released the punt gun and shrank back into his narrow cockpit. Ben leaned over Bolton's boat, grabbed the heavy punt gun, and lifted it out. He raised the barrel, pulled the stock toward his chest, and then heaved the weapon into the air on the other side of the rowboat, where it splashed into the water. Ben reloaded his shotgun while Robert kept Bolton still and then blasted two holes in the bottom of the punt boat. Ben and Robert pushed away while Bolton sank into the water with his boat.

"I hope he can swim," Robert said.

"It's only about six feet deep here, but Bolton

can't be more than five and a half. He'll make it to shore, but it will be a while until he gets his gun back."

When Ben and Robert returned to Havre de Grace, several duck hunters who had watched the incident in the cove stood to clap and whistle.

"Gentlemen," Robert called out to them, pointing to the cove. "There is a sunken punt boat and a punt gun in the water over there. Perhaps one among you might be interested in seeing them gone altogether."

From the dock, Ben and Robert watched several duck hunters row across toward the cove.

Robert sighed. "I was afraid you were actually going to shoot that man, Ben."

"I was."

While Ben and Robert were rowing across the Susquehanna Flats searching for their first ducks that morning, Mickey stood beside Sonja on the porch in Lapidum. His gaze was fixed over the river, unfocused.

"Mmm?" he asked, not turning to respond.

"I said, 'I will need to go into Havre de Grace this morning'," Sonja said, punching his side with her finger. "You are as bad as Ben, pretending to give an answer when you're not listening."

He gave her a half-smile. "I was listening."

"You were not. What did I say?"

"Said I was as bad as Ben."

She folded her arms and scoffed. "So, do you want to go with me?"

"Where?"

She punched him in his side and walked away. Mickey feigned an injury from her and followed her into the kitchen, limping and moaning.

"Oh, stop it, Mickey. You did not hear a word I said."

He pulled out a chair at the small kitchen table, taking up his abandoned coffee cup. "Sometimes I hear unspoken words."

She tossed the dishtowel over her shoulder and turned to face him. "Another feeling?"

"Yes."

She tsked. "Ben? Me? Who?"

It was little more than a whisper. "I don't always know." He smiled. "Sometimes, it's just dyspepsia."

Sonja placed her fingertips on the coffee pot, then used her dishtowel to grab the handle and pour more coffee in his cup and then hers. She sat down across from him and sighed.

"You and Ben are at odds a lot," he said.

"Is that your famous feelings again?"

"No, it's my Irish eyes watching two people circle each other, always ready for a fight."

She blew out her breath. "Sometimes he acts like he just doesn't give a damn about things."

Mickey ran his fingertip along the rim of his cup, peering at her from under his eyebrows.

She sipped her coffee. "Isaac has been dead three months. When we sat trying to remember him on our first day back, he could only talk about the little dock Isaac built as a boy. I had to wait until Ben got in a loud argument with Franklin Curtis last night to hear any word from him about how he honestly felt losing our son."

"My father was like that, Sonja."

"And you always told us he was an ass, so that doesn't help me."

Mickey chuckled. "I did say that. And he was. What do you want Ben to tell you?"

She stood and moved to the sink, resting her hand on the water pump, peering out the back window overlooking their field. The morning light outlined her profile.

"Sometimes you see my soul better than I do, and I feel as if my secrets are already known to you even before I say them."

"And yet, my spiritual sister, say them you must. Not for me to hear, but for you to get them out."

She glanced down at her hands and sighed. "You sound like Franklin."

"It's the mournful Irish in me." Mickey stood and motioned toward the dining room, then led her out onto the porch.

"Sometimes," he said, "big problems need more room to let them out, to air them out."

They sat side by side.

"You are like a brother to me, Mickey."

He patted her hand.

"I almost left him several years ago," Sonja said, "but I couldn't do it. There was another place I could have gone, would have been accepted there, but I could not."

"Do you want to go away now?"

"No. The urge is gone, but the feeling of it remains."

"When you thought you had lost Alisha, and I was crazy in grief of losing wife and child, something kept us from taking the wrong step."

Sonja released a hollow laugh. "You did. Not me." She sighed. "But, this is not that."

He examined his coffee cup in silence. She rose and stood behind her chair, gripping the ladderback posts.

"I'm tired of always waiting for the anger to erupt," she said.

"He will mellow, Sonja."

"I'm beginning to think he will not...and what I have of him is all I will have."

"Is that not enough?"

"Mickey, sometimes I wonder if Ben and I have gone too far from our original lives to get back there, to the memory of us in the beginning."

"You did it when he came back from China. For three years, you thought he was dead. You thought Alisha was dead."

"I didn't come back from that, Mickey. He and I were both different because of that. We had to start over, but I don't know if I can make such a weary journey again."

They watched the returning heron briefly circle the canal again, listened to the wind rushing through the trees and the river gurgle around the boulders standing in the water.

Creaking from Mickey's chair ended the silence as he straightened his back. "So, where would you like me to accompany you?"

"Never mind that. I think the walk into town will do me good. I have to meet with the lawyer, Lester Watkins."

"What about?"

"I don't know, but meeting with him is as unpleasant as cleaning out the stables."

Mickey chuckled.

Sonja entered Lester's office while Ben was rowing back from the cove with Turner. She wrung her hands and took in a deep breath as she sat. He gave a mumbled morning greeting, and she had barely settled onto her chair before his desk when he pulled up several documents.

There was a dark wood box with brass fittings sitting prominently on his desk.

"Is this about the case against Ben?" She asked.

"Oh, no, Mrs. Pulaski. There are still several

assets of the Binterfield estate to settle."

"More for me to sign?"

"I need your authorization to liquidate the remaining assets. Cattle, sheep, land, the building that once housed Mr. Binterfield's bank, some stocks, et cetera. Do recall that you bade me not give you a detailed list of assets when I informed you of your inheritance, but now, there are taxes to pay and debts to resolve."

"I would like our own lawyer to review those papers first," she said.

"I see. Well, Mrs. Binterfield charged me with officiating the settlement of her estate. I cannot abdicate from those duties, but you are certainly within your rights, and your husband's rights, to retain additional counsel," he said, setting the papers to the side and sliding the box toward her.

Sonja leaned closer to the box but did not move to open it, glancing at him, her eyebrows raised in question.

"This box contains some items that were discovered on the property previously owned by Mrs. Mamie Stewart and currently managed by the negro, Tobias Bond."

He opened the box, but Sonja did not peer into it. She kept her eyes fixed coldly on Watkins.

"There are three bones in this box and a delicate ivory button. The kind of button one would find on a lady's stylish dress."

Sonja sat motionless, allowing no expression on her face as it flushed. Her mind flashed the image of Lydia, her face naturally pale under her immaculate raven black hair. She stood perfectly erect in her deep green satin dress. The line of dainty white ivory buttons dotted the space between the pleats over her bosom, trailing from her neck to her narrow waist.

"Did you know, Mrs. Pulaski, that our honorable undertaker, Bartholomew Lister, was schooled as an osteologist before entering his current trade? He knows a great deal about bones, human bones that have been buried in the ground, and he has studied these bones at length."

Sonja swallowed, keeping her eyes on Watkin's face. The clock on the mantle across the room struck ten times, sounding so loud. Watkins' eyes sparkled as he smiled, showing large yellow teeth. Sonja's face paled, her throat was dry, and her breathing shallow.

"Bartholomew has determined that the bones in this box are from a woman, likely a white woman of an easy life, whose bones went into the ground possibly as recently as twenty years ago. Into ground where today sits a modified barn adjacent to an old garden, once owned by Mrs. Stewart."

Sonja squeezed her hands together on her lap, digging her fingernails into the back of the other hand. Delicate beads of blood arouse at the tips of her fingernails. Her throat tightened, and she pressed her lips together in a thin line.

Watkin's smile broadened. "It even seems probable that these discovered bones went into the ground near the time of Mrs. Binterfield's abrupt departure to Spain."

Sonja remained silent, her attention focused on his face. Watkins closed the box and tapped his fingertips casually on its top.

"Yes, well, it is an amusing little mystery for us to contemplate. Nothing more." He pulled a large envelope from his desk, offering it to her. "I assumed you would wish the sage advice of Mr. Milton again. Please obtain it today and let me know your decision. There are other actions I must take in resolving the Binterfield estate, legal actions, and I must act quickly. And there is, of course, the court case regarding your husband that I must prepare for."

Sonja left the office without speaking, hearing Watkin's last words to her as she closed the door behind her. "Today, Mrs. Pulaski. Today."

She wandered without direction, meandering toward the water's edge, to the end of St. Clair Street, where once the steamship met the train to take it across the river. The wind had increased and snatched the fur hat from her head, taking it up beyond retrieval. Her skirt whipped around her ankles. Men leaned into the wind, holding on to their own hats, while others surrendered to it and held their hats in their hands. Woman's shawls snapped like unfurled flags. Out on the water, a few duck hunters struggled in rowboats against the growing waves, working their way across to the cove on the Cecil County shore. Whirlpools edged in froth formed in the middle of the Susquehanna Flats, where river water and bay water contested ownership of the space, each straining to push the other back. Chill seeped within her clothes, and points of pain on the back of her hand throbbed.

Sonja made her way to the protection of the Oyster Street Tavern, not driven by hunger but seeking a place to sit and collect her thoughts. Rebecca came to her table as soon as she settled, and she ordered oyster soup and tea, though not expecting to eat any of it. When it arrived, Sonja's stomach growled from the aroma, and she gave into the salty, buttery flavor with determination. She finished the bowl, drinking the tea, and requesting a second cup. She focused on her meal and her thoughts, not making eye contact with other patrons who were driven into the warm tavern and delicious smells. The clock near the corner by the tavern struck twelve when Sonja emerged, her mind decided, and her steps determined. Moments later, she sat before Watkin's desk again. He set the documents and an ink well before her on the edge of the desk.

"What do you gain by my signature?" she asked.

He allowed a faint smile on his lips. "You did not visit with Mr. Milton?"

She remained silent, her head up and her gaze steady.

"Essentially, you will grant me full authorization to dispose of the assets as I see fit."

"And what will you do with the proceeds?"

He shrugged his shoulders and broadened his smile. "Administrative costs."

Sonja frowned, taking in a deep breath and slowly releasing it while he waited. She wanted him to wait. "Seventy-five percent comes to me; you give me the bones. Then and you sign a document stating what you believe the bones to represent and that you willingly conceal that information in cooperation with me."

He shook his head no. "All to me, the bones to you, and no signed statement."

"Lister knows about the bones," Sonja said. "I will offer him half of my assets from Lydia to testify against your attempted bribery at 'our' trial."

"All to me," Watkins said, "the bones to you,

and I will sign the statement."

She tapped the papers with her fingertip. "That is robbery, Mr. Watkins."

He tapped the wooden box. "That is evidence of a murder, Mrs. Pulaski."

Sonja raised her chin. "What is actually in there that connects me to...that."

Watkins sighed and leaned back in his chair. Sonja raised her eyebrows and gazed at him with sky blue eyes. Watkins pulled open a desk drawer, withdrew several sheets of paper, and laid them on top of the power of attorney documents. He displayed a broad smile and motioned to the papers.

"I have a written statement from our American Consulate in Spain that no Lydia Binterfield ever resided there, married there, died there, or was buried there. And no record of Lydia Binterfield ever sailing to Spain."

Sonja swallowed a large lump in her throat.

Watkins continued. "The note provided me by Mamie Stewart to settle her estate for Tobias Bond has the same handwriting as that purportedly signed by Lydia Binterfield. The handwriting is not of a woman dead twenty years and lying in Mrs. Stewart's garden. It is the handwriting of Mrs. Mamie Stewart. And though that could incriminate Mrs. Stewart, she inexplicably gave all those Binterfield assets to another person. You."

Watkins' butler tapped on the door and poked his head in. "Mr. Bolton is here for his appointment, suh."

"Tell him to come back in half an hour," Watkins said, then waited until the butler had closed the door then faced Sonja."

Sonja shook her head no.

Watkins sighed. "Seventy-five percent to me, you get the bones, and I sign the paper."

Sonja stood. "I will have Mr. Milton come see you about your attempted extortion, and he will find a doctor to refute the undertaker's learned opinion."

Watkins folded his arms and displayed a frown. "Damn, madam. Fifty percent, you get the bones, and I sign the statement."

"Very well," Sonja said, standing before the desk. "I will take the box now."

"Certainly not, madam."

"I will return Monday to see your statement. If I am satisfied, you will sign it before a witness who can swear only they saw you sign the document. Then you will hand me the document and the bones. After that, I will sign your papers."

The butler opened the door, "I am sorry, Mr. Watkins–"

Bolton barged past the butler, his clothes dripping water. "Watkins, we gotta talk."

Watkins indicated Sonja standing in the room. Bolton glared at her but remained where he stood.

Sonja turned to leave as Bolton asked Watkins about the box on the desk. "Don't touch it," Watkins said, peering at Sonja. "It's worth a fortune to me."

Sonja then visited George Milton in his office, where she described an oversimplified version of her arrangement with Watkins. She did not mention the bones nor any of her secrets relating to them. She handed him the envelope Watkins had given her earlier.

"I want to be shed of all connections to the Binterfield estate as well as Watkins," she said. "I am willing to give Watkins half of what I didn't know I had, but I need you to look at these to confirm that is what I will be doing."

He scratched his head. "And go with you...to watch you sign these and watch him sign another document...which I will not read either before or after he signs it."

"Yes, George. That's right. Will you do that?"

He rubbed his chin and forehead, then folded his arms and sighed. "For you? Yes. But I don't like doing it. And, I don't like Lester Watkins."

"That's one of my reasons why I trust you to do it, George."

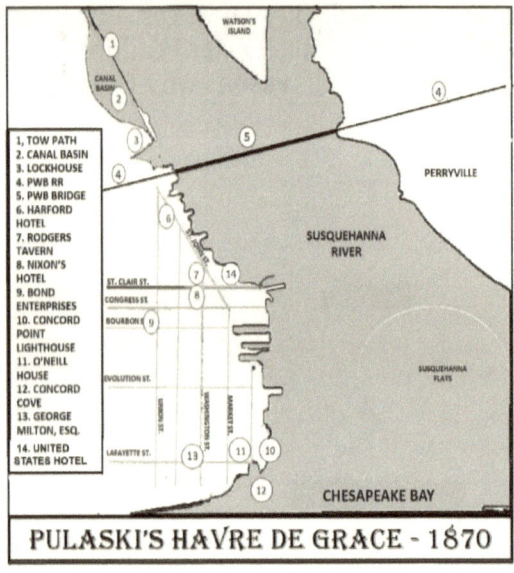

1, TOW PATH
2. CANAL BASIN
3. LOCKHOUSE
4. PWB RR
5. PWB BRIDGE
6. HARFORD HOTEL
7. RODGERS TAVERN
8. NIXON'S HOTEL
9. BOND ENTERPRISES
10. CONCORD POINT LIGHTHOUSE
11. O'NEILL HOUSE
12. CONCORD COVE
13. GEORGE MILTON, ESQ.
14. UNITED STATES HOTEL

PULASKI'S HAVRE DE GRACE - 1870

Bolton gazed at the wooden box on Watkins' desk. His black hair was greasy and matted to his head. He was unshaven and poorly bathed, though recently dunked, still dripping water as he entered. His checked flannel shirt was tattered at the ends of his sleeve, and animal blood stained his canvas trousers. Watkins blinked as he noticed Bolton's highly shined shoes, which explained the shoe black outlining Bolton's dirty fingernails, but not the oddity of the sight.

"What do you want, Bolton? You did not have an appointment with me today."

"I told your man that so I could get in to see you."

Watkins scowled at him. "You are dripping on my wool carpet. What do you want?"

"Pulaski just stole my punt gun and sank my boat, then he sent ruffians to keep me from finding my gun. That's my livelihood. It's all I have, damn him."

"He knows you are the one that tried to kill him with that punt gun. I hardly blame him."

"He can't know. It was dark."

Watkins gazed at him with his mouth open. "You did do it? You fool."

"I didn't mean to kill him. I just wanted to shoot his horse."

"I can't believe you are actually telling me that."

Bolton shrugged his shoulders, his eyes fixed on the box. "What's in there?"

Watkins dug into one of his desk drawers. "None of your business." He withdrew a small brass padlock and attached it to the clasp on the box. Then he took the box to a glass front bookcase behind him, moved several books, and slipped the box inside. He then closed and locked the bookcase.

"You need to get out of town, Bolton."

"I need money."

Watkins sighed, pulled open his center drawer, and withdrew a five-dollar bill, tossing it in front of Bolton.

"I need more than that," Bolton said, snatching

the bill. "I got no punt gun and no boat. What am I gonna do? Can't we sue Pulaski?"

"Sue him for what, you imbecile?"

"He ruined my gun and boat. He took away my livelihood."

"You. Tried. To. Kill. Him."

"Folks don't know that," Bolton said, sitting in the padded chair before the desk.

"Don't sit there, Bolton. You're soaking the cloth."

"What am I gonna do without my punt gun?"

Watkins scratched his ear. He did not look directly at Bolton as he spoke. "I'm pretty sure I heard Pulaski tell someone he found a witness saying they saw you do it."

"Who?"

"Mmm, Franklin Curtis."

"That n–"

The door to the office burst open. George Milton charged in. His face was ruby red as he pointed a finger at Watkins. His other hand was balled into a fist, gripping a large crumpled envelope.

Watkins yelled. "Can no one get an appointment to see me? Wallace. Wallace! Get in here. Where is that damned butler?"

"I told him to go for a walk," Milton said.

Bolton's eyes flew from lawyer to lawyer.

"What do you want, George?" Watkins asked.

Milton rushed to the desk, waving the crumpled envelope before Watkins' face. Watkins leaned away from him with his arm raised for protection. Bolton shrank back in his chair.

"Want?" Milton said. "I want to stop you from cheating Sonja Pulaski."

"That is legal business between me and my client, George. It is none of yours."

Milton held up the envelope. "This is grand larceny. She would be signing everything over to you without any requirement for accountability or revenue. She would be giving away over two hundred thousand dollars in assets."

Watkins relaxed in his chair and straightened his spine. "It is our agreement for all I have done for her and Mrs. Binterfield. And, by the way, you are ignorant of true values. You underestimate the assets by half."

Bolton's eyes flew wide open, his jaw dropped, and his eyes flicked to the wooden box locked in the bookcase. Then he lowered his eyes back to Watkins.

"What are you doing, Watkins?" Milton asked. "What are you going to give her in return for all that money?"

Watkins peered at the bookcase and showed a delicate smile. Bolton noticed the tell. "Something she values even more than that," Watkins said.

"I will get an injunction to stop you," Milton said.

"Today is Saturday, George. Mrs. Pulaski has promised to sign our agreement Monday morning. You have until then to stir up trouble. However, you should be preparing to defend Benjamin Pulaski for assault on poor Bartholomew Lister. Pulaski is going before a Judge in Bel Air on Tuesday."

Milton's face was without expression, the color fading to pale.

Watkin's smile broadened. "You didn't know?"

Milton stormed out of the office. Watkins folded deep in his chair, his hands trembling, his elbows resting on his knees, his voice dry and speaking to the floor. "Get out, Bolton."

Watkins' butler stood in the doorway, ebony black, tall and slender with rounded shoulders. He had the lines of a perpetual smile on his face and lips surrounding perfectly white teeth. "You all right, Mr. Watkins?"

"No thanks to you, Wallace. I will speak to you about your desertion later. For now, escort this person out of my house, through the servants' entrance. Then get some rags to sop up the puddle he has made in my carpet like some stray dog."

Bolton scowled at Watkins as Wallace pulled him from the chair. Bolton glanced back at the bookcase as Wallace escorted him from the room, noticing the nearby window and flimsy construction of the glass bookcase as he crossed the threshold.

Bolton jerked his arm from Wallace as he left through a side door, then he stopped in the road, fingering in his pockets. He smiled to himself and headed to his rented room for dry clothes. An hour later, Bolton entered the United States Hotel near the end of St. Clair Street and settled onto a bar stool in its tavern. He received a few smirks and bold stares from the patrons, making him conscious of their fashionable dress compared to the tattered and stained clothes he wore. Bolton glared at them with his chin up, then turned his attention to his drinks. Shortly, with his third glass of whiskey in his hand, he wandered into the lobby where one of the large windows offered a narrow view of the river and the docks. The waves were whipped into whitecaps by the wind, and the ducks were huddled in the shallows, but no duck hunters ventured out in rowboats. Waves rushing north crashed against the posts of the docks throwing water spray into the air. He waved for a passing waiter and ordered another whiskey. The grand clock in the lobby struck five times. Couples descended the center stairs to amble into the tavern for the roasted duck and boiled potatoes that scented the air.

The waiter delivered a fresh glass of whiskey, then lingered, clearing his throat. "I beg your pardon, sir, but the tavern manager requests you pay for your drinks now. Your bill is already at two dollars."

"Two dollars?" Bolton pointed to the glass just set beside him. "That's only my fourth glass. Two dollars? That's fifty cents a glass. That's, that's grand larceny."

He reached into his pocket and withdrew the crumpled five-dollar bill. "Here, take your blood money from this and be sure you bring me the correct change, you hear? I'll have my change in silver."

The waiter skittered away. Out on the water, a sloop raced in before the wind, its sails only half raised and shorted, but still, the stress lines ran across the canvas from its tied battens. Closing to the docks, as sailors ran to the ropes to loosen sail, a stronger gust of wind slammed the sloop against the pier, snapping the mainmast. Bolton laughed as the waiter brought his change, and he left the hotel.

The rough water driven by the increasing wind slammed the *Jester* against the dock a second time before the crewmen could scramble to release the mainsail from the broken mast. The wind found its way under the canvas yanking against the mast.

Jimmy retrieved a hand ax and began hacking the tie ropes between the sail edges and the wooden loops that held the sail to the mast. He yelled for Tobias to help fold the sail and for Garrett to loop the mooring line around the dock's posts. The two tongers who had come from the oyster beds with them did all they could to assist. The ship smashed against the pier again. Other men from a ship already moored at the dock ran to pull the mooring line around the bollards and cleats on the dock. It took several minutes to secure the wayward sails from the broken mast and set the mast aside off the cargo hold. Tobias and Jimmy rigged a temporary boom to the remaining mast above deck. They focused their efforts on raising the oysters from the cargo hold as the others grabbed bushel baskets and barrels to receive the oysters.

The evening train was due at six. As the packers neared the end of filling shipping containers, Garrett dashed off to borrow a cargo trailer. Not wanting to waste time renting a horse at the livery stable, the men pushed and pulled the trailer the blocks to the train station. The train was waiting in the station, and the locomotive raising steam for the pull across the bridge. The railroad clerk waited anxiously at the open boxcar when the near-breathless men shoved the trailer next to it. Moving like zombies, they pushed themselves further to unload the containers from the trailer and up onto the boxcar floor. Then, wearily they climbed into the car to restack the barrels and bushel baskets for the trip to Philadelphia. It was already New Year's Day, and the prices paid New Year's Eve would not be duplicated. Still, most of the oysters would wind up as late evening meals that day, so the prices almost doubled from the previous week. The railroad clerk inspected each container for quality and volume, then signed the company payment note Tobias could deposit on Monday. The group collapsed on the cargo trailer catching their breath as the train blew its whistle and chugged its way north.

Tobias bought beer for them all at a colored tavern nearby that was one of his regular customers. He saw to it that the tavern had plenty of fresh oysters for their own customers and asked that the beer be sent out to the trailer. However, the tavern owner invited them all inside to get warm and have a little oyster stew. The tavern was little more than a shack near the train station, but anyone pausing from a train passing through Havre de Grace who had a hunger and a nose for good food, took their business there.

"Good as the Oyster Street Tavern," the owner proclaimed, and he had every right to the boast since he also owned the goats that provided Franklin his not-so-secret ingredient. People who live together in small towns are always linked in so many ways.

Tobias then hired an empty cargo wagon to pull the trailer back to the docks. One of the tongers lived in a modest house near the train station and left them to spend the night with his wife. Back at the pier near the *Jester*, Tobias, Garrett, and Jimmy untied the rope to the trailer and went to the sloop. The other tonger rode with the wagon driver who lived near him.

Jimmy halted, gawking at the sloop. "I've never seen her so high in the water. Come to it, I've never seen her on such a high tide."

Waves ran just under the dock boarding, splashing water up between the planks when it usually would have been two to three feet below them. With the heavy ballast rocks tossed overboard at the Bush River to allow for more oysters, the sloop rocked drunkenly.

Jimmy rubbed his head. "We need to tie additional mooring lines to her, or she'll beat herself to death during the night."

They added more lines to bow and stern, then more hemp fenders between the hull and the dock until the rocking was reasonable and the damage halted.

"Tobias," Jimmy said, "Doesn't look like we're going back to the oyster beds in the morning."

"We have to, Jimmy. We've got to pick up my men to bring them home. They'll never make it back through the waves out there in boats designed to sit low so they can tong oysters through calm water."

"This sloop is in no condition to sail, Tobias."

"Jimmy, they agreed to stay out there, twenty miles from their homes and families on New Year's day, another day in cold weather, to haul in more oysters."

"That's not my fault."

"You're the damned captain, Jimmy. Sonja said for you to work out the details. So, work them out."

Garrett turned away in silence to walk up the dock. Jimmy and Tobias continued to challenge each other for a solution to retrieve the oystermen. Thought after thought succumbed to reality and fell into impossibility. Finally, Jimmy recalled that the old ship originally had a more vertical mainmast than the one presently raked back several degrees to better brace against the wind's power.

"The slot the original mast set in is still there, unused space. If we can get a slightly slimmer mast to slip in there. And cut away some of the splinters, but leaving some of it as an angle brace, we could step a new mast tonight."

"Three men could do that?"

"It couldn't be a tall mast, but it could hold enough sail to run before the wind." He pointed up to the darkened sky. "We wouldn't need much sail to run before this wind."

"What about tacking, back and forth to get there?" Tobias asked.

Crestfallen, Jimmy's shoulders sagged as reality overwhelmed his idea. "No. It could never do that."

Garrett returned to the dock. "Don't need no tacking to get to the Bush River."

"Since when can we sail against the wind?" Jimmy asked.

Garrett pointed to the ship moored in front of them. "See that schooner? Her captain had a steam engine put in her last year."

"I saw the smokestack but didn't see any paddlewheels," Jimmy said. "I thought she was a little whaler."

Garrett stuck his thumbs in his suspenders, giving a rare smile in the lantern light. "Nope. She's got a screw in her stern. She runs into the wind like a rabbit. What's more, the captain agreed to tow us at first light, up to the mouth of the Bush River."

Tobias gave Garrett a bright smile. "How do you know all this?"

"Her first mate is an old friend of mine, Amos Morton. Knew him long before the war. He married my first cousin. So, he asked his captain, cause they gotta be in Annapolis tomorrow morning anyway."

"How much does he want to do it?"

Garrett gave them a lopsided smile, puckering his cheek where the scar remained stiff. "Six bushels of fresh oysters."

Tobias and Jimmy patted him on each shoulder.

"I'll give him ten bushels," Tobias said.

"No, you won't," Garrett said. "Them other four bushels go toward my bonus."

Ben and Mickey were by the barn plucking duck feathers when Sonja came home. Her back was stiff and straight, the gait more of a march, and she made no effort to greet the men.

Ben waved with feather-coated fingers. "How was your meeting with Watkins?"

Sonja stepped closer to examine the ducks, speaking without a smile. "Are you going to cook all three of them?"

Ben and Mickey glanced at each other.

"We, um," Ben said, "We were hoping you would."

She showed a smirk. "I'd better if they're going to be worth eating. Don't pluck the other two, just hang them on the side of the barn a couple days, so they'll be tender."

Ben held up the one he had been plucking, showing it to Sonja.

She shook her head. "I'll soak it in salt and rosemary until tomorrow."

"You can't cook it tonight?" Ben asked.

Mickey smiled at Sonja. "Men don't wait for meat to grow tender. They want it fire cooked and still bloody in the middle."

Sonja rolled her eyes and turned away, speaking as she walked to the porch. "Then you cook it."

"We can do that, woman. Don't bother yourself," Ben said to her back as he began making a fire pit while Mickey gathered kindling. With enough kindling, Mickey gathered split wood while Ben went to the barn to bring out a roasting crank and iron support rods. Soon a substantial fire was burning. The duck was salted and peppered and skewered above the flames. Mickey turned the spit on one side while Ben smoked his pipe on the other. Sonja emerged from the house carrying a small whiskey jug and two glasses, marched to the fire pit, handed Ben the jug and glasses in silence, then returned to the house. Ben smiled to himself, nodded his head in satisfaction and filled the glasses, then offered one to Mickey, who held his up in salute, as did Ben.

"Tonight, the men cook."

The duck turned golden as it began to cook and sizzle. Ben took his turn with the spit as Mickey smoked his cigar and refilled their glasses.

"I once had brandied duck in the officer's mess at Fort Monroe," Mickey said.

"I've heard of that," Ben said, "but never tasted it."

Mickey regarded the whiskey in his glass. "Don't see why we couldn't use whiskey. Should be about the same."

Ben had his attention on the flames when he spoke. "I think brandy would be a sweeter drink than corn whiskey."

Mickey stood and moved close to the fire as Ben glanced up to him. Mickey leaned over the duck extending his hand with the whiskey glass as recognition filled Ben's face with surprise. Ben opened his mouth to speak as Mickey's whiskey splashed on the duck, mixing with the volatile duck fat weeping from the skin, and the duck erupted into flames. Ben roared a series of profanities and grabbed at the spit handle, which was also covered in duck fat, and as he raised the duck from the fire, the flames spread to the crank handle. Ben yanked back from the burning rod, tossing the flaming duck into the air like a flying torch that landed on the pile of split wood gathered for cooking. The duck fat coated the wood, igniting instantly with both the wood and the charring duck feeding the flames higher. The front yard lit up like a great whale oil lamp as the first of the sleet began to fall from the heavy clouds above. The sleet grew thick and included pieces of ice growing into hail, pelting the men and hissing onto the duck's funeral pyre.

"Leave it," Ben said, pulling Mickey by his coat sleeve.

They dashed to the porch dodging hail, then onto planks stomping the mud from their boots and shaking rain and ice from their coats as the air filled with a downpour of sleet and rain. Sonja opened the front door, releasing the aroma of the heated venison stew, and peered beyond them to the burning duck carcass. Her face was illuminated by the pulsing flames still burning despite the falling sleet. Without expression, she fixed her eyes on Ben's.

"Is it done yet?"

Moments later, after toweling off, Ben and Mickey sat at the kitchen table while Sonja said a blessing over the stew. After saying, "Amen," she added, "You gentlemen need to bring my glasses back inside when the rain stops."

They ate in silence until Sonja slammed her

spoon onto the table. Her expression was fierce and directed to Ben. Mickey stood from the table and left the room.

"I heard men in town talking," Sonja said, her teeth clenched, "about Ben Pulaski shooting a hole in a punt boat."

Ben returned her gaze in silence.

"Did you kill him?"

"No."

"Did you shoot at him?"

"No."

"I don't believe you, Ben. You have done horrible things when you thought you had to, but you've never lied to me...until now."

"I wanted to kill him. He almost killed you, and he deserved it."

"They said you went after him. Crossed the river to get to him."

"Yes. I did that."

"And then what? You forgave him? Ben Pulaski does not forgive."

"NO. I will never forgive that bastard, Sonja. I had my shotgun pointed at the back of his head, but I did not shoot."

"Why?"

He gazed at her eyes.

"Why, Ben?"

"I...I heard your voice."

She scoffed. "What did my voice say?"

"I heard you breathing. You said my name."

She bit her lip and turned her face away. Then she stood and moved to the sink, resting her hands on the metal rim, looking out the window into the fading light.

"I am so sick of these clouds," she said. "It's

dark even when it isn't. This winter that never comes, it only threatens."

She turned to face him. "Watkins told me you were going to court again for attacking Bartholomew Lister, but this time in Bel Air."

"Yes. I'm sorry about all the trouble that has caused."

"I don't want your sadness. I am so sick of sadness and worry, and guilt. I ache for all the evil I have let myself sink into. I ache for my lost son. I ache to know my husband, the father of my lost son, feels that loss. I ache for a man that knows more than anger and violence, that can admit to himself a tragedy that overwhelms his family."

Ben gave his attention to the spoon next to his bowl, unable to meet her eyes.

She grabbed a dishcloth and threw it at Ben. "I need you to talk to me about how you feel. I need more than just listening to you yell at Franklin in his tavern."

Ben cleared his throat but said nothing, refusing to raise his face to hers.'

"You can tell him," she said, "but you cannot tell your own wife, the mother of our dead son."

Ben faced her with a frown, "Don't do that."

"I don't want your anger," she said. "You have given me far too much of that."

She crossed the room to him, grabbing his face, pulling it up to hers. "Don't you mourn him?"

Ben pulled her hands down. "I cannot dig up his rotting body, Sonja, and bring him back to your arms. I did not kill him. He killed himself. But, but if I could, I would walk into Hell itself and trade places with him this instant! He and I both would be better off, as would you woman! Because my

Hell has already come. It is a living one."

He stormed out of the kitchen.

"No," she yelled after him. "I want you both!"

Ben charged out of the house, passing Mickey on the porch, stepping into the thinning rain and sleet. Ben searched the ground near the fire pit until he found the dropped glasses. He stood still a moment, his chest heaving, then he raised both glasses above his head, turned his face to the falling rain, and bellowed, releasing a long anguished animal roar that continued until his lungs were empty. Ben smashed the glasses into the woodpile and marched down the slope to the canal, then crossed the muddy bottom ankle deep in rainwater. He crawled up the other side onto the towpath, where he walked in circles before heading south, out of view.

Mickey stood at the edge of the porch, tears slipping down his cheeks, muttering to himself. "Let it out, Ben. Let it out at last."

Sobbing drifted from Sonja's bedroom window as Mickey wiped his eyes. The rain and sleet stopped, but the wind from the south stiffened. Mickey took the top steps from the porch then paused, gazing up at the charcoal sky.

"If this is what you brought me here for, to witness this...you're a sick bastard, your Lordship...begging your pardon."

Two miles along the towpath, where the trees were thick and formed a dark tunnel with only a thin promise of gray at each end, Ben stopped his march and fell to his knees. He raised his face to the last falling sleet finding its way through the leafless branches, wetting his face with chilled water. Tears flooded his eyes, mixing saltwater with the melting sleet, then he began slapping the sides of his own face. His hands curled into fists, and he continued to beat his face until he leaned back on his ankles and screamed up into the darkness.

"Isaac. I-i-i-i-i-s-s-s-a-a-a-c-c-c!"

In the silence that followed the cry, a heron huddling among the trees stepped awkwardly toward the strange human that knelt in the mud, stood near him, and bowed its head.

Bolton had drifted to cheaper taverns, drinking and swearing until he was told to leave and had only a dollar left. Four silver quarters. He stood in the middle of the street, left muddy by rain and sleet moving away. He returned to the boarding house where he rented his room, but the housekeeper and her husband met him in the front room, blocking his way.

"You owe for your room," the husband said.

"I'm good for it," Bolton said.

The husband held out his hand. "Not hardly. Your boat's sunk, and your gun's gone. You ain't getting in your room lest you pay."

Bolton dug his four silver quarters from his pocket and slapped them into the man's hand.

"That'll get you in tonight. Tomorrow you pay up, or we lock you out and sell whatever is left in your room."

Bolton shouldered his way past the man and climbed the stairs to his attic room. The wet clothes from his morning dunking had dried and were in slightly better condition than those he wore. He changed into those and examined the top drawer of his chest. Inside there was a nearly empty pint bottle of whiskey, a tiny silver Saint Christopher medal he once stole from a drunk, and his deer horn handled knife. He drained the bottle, pocketed the medal, pissed in the corner of the room, and left with his knife.

Minutes later, Bolton knocked on the business door of Bartholomew Lister's house. After he knocked several times, Nadja Lister opened the door.

"Need to talk to Bart," Bolton said, pushing his way past her and found his way to Lister's private office. "This is all your fault," Bolton said as he dropped onto the chair beside the desk.

Lister glanced up from his magnifying glass, sighing at his visitor through clenched teeth.

"If you hadn't told me Pulaski had money, I wouldn't be in this poor situation."

"What have you done, Harris?"

"Pulaski and I are enemies because of me bringing charges against him at your insistence."

"You agreed to do that."

"Yeah, for the money. That never happened, and now Pulaski has thrown my punt gun into the bay and shot up my rowboat, and I have lost my room. This is all your fault."

"You tried to shoot him with that punt gun, you fool, and all you did was kill his horse. Of course, he is your enemy, now. Maybe I can help you some after my suit against him Tuesday."

"I can't wait until Tuesday. Where am I gonna sleep?"

Lister sighed. "All right, I knew Pulaski had money, and when he hit you in the tavern, I knew you could take him to court if I helped. Now Pulaski has attacked me too, damn him. I'll get you some money, Bolton. I'll have more after going to court in

Bel Air, but you will owe me. Wait here."

Lister went into another room, where a casket was on display. Bolton heard him arguing with his wife.

"You are not giving him any of our money," she said.

"Hold your tongue, woman."

The anger in her voice drove it to a shrill. "No. You are not giving him any of that money."

Bolton followed the voices and found them struggling over a small wooden box. As they fought for the little box, it sprang open, losing several bills onto the carpet. Bolton swooped between them, grabbing the bills. Nadja pounced on him with a flurry of slaps and hits. Bolton hit her face with his fist, knocking her to the floor. Lister grabbed a nearby brass candlestick and swung it at Bolton, who blocked it with his arm, crying out in pain. Lister raised the candlestick to strike again. Bolton pulled his knife and thrust it at Lister's forearm, missing his mark and driving the blade into Lister's armpit. Bolton yanked the knife back as Lister gasped in pain, gazing wide-eyed at the spraying blood and the knife in his own hand.

"You caused this," Bolton said.

Bright red blood spurted from Lister's armpit, soaking his shirt. Lister's face paled, and he fell back against the casket, blood pouring from his sleeve dripping to the floor as he collapsed.

Nadja screamed. "Murder! Murder!"

She flew against Bolton, pounding him with her fists, driving him against the casket.

Bolton snarled. "Shut up, woman. He caused it."

He jabbed a fist against her face. Nadja spun

under his arms, clawing at his eyes, screaming at him. They fell against the casket, knocking it to the floor in a resounding crash, with them on top of it. She scratched at his face. He grabbed her hair, pulling her head back, and drove his knife into her throat. She screamed with bloody foam from her mouth and neck wounds.

Bolton shoved Nadja onto her husband, "All I want is the money, bitch. You brought this on yourself."

Bolton settled onto his knees to grab the money. Lister grabbed at his ankles. Bolton kicked his heel into Lister's chin, causing him to scream in pain. Lister screamed, grabbing for the fallen candlestick.

"You'll hang," Lister said.

"Not by your word," Bolton said, then stabbed him in the throat, pushing the horn handle with both hands.

"It's all your fault," Bolton said to Lister's bloody face. "You stupid people. Look what you made me do. All I wanted was some money. You got me into all this. It's your fault I shot at Pulaski. I only wanted to shoot his horse. It's all your fault. You got what you deserved."

Bolton stood, kicked both dead bodies, and ran out the door, shoving the money into his coat pockets. He ran toward the water, his clothes soaked in blood, seeking a rowboat to cross the river. The smaller boats had been pulled ashore from the churning river and lashed to posts, while the bigger ones were chained.

The wind howled through the streets, flipping store signs and snapping canvas awnings over the doorways of closed stores. Bolton ran on, passing the Bachrach's clothing store and the office of Turner Enterprises. Glancing in the windows as he ran, he halted before Turner's office. Peeking through the window, he muttered to himself.

"I oughta set fire to this place. English bastard put a shotgun to my cheek before that crazy Pulaski holed my boat. Same stupid people like them Listers. It was their own damned fault. I wasn't looking for all that. It come to me, and I dealt with it. Had to."

The closet door in the back of the office was open, showing the Purdy shotgun leaning in the corner.

"Oh, yes," he said, spotting the shotgun. "You're mine. He owes me that much."

Bolton pried the front door latch with his knife and dashed to the closet to snatch the shotgun, then back outside to survey the street. No one was there. He glanced at the next shop where new suits and watches were on display in the front window.

"I'll burn you later," he said to Turner's office, then stepped in front of Bachrach's store to pry that door open as well. Once out of the wind, he peeked to see if anyone had seen him, then he dashed through the store looking for whatever he could find of value. He scooped up four new watches, then noticed the wool clothing hanging on racks. Glancing outside again to ensure he was safe, he dressed in a new wool shirt and pants, then yanked down a long wool coat with big pockets. He threw his bloody clothes into a corner, stuffed the money and the watches in the coat pockets, then grabbed new leather gloves and a new bowler hat for his head. Bolton explored the store's rear finding a back door to the shop locked by latch from the inside. He left through that door and into a service lane. The lane was darkening as evening drew on, which gave him a way out without being observed. After hurried strides along the route, he slowed his pace, sure no one would recognize him.

"Just a gentleman duck hunter coming home," he said to himself, then stopped in mid-stride. "But where is home now?" Then he smiled. "That box of valuables in Watkins' bookcase. Bet there's a bunch of money in that. Maybe even gold."

At the lower end of the canal basin near the lockhouse, several barges were sitting in low water, tied side by side, waiting for spring. Ben's gait was awkward as he stepped onto the closest barge. One of his bargemen was wintering in that first cabin, so Ben made his way to the barge beyond, which was not occupied. Boots clomped within the cabin stairwell of the first barge, and just as Ben stepped over onto the next one, the cabin hatch flew open, and an oil lamp lit the area.

"Who is that?" a voice demanded. "What are you doing on Pulaski barges?"

Ben stopped and turned to face the man. "I own them."

Claude Haney held up the lantern to see the intruder's face. "Lord a'mighty, Ben. What happened to your face?"

"Some crazy man beat me on the towpath, but I'll be all right."

"You want me to go for the deputy? Or get some of our men to go after him."

"I did some pretty stupid things tonight, Claude. I expect I had it coming."

Ben turned toward the cabin of the next barge.

Claude called after him as Ben lifted the hatch to the cabin stairs. "If you're going to bunk up in the old *Sarah,* Ben, Cap'n Holter always keeps a little jug of whiskey in the right-hand cabinet below his bunk. I'm sure he wouldn't mind."

"That's good to know, Claude. I'll replace it before he comes back in the spring."

Ben's ache for Isaac was joined by the thought of Aaron's first child, Sarah, who the barge was named for. Little Sarah had died with her mother, Maggie, on her only day of life. It was hard to think of a canal barge once newly named for an infant to now be considered old. He thought about Maggie and the baby as he descended the steps into the darkness.

"Twenty- five years ago," he said. "That poor baby died right after her first cry."

Ben lit an oil lamp in the musty air, scented with coal dust from a thousand trips up the canal and long ago fried meat. He reached for the cabinet under the first bunk and pulled out the whisky jug. He set it on the narrow table in front of him, rested his forehead onto his arms, and cried again.

Bolton knocked at the servant's entrance to Watkins' mansion. When Wallace opened the door, Bolton put the shotgun to his face.

"Step out here, boy."

Wallace slowly emerged as Bolton guided him with pressure from the gun and body motion. "You got people in town?"

"Yes, suh."

"You go stay with them, and don't you come back until tomorrow. You hear me?"

"Yes, suh."

"Anyone else in there besides Watkins?"

"No, suh."

"Git."

Wallace hurried away as Bolton made his way into the house and crept to the office, where he tried the door to the bookcase. The door was still locked. There was still enough remaining light from the window to see that the box was still inside. He heard Watkins cough in another room, so he returned to the foyer. Lamplight from the parlor illuminated the carpet in the main entrance. Bolton crept to the doorway, where the door was slightly ajar, and peeked in. Watkins sat in a padded wing chair before the fireplace, reading a book by an oil lamp sitting on the table beside him. A crystal brandy decanter sat on the table next to the lamp, and a dainty brandy snifter sat next to it. The glass was empty.

Watkins lifted the glass to examine it in the lamplight. Then set it down to pick up a silver bell, which he rang several times. Watkins released a heavy sigh, saying, "Where is that useless man?", then yelled out, "Wallace. Wallace, get in here."

Bolton grinned, stepping close behind Watkins' chair, "Yassuh?"

Watkins held up his glass for Wallace to refill it. Still grinning, Bolton picked up the decanter and drank from it with exaggerated gulping swallows. Watkins spun around in his seat, "What th–" his face screwed up in fury until Bolton put the barrel of the shotgun against his nose. Bolton pirouetted around Watkins, keeping the barrels against his nose, until Bolton stood before him, still holding the decanter in his left hand. Watkins still held the snifter. Bolton took another drink from the decanter then giggled as he refilled Watkins' glass.

"Swallow it down, Lester. We got work to do in

your office."

Watkins took a trembling sip.

Bolton withdrew the shotgun several inches to give him room. "Oh, drink it like a man, Lester."

Watkins took a modest drink, and Bolton knocked the glass from his hand with the barrel.

"Get up. Let's go to your office. I want that box and whatever money you have in there."

"You don't understand, Bolton."

Bolton poked the barrels into Watkins' nose, making it bleed. "No. You don't understand. You do what I tell you to do, or I will blow your damned head off. You and Lister got me into trouble with Pulaski, and now he's after me, so you're gonna help me get outta town. Now move."

Bolton guided Watkins into the office and to the bookcase. "Open it."

Watkins turned to face him. "There's nothing in it–"

Bolton poked him in the face again. Blood poured from his nose, dripping on his vest."

"Now unlock it."

Watkins fumbled with keys from his vest pocket, his hand trembling as he unlocked the bookcase.

"Put it on the desk."

Watkins' shoulders sagged, his back bowed. "You don't understand."

"I told you to shut up," Bolton said as he swung the buttstock around and smashed it into Watkins' face, dropping him to the floor.

Bolton pulled the keys from the unconscious man's hand and began examining the keys for the one to the lock until he heard voices outside. He dashed to the window, pulling back the heavy drapes just enough to peek into the yard. Several black men and a white man had gathered at the yard's edge, pointing to the house. Wallace was among them standing beside Deputy Hopkins.

"Shit."

Bolton scooped up the box, shattering an empty brandy snifter sitting on the desk, and grabbed the shotgun, heading for the door to the carriage house in the rear, then out through the bushes near the old outhouse onto the lane he had used from the shops. The keys he had taken from Watkins jumped unnoticed from his pocket as he sprinted as fast as his legs could carry him. He flew onto another lane at the end of the next block and pumped his legs to get farther away, finally stopping for breaths behind the Oyster Street Tavern.

Inside the tavern, Franklin Curtis locked the doors. He closed early on Saturday evenings. He lost business by doing that, but he had a schedule to keep for his church. He and Rebecca would row to Watson's Island every Saturday evening, so he could cook for his parishioners. Sunday morning breakfast. The word of the Lord was food for their souls, but the ham and eggs and grits and biscuits he cooked for them was to bring them across the river to fill their bellies. He cooked all night each Saturday and fed the people before worship service. He slept only briefly since the war and losing his leg. The nightmares that took him to Jesus still raged in his sleep, so he fought it off until utter exhaustion drove him down, and he could find peace in nothingness. Franklin also fed his flock lunch before they went home. It was the secret to the success of the little chapel on Watson's Island. Even though the word of the Lord was gift enough, having full bellies helped people pay attention to the word. Sunday afternoons, when everyone but Rebecca was gone, he would lay on a pad of old blankets in the back of the church and surrender his body while God and his daughter watched over him. He and Rebecca began gathering the meat, flour, and grain from the tavern kitchen, preparing their load for the trip to the island before full darkness came.

They had a full cart of supplies when they left the tavern heading for the little dock near the canal basin's outlet lock. The river's surface was high and angry, but the twenty-foot boat Tobias had acquired for them would be safe, and Franklin's massive arms would take them to the island in short order. Franklin tied the emptied cart to a nearby post, then helped Rebecca on board as Bolton stepped onto the modest dock.

He set the box at his feet. "Got room for another passenger, preacher?"

Franklin did not recognize him in his suit and bowler hat but glanced around the contents of the boat and pointed to an open spot in the stern as he settled between the oars. "Sure, we can take you to the island. Untie that last rope for me as you get in."

"I need to go to the other side of the river," Bolton said.

"I'm sorry, Mister. But we're going to the island."

Bolton drew the shotgun from under his long coat and pointed it at Franklin. "Don't argue with me, cook. Just take me to the other side of the river, and I'll be gone, and you and missy there will still be unharmed."

Bolton kept the gun pointed at Franklin as he handed him the box and pointed to the stern seat where Franklin set it. Bolton slipped the loop of rope from the post, stepped into the boat, and settled onto the stern seat with his feet on either side of the box.

"Row."

The boat slewed around first from the river current, then from the tide's resistance force, turning the boat entirely around.

"Can't you row a damned boat?"

"There's a lot of power around those whirlpools," Franklin said." Got to stay away from them. Never seen the river like this before."

"Just row the damned boat."

The boat slewed again in the opposite direction. The waves slapped against the boat from all angles as the rowboat spun. Franklin groaned as he strained to pull the boat farther away from the vortex spinning in the water.

Bolton kept the gun pointed at Franklin but centered his attention to the brass lock on the box and felt his pockets for Watkins' keys. He cursed when he could not find them. Bolton turned the box on its side, so the little lock hung down and then smashed it three times with the butt of the shotgun. The lock shattered, and the box flew open, spilling its contents onto the bottom of the boat.

Bolton sputtered in disbelief, "What the hell? A couple broken pieces of bones and a piece of wood." He snatched up the box to see better and ran his hands around inside. "What the hell? He said it was valuable." Bolton glared at Franklin. "The bastard must have switched it. Knew I was coming."

Bolton scooped up the bones, threw them back into the box and slammed the lid shut, jamming it closed. Then he tossed it into the water, cursing the box as it sat high in the water, drifting primly away.

"Nothing," he said. "Not a damned thing in there worth any money."

Bolton raised his rifle to shoot the box then glanced up as Franklin flew at him. Franklin grabbed Bolton's shoulders and tossed him into the water, the rifle clattered into the bottom of the boat. Bolton's new wool clothing sucked up pounds of water as he thrashed around, trying to get back to the boat, but it slipped beyond his reach. His knuckles jammed against the box sitting on the surface. "Damn it."

A rope splashed into the turbulent water near Bolton.

Franklin yelled to him. "Grab the line."

Bolton found the rope and was slipping under the water himself when Franklin pulled him up to the surface.

"Hold on to it, so I can row us to shore," Franklin told him.

Moments later, the rowboat slipped up onto the southern end of Watson's Island, several yards closer to the buildings than Franklin had ever seen it. The wind from the south was approaching gale strength. The froth had the appearance of ocean turmoil. The only remaining posts to tie the boat to were the church foundation's corners, usually fifteen yards beyond the waterline. Bolton crawled on his hand and knees in the surf, coughing water from his lungs.

Franklin stood over him. "Now you settle

down, Mister. You behave yourself, and maybe in the morning when this storm quits, one of the parishioners will take you back with them to the Cecil County shore. But don't you ever point a gun at my daughter or me again. God hasn't given me enough patience for that yet, and I expect it will be a long time coming."

Bolton slipped from his wet coat, pulled his knife from his belt, and charged Franklin, screaming. "I'm going to kill you."

Franklin turned to face him, but his artificial leg caught among the loosened rocks, and he stumbled, crashing onto his left elbow as he fell. Bolton threw himself on top of Franklin, driving the knife toward the man's chest with both hands. Franklin twisted to his side, pushing Bolton's blade away, then smashed his fist into Bolton's face. Another form flew against both of them, knocking Bolton onto his side. Blood spewed from the man's nose. Franklin rose up on one knee, giving his right arm full swing, and pounded his fist against Bolton's face again. The crack of cheekbones was audible. Blood from Bolton's nose gushed over both of them. Franklin punched Bolton's face a third time, and the light in his eyes turned to steel then went out.

Franklin pushed up onto his knees to find his daughter kneeling next to him, and she wrapped him in her arms.

"I couldn't just stand by, Papa. I had to do something, so I just flung myself into him. I didn't know what else to do."

He folded his right arm around her shoulder and kissed her cheek. "You did good, daughter. Momma would be proud. You have her spirit."

She peered at the bloody face of Harris Bolton lying on his back, staring up at the black sky with unconscious empty eyes.

"I'll tie him up," Franklin said, "and put him in the boat for safekeeping, for now. Then we'll take him to Deputy Hopkins and tell him about all this as soon as possible. For now, he can just lay in the rowboat. I'll put his coat over him, so he won't freeze, but I'm not having him in my church, even tied up."

"He doesn't deserve that, Papa. He was an evil man."

"Maybe so in the end, daughter. But he is some mother's child, some father's son, maybe some woman's husband, maybe even a father to his own children. He was also a child of God, and he deserves to be treated as such."

Rebecca retrieved Bolton's wool coat while Franklin tied the man's hands and arms. They laid him in the rowboat that brought him to the island. Then Franklin retrieved the shotgun from the boat, speaking to the unconscious Bolton.

"You don't need to get your hands on this again."

As the night advanced, the Susquehanna Flats' turbulence was kicked up by the strengthening southern wind. Garrett's friend Amos from the steam-powered schooner requested permission to come aboard the *Jester,* where the three crewmen gathered around him.

"Captain says he has to leave tonight," Amos said. "He wants plenty of time to negotiate the point coming into Annapolis with all this crazy weather and cantankerous tides. He says he'll still honor his promise of a tow, but you'll have to leave tonight."

"How is he going to see at night?" Asked Jimmy.

"The ship has a quicklime searchlight," Amos said. "That thing will make a beam brighter than the sun."

"How does it work?" Tobias asked, but the man only shrugged his shoulders.

"We still haven't stepped a replacement mast," Jimmy said. "The spar your captain sold us will work well for the run back, but we haven't finished preparing the bracing."

"Captain says one hour," Amos said.

"The mouth of the Bush is sheltered, some,"

Garrett said. "We ought to be able to step the mast there and have it rigged before dawn."

Jimmy turned to the visitor. "Tell your captain 'thank you,' and we'll be ready."

"He wants to leave within the hour," the visitor said.

Garrett and Tobias scrambled to tie down or stow everything they could while Jimmy went in search of the two tongers who would lose their precious time at home. It took Jimmy a half hour to bring the two additional men. One was resentful but determined, while the other was heavily inebriated, suspended between the other two, half walking, half stumbling, and mumbling curses. Jimmy shared his uninjured arm to support the drunken man. The tongers were brought on board and sent below to get some sleep, while the other three made fast the tow line for the steam schooner. Jimmy used his good hand as effectively as many used two. The schooner's sails laid unfurled and wrapped tight and tied down, securing them to their spars to prevent catching any wind.

Both ships were facing north along the dock. The steamer warped out away from the wharf to make a complete rotation to face south, then moved beside the *Jester*. Jimmy stood in the bow of the *Jester* to toss the heavy tow rope to the steamer as Tobias and Garrett slipped the last mooring lines from the bollards, freeing the *Jester* from the dock, so she could follow the steamer. The incoming waves shoved *Jester's* stern against the pier again with a crash that shuddered the interior of the *Jester*. The schooner took up the slack in the tow line as she moved south, gently swinging the *Jester* around to follow her.

As the ships passed the Concord Point Lighthouse, the schooner's searchlight shone a mile ahead, lancing out with a narrow white beam. Driven by its steam engine, with the darkness cut away before it, the schooner shoved its way into the teeth of the wind, bringing the *Jester* behind her on a sleigh ride. Faces on the *Jester* showed excitement and childish glee at such a ride against the wind.

Three hours later, after shouldering her way through the rough waves and pulling the *Jester* behind her, the steamer steered her bow into the mouth of the Bush River. There the steamer's crew tossed the towline overboard at the apex of her route. The *Jester* continued her headway from the tow, running farther into the mouth as the schooner turned back toward the bay. As she turned, the shoreline lit into day, where the beam swept along it. The captain knowingly forfeited his six bushels of oysters in his need to reach Annapolis.

Jester's crew was relieved to be within the protection of the Bush River. They dropped her stern anchor as she lost her headway, followed quickly by dropping the bow anchor to keep her facing the river current. Filling her hold in the morning with oysters would replace the lost ballast and stabilize the exaggerated rolling and yawing she suffered at that moment. Without moon or stars overhead and no land lights around her, the *Jester* was cloaked in darkness, only pushed away by the glow of her oil lanterns. She was a small island of faint yellow light in a world of black, her inhabitants swarming her deck hammering and sawing to give her a mast for her sails, to give her life again.

"A spar is just a lesser version of a mast," Jimmy said to Tobias. "It's usually used in a secondary role as a top or bottom boom for a sail. But, once the spar is been placed snugly in the deck, the *Jester* will have received a smaller version of her mast."

Afterward, the *Jester* was ready to receive shortened sails."

Jimmy passed the sails to Tobias and Garrett. "These should be sufficient to run before the wind that blew toward Havre de Grace without significant difficulty."

When the sails were rigged, Tobias offered to send his tongers below to get some sleep since they would have a hard final day of oystering.

"We'd just as soon row back to our camp," Lawrence said. He was becoming a spokesperson among the tongers. "We'd rather take the oyster boat tied beside the *Jester's* and return with the others and sleep on the cots instead of rocking in the sloop."

Even Jimmy admitted to suffering the ungainly motion of the ship without sufficient ballast weight in the bottom. Still, the absence of the stones would allow another ton of oysters to sell the following night.

Some additional weight had already accumulated in the ship's bilge, though not enough yet to make a noticeable difference in the *Jester*'s wallow. One of the hull planks just above the water line had suffered a severe blow when the thirty-year-old ship slammed into the dock in Havre de Grace. The impact caused a thin split along the grain of the old wood. Water seeped in steadily, saturating the wood grain within the break, slowly driving the opening farther along the plank as the ship rocked. As water collected in the bilge through the split hull plank, the sloop settled lower into the water, bringing the plank below the surface.

As the night progressed, the three men labored to reattach the boom to the short replacement mast to hold the sail at its base. They had to repair the wooden sail loops that slipped up and down the mast to carry the edge of the sail aloft or bring it down as needed to work the ship. Then the lines had to be run to hold the mast in place, securing them to the deck and ship's sides run. Finally, more lines were run through blocks and tackle to raise and lower the sails. Their experience had long taught them that taming the wind was a complicated task, and the workings of a sailboat belied its complexity.

Their muscles and joints ached from the feverish activity to remake the ship able to run before the wind in the morning, as morning came closer and closer. At last, they stumbled from the cold to their bunks, wrapping in wool blankets for brief hours sleep, far too exhausted to notice the lull in the ship's wallow.

Jimmy examined the finished work on the *Jester*. "You can't trust the appearance of the bay," he said at large. "She often hides the moving forces below the surface, even when she appears at rest."

"She can surprise ya," Garrett said. "Winter waters here in the upper bay didn't freeze because of that warm southerly wind. But Pennsylvania and New York, where most of the water for the Susquehanna come from, had no such mild winter. The river farther north has been freezing. That reduces some flow into Maryland."

Jimmy nodded at Garrett's comment. "The cold Susquehanna that feeds the Chesapeake slides across the warming bottom of the Susquehanna Flats near Havre de Grace, but then falls into a deep trench carved by an ancient hurricane."

"Which matters how?" Asked Tobias.

Jimmy pointed out beyond the mouth of the Bush River.

"The cold channel flows along the bottom like a tunnel under the bay, even when the two high tides a day raises the surface water. The battle between river force and tidal force can be worse under a strong wind. Steady winds working with the river water flow can sometimes push the high tide away, keeping the bay from rising as much as usual."

Jimmy used his hands to show the push of the wind and water.

"But when the wind blows with the tide, instead of against it, the tide has added strength. The bay can rise above a normal high tide. Like a broom sweeping a puddle of water on the floor, the wind alone could stack up the water in the bay; damming it at a level higher than usual."

Jimmy spoke with the confidence of a true sailor. "The wind's been southerly for several days. The tides are growing higher each time, coming in with more force. That's not a good sign."

Meager dawn crept into the sky, highlighting clouds like tarnished silver. The wind-driven tidal wave swept into the Bush River, stacking upon the imprisoned cold water, flooding over docks, and rushing inland like an angry animal. The tonger boats were snatched away from their mooring or sunk immediately. The tonger's camp was inundated at the same time. Water ran into the tents, rising quickly into their cots, driving the men out with no time to recover clothing or boots. They scrambled out, yelling to each other to ensure they were on their feet. The water came to their knees, flowing from the river, and thoughts of getting to the boats were abandoned.

"We gotta get to higher land," Lawrence yelled. "This water's coming from the bay."

They dashed shivering and half-awake, splashing up the trail to the little village farther inland, hoping to outrun the menacing tide. The tide rose to their waists, the cold water taking their breath, running beyond them, ahead of them, reaching the village before them. The icy water climbed up to their armpits. The men yelled out alarms to awaken the villagers, but most of the modest houses were already empty, and the people were gone when the men arrived.

"They're all gone." Lawrence said. "Keep going!"

The village was on a slight rise, letting the men climb to a lower water level that fell to their waist as they discovered the water already flowing through the houses. Those houses with front and back doors were left open to save the humble structures from the strength of the flood. Tables and chairs floated into the bushes where the current took them, perhaps held for the living to reclaim them later.

Lawrence and the other tongers from the *Jester* caught up with the fleeing villagers, and the crowd grew, moving farther inland. Men and women banged on pots and pans for an alarm to others, sloshing away with whatever they could grab. Women carried their babies. Lawrence and the other tongers joined in with them, lifting up the children too old for their mothers to carry them but not yet tall or strong enough to fight the tide. Older children and men brought whatever would help them survive.

In the river, the *Jester* sat low in the water as the surface rose. The bilgewater already found its way from the cargo hold into the tiny bunk room. Silently, the ship rose with the high tide, taking up the chains from fore and aft, wasting what little slack was allowed between ship and anchors. The grip from the bottom with the sloop anchored to face a river current becoming inconsequential would become a trap in the flow of the catastrophic tide coming to breach the *Jester*.

The tide shoved the ship up to the ends of its anchor chains, sending a jolt through the hull. The three men arose, stepping into cold ankle-deep water, reaching for boots and coats, and scrambling up the narrow ladder to the main deck. There they saw the flooded river and the danger the ship faced. The tidal water rose fast as they struggled to free the sloop from its anchor chains, held fast by iron stakes driven deep to hold the ship. Jimmy grabbed a speaking horn and yelled a warning to the men at the camp, hoping they would hear it, not knowing they were already gone inland.

The river water level was well above the split plank, and the mounting pressure on the hull sprang the plank, opening a waterfall into the hull. Water rushed up within the hold even as the tidal water rose in the river. Within seconds, water crept from the hold onto the main deck and was immediately joined by river water coming over the ship's sides.

Jimmy called to the others, "She's going down," and pointed to the *Jester's* rowboat at the stern.

They dashed to the sinking stern, scrambling into the rowboat. Garrett took up the oars. Tobias tried frantically to untie the rowboat's bowline, its painter, from the ship, but it had fouled. The sloop was sinking stern-first, taking the eyebolt and the knot under the surface. Jimmy handed Tobias his knife as the rowboat's bow began to dip, pulled down by the ship. Tobias cut at the line, nearly berserk in a panic of going under, as the bow went closer to the surface of the water.

The last fiber fell to the knife, letting the bow spring back up to the others' guttural approval. Water in the river's mouth swirled, spinning the boat between pressures of the river current and the tidal wave. The crest of the wave had moved inland, but the tide's force pushed them toward the northern shore, opposite from the tonger's campsite.

"We'll get trapped in the bushes on that side," Jimmy said. "And there's no land there, even above low tide, its nothing but marsh. We've gotta go out into the bay and ride this north.

"But my men at the camp," Tobias said.

"That camp is long underwater," Garrett said. "They likely skedaddled even before we started sinking. They got hard ground away from there and places they can go."

Garrett pulled against the oars, fighting against the tide's strong push, turning the bow due south just to keep the boat moving east toward the bay.

When they finally made their way past Abbey Point out into the bay, the tidal force flew them north, the faint light of the Pooles Island Lighthouse fading on the southern horizon. They were twelve miles north of the Bush River in less than an hour, slipping past Spesutie Island. Much of the island was underwater, and the tidal wave moving north was filled with lumber, barrels, and bodies.

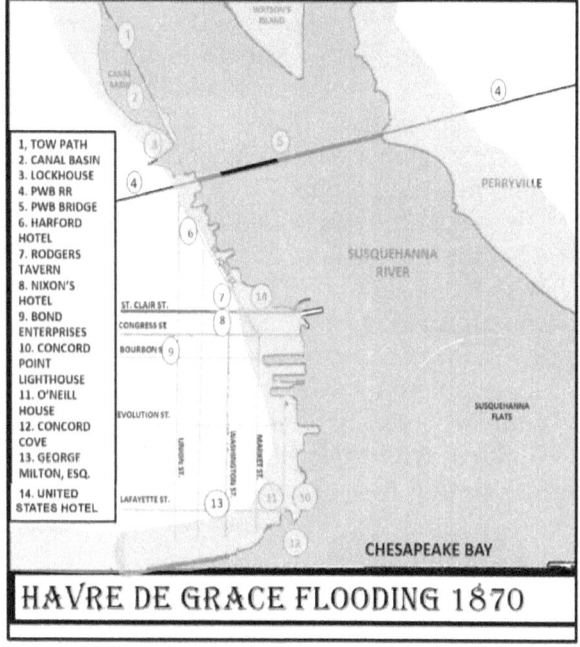

1. TOW PATH
2. CANAL BASIN
3. LOCKHOUSE
4. PWB RR
5. PWB BRIDGE
6. HARFORD HOTEL
7. RODGERS TAVERN
8. NIXON'S HOTEL
9. BOND ENTERPRISES
10. CONCORD POINT LIGHTHOUSE
11. O'NEILL HOUSE
12. CONCORD COVE
13. GEORGE MILTON, ESQ.
14. UNITED STATES HOTEL

HAVRE DE GRACE FLOODING 1870

Deputy Hopkins stepped to the front of the Watkins' Mansion, punched the brass knocker several times against the door, and then listened for sounds from inside but heard nothing. He turned to Wallace standing behind him.

"I will knock once more, and if Mr. Watkins

does not arouse to answer it, I will ask you to let me in through the servant's entrance."

After repeating the knock, Hopkins and Wallace moved to the side entrance. The door there was still unlocked. Hopkins told Wallace to stay outside, to be watchful for anyone running out.

"Only to identify such a person," Hopkins said, "Not to endanger yourself by trying to stop them. That is my job."

"No suh, but dep'ty, you don't know which room is which, and I do. I know which room is most likely where Mr. Watkins would be and which rooms he is not likely to be."

Hopkins glanced at Wallace. "Does Harris Bolton know which rooms?"

"Oh, yes, suh. He's done work for Mr. Watkins before he became a client. He knows most places in the house."

Hopkin nodded in agreement. "All right, then, Thank you for your help, Wallace. Just please keep behind me, since you said Bolton has a rifle."

"Double barrel," Wallace said.

Hopkins withdrew his revolver before they entered the side door. Inside they soon discovered Lester Watkins lying unconscious in his office, his face bloodied and bruised.

"He's a grouchy person," Wallace said, looking down at his employer. "but he didn't deserve having that done to him. Maybe we ought to carry him up to his bed."

"You're a good man Wallace. I've known Watkins several years, and you are much better than he deserves. He seems to be breathing, so let's check the rest of the house," Hopkins said, "but seeing the damage in this room, I suspect Bolton already got what he wanted."

It took them thirty minutes to check the other rooms of the grand house to ensure no one was hiding within it. Back down in the office, Hopkins asked Wallace to stay with Watkins while asking one of the men outside to go for Dr. Silver, who was in town for the holiday. Wallace and Hopkins then took Watkins up to his bedroom. He regained consciousness but was confused and disoriented, recalling only little. Hopkins returned to the office to examine the details. Beneath the broken glass on Watsons' desk was a set of documents naming Sonja Pulaski as signaturee. While considering the coincidence of another Pulaski involvement, Hopkins was approached by Bartholomew and Nadja Lister's frantic housekeeper.

Tears streamed down her face, and she sobbed as she spoke. "They're dead, Mr. Hopkins. They've been butchered in their own house. Come see."

"Good Lord above," Hopkins said, "will our year 1869 end in a pool of blood?"

Hopkins followed the distraught lady to the residence and funeral home of Bartholomew Lister. Bartholomew's body lay crumpled on his face in his casket room. Hopkins rolled him onto his back. His face had been battered, but the terminal knife wounds to his arm and neck were vicious. Lister's shirt was soaked in blood that had pooled around him, and the nearby wall was splattered with bloody spray. Nadja's body was lying nearby, her face immobilized in a perpetual snarl as she too had been stabbed in the neck, lying in her own blood with blood spray on the walls, floor, and casket.

The housekeeper stuttered, and her body shook as she recounted her discovery as she entered. The murders had been committed before her arrival, and she had seen no one near the property. The Lister's neighbor, who had long complained of the undertaker business being provided at the edge of his own lot, identified Harris Bolton as an evening visitor to the Lister home.

"That Bolton is on a rampage," Hopkins said.

Wallace and most of the men who had gathered outside the Watkins house arrived at the Lister house, joined by others. Hopkins identified four to help him as temporary deputies, asking them and others to search the town for Bolton. Searches in the growing morning light among the yards of the homes and the town's shops discovered the break-ins at Turner's office and Bachrach's store. Hopkins sent for the shop owners to assess missing items or damage.

Wallace joined the deputies moving along the waterfront businesses, finding the water rising over the tops of the docks as the tidal wave surged into town. Stacked lumber along the waterfront separated and began floating away, storage buildings were inundated, and steam engines to drive the sawmills were flooded. Rowboats that had pulled safely ashore away from the choppy water and left upside-down were snatched from their ties. The buoyancy of the trapped air inside, rolled them allowing the water to fill and sink them. Some boats luckily righted but were then stolen away in the unrelenting current. Lumber, barrels, and crates joined the rowboats, and debris already caught up in the water flow of the river.

The water continued to rise into town. A schooner moored at the DuBois Lumber dock was raised, dragging her anchor and pushed up onto the pier by the flood. It teetered on its keel, leaning precariously toward its side and terrifying its few remaining crewmembers. The yells that erupted from the crewmen when she nearly capsized turned to cheers as the water level rose further, righting the ship at the last moment, carrying her farther toward town.

Farther north along the shore, water flooded into McCombs Iron Foundry sitting at the river's edge. The water extinguished the foundry's coal furnace, kept burning at a lower level even at night to allow early morning resumption. Billowing vapor and soot spewed high into the sky and over the streets. The brick furnace exploded from the steam's fiery combustion, rocketing loose bricks into the air in all directions. Wallace and onlookers in the foundry's vicinity dashed to cover, splashing through streets never before covered in brackish water. Men ran to pull horses and mules from the livery stable, taking them to higher ground for safety. Some used the open lot on Union Avenue that was once the site of Mamie Stewart's boarding house. Flooding washed along all the eastern streets of town, leaving only Market Street and St. Johns Street above water. Water lapped at the Harford Hotel base, although the United States Hotel on St. Clair Street was not so lucky, seeing several feet of water in its lobby as guests took to the stairs abandoning their breakfasts to seek safety in their rooms above the water level.

Wallace joined Hopkins on Market Street to describe the explosion at the foundry. One of the deputies approached Hopkins, with another man pulled along by his sleeve.

"This is Warren Cable, Deputy Hopkins. He saw Bolton earlier."

Hopkins faced the man. "You sure it was Harris Bolton."

"Yep," Warren said. "Known him since before the war. Owes me money. I saw him at the docks below Water Street."

"When?"

"Before the flood hit. He was talking to Franklin Curtis. Curtis and his daughter were getting in their boat. Bolton got in with them."

"Where did they go, Cable?"

"Out across. Curtis has that little church on Watson's Island. I wasn't close enough to hear what they said, but he went with them in that boat."

"What about–"

"Deputy, I can't say anything after that moment he got in that boat, the floodwaters hit where I was, and I skedaddled."

"I need to go after him," Hopkins said. "He could kill those people. Find me a ferry man."

"Ain't nobody going out in this flood, Deputy. Maybe in the morning, if it lets up by then, and we ain't all been drowned."

"Then I will require a ferry as soon as the water recedes. I must pursue that man before he murders again."

⸺⸺ ⟶⊙⟵ ⸺⸺

In the early gray morning light of the previous morning, Sonja emerged from the bedroom to find Mickey fully dressed and making coffee in the kitchen.

She smiled. "At least you can fend for yourself without waiting on a doting wife." Her smile faded as soon as she uttered the words.

He saw her expression change and waved it away. "I have not had any doting to rely on in many years, Sonja. Though your daughter Alisha treats me far better than I deserve. Having my medical practice at her property in York Furnace has given me a family in my life at last. And your granddaughter Cathy is pleasant company when Alisha can pull her down from climbing trees."

Sonja poured coffee into her cup. "Has Ben returned?"

"No, and I am concerned, Sonja."

"Don't be," she said. "We have four of our barges waiting for spring in the canal basin, and only one has a winter resident. When Ben gets angry, sometimes he will spend the night in one of the barges. He says 'it's better for both of us.'"

She sighed. "Sometimes yes, but then sometimes he comes back silent, and we never finish what started the argument."

Mickey smiled and raised his eyebrows. "Ben doesn't argue enough?"

She crossed her arms and peered at him under hooded eyes. "Have you ever known Ben to avoid an argument or a fight?"

Mickey chuckled. "Don't believe I have."

Sonja pulled down a smoked ham hanging in the corner and pulled out some biscuits cooked the previous day but wrapped in a dishtowel and still soft enough to eat. "Let's take him some breakfast," she said.

"I'll hitch up the buggy," Mickey said as he left the room.

Minutes later, they sat in the buggy as the new mare took them across the arched bridge over the canal to the towpath, then turned south at a trot with barely enough light to see. Sonja held the breakfast food for Ben as Mickey held the reins. Beyond the towpath, an old tree had fallen into the river, drifting lazily in the water.

"That's odd," Sonja said. "That big old tree floating in the river."

Mickey gave the river a mere glance. "What's odd about that. Happens all the time. Back when I worked the canal with Ben–"

"It's not hardly moving, Mickey. Like the river has no current."

Mickey gave the tree another look. "Mmm. You're right. It's just wallowing there. Maybe one of its branches underwater is dragging the bottom."

"Maybe so...but look at the loose leaves on the surface near it. They're hardly moving."

"That is odd," Mickey said as the buggy moved away from the tree, heading on, overtaking the tree's drift. He shrugged his shoulders, but a moment later, he flicked the reins on the horse's haunches, increasing the speed of her trot. "Something doesn't feel right, Sonja."

The increasing speed against the wind coming up from the south pushed Sonja's fur cap higher on her forehead. She clapped her hand on the hat to push it back down. The light in the sky increased, showing more flotsam on the river's surface, natural debris that typically flew along toward the bay when the winter river was without ice.

"Maybe the Flats are finally freezing, Mickey. The air feels cold enough."

"Seems like the river would still run under the ice. It would be thin yet."

The mare trotted farther down the towpath. The canal basin was close; the towpath reached near the end trees and foliage at the basin's northern limit. The basin came into view. Mickey halted the horse.

"What in the name of heaven," he said.

Sonja placed the food basket on the seat beside her and stood to observe the strange sight.

The basin was filled with water, and the barges floated high on summer levels. Water flowed from the basin into the canal. Barges that yesterday sat in the muddy shallows near the lockhouse were free-floating and had drifted to the northernmost part of the basin. They rode high in the water, nudging against the perimeter towpath separating the basin from the river. Mickey and Sonja left the buggy to move toward the strange sight, stepping to the end of the narrow manmade pathway. People were standing on the canal boat decks gazing around them and exchanging excited comments about the phenomena. The closest barges belonged to Pulaski

Shipping.

A woman Sonja knew as Mrs. Haney stood on the deck of the closest boat holding her baby wrapped in a blanket. Coal smoke drifted from the stovepipe from the low central cabin behind her. Her husband, the Pulaski winter watchman, stood near the barge's far edge, speaking with someone on the next boat pushed against theirs. It was Ben.

Sonja called out, "Ben."

He peered at her then waved. "Morning. Such a sight, isn't it? We will need to pole the barges back toward the lockhouse before the basin drains again."

Sonja held up the basket, "Ham and biscuits," she said, handing it up to Mrs. Haney, who took it with her free hand.

"Thank you, Mrs. Pulaski," she said.

Ben stepped onto the deck of the Haney barge as they peeked into the basket and smiled. He stood in wool socks, his boots left in his cabin when Claude had called out for him. Ben sniffed the aroma as he passed the basket and neared Sonja.

Ben pointed back to the barge he had just left. "I have coffee in my cabin. You and Mickey come aboard as soon as I slide down a gangplank to the path. Looks like we have some water flowing into the basin from the outlet lock, pushing us here for now, but we're not going any further. We can grab a couple biscuits and take them over there. Cabins are too small for all of us. That way, the Haneys can eat together on this one."

Ben grabbed the plank from the deck and slipped it over the side onto the path. Sonja smiled up at him, putting away her concerns about the previous night, for the moment. The Haney barge still contained most of her coal load, so the gangplank was not too steep. Ben held out his hand for her, and she reached for it.

Mickey slapped Sonja's shoulder, pointing south toward the lockhouse and the wall of water charging toward them, yelling, "FLOOD! FLOOD!"

Ben glanced over his shoulder then yanked Sonja off her feet up onto the barge. Mickey dashed away from the wave. The massive wave charged upon them, lifting the series of barges in succession as it came, crashing them into each other. Ben wrapped his arms around Sonja, throwing them both to the deck, grabbing the edge of the cargo hatch to anchor them. The Haney's barge shuddered from the blow of Ben's barge smashing into it. Then Ben's barge flipped in the air, the barge rolling on its side as the wave shoved under them. The barge returned upright with a jerk as the swell lifted them onto its back, bucking them like a bull. The flood engulfed the canal boats, surging from below and over the decks with a wall of water.

The two barges were catapulted over the towpath into the river. Mickey tried to climb a tree but was swallowed by the wave, clinging to a limb as it engulfed him. Mrs. Haney screamed as her infant slipped from the blanket she clutched, sliding through the water on the deck. Sonja broke from Ben's embrace to grab the infant's arm as Ben grabbed Sonja's ankle.

Mrs. Haney scrambled on her hands and knees to retrieve her baby. Claude grabbed them both in a bear hug, his leg hooked within the cabin entrance. The barge rocked violently in the opposite direction, shoved farther out into the river.

Sonja slid in the deck water toward the bow,

washed away from Ben. Ben clawed to her along the edges of the cargo hatches, grabbing her arm, pulling her back toward him.

The barge canted again. The world was a dizzied flash of water. Sonja slipped from Ben's hand as the sixty-ton barge rose up on its side. He wiped the water from his eyes to see her, but she was gone. She screamed out, "Ben! B–" He pulled himself to the railing. She was in the water, going under the surface.

Ben yanked on the railing, throwing himself from the barge into the water. Sonja's head rose, spitting water. He reached for her, but she flew away in the swirling water as he slipped under its surface. He kicked his feet, grabbing at the water pulling himself to the turbulent surface. The cold water pricked his skin, and the air was colder when he broached the surface.

With his first breath, Ben called her name. His mind was insane with anguish. She answered him from behind. He kicked around, saw her head, her hands clawing at the water to stay afloat. He lunged for her, touched her hair, but she spun away. He kicked the water, pulled at it, pulled at it, and pulled again. He felt for her hand. Sonja grabbed him with frenetic fingers. Ben pulled her to him, but she slipped under. He kicked harder, driving them up again.

She stuttered. "Boots."

"Deep breath," he said, then gobbled a breath himself.

Keeping hold of her, he slipped under the surface along her struggling body to her legs. The leather boots were hellish to take off her. They clung to her skin. He managed to pull off one then had to resurface for air. They had both dropped farther into the rolling current. Colored spots were flashing in his eyes when he finally reached air again, pushing her up too. The cold was numbing their muscles, even as they worked them frantically—three deep breaths.

"All right?" He asked.

Her word shivered. "Yes."

The hateful boot resisted, determined to remain where it was. Ben grabbed as a demon to pull it off, knowing it cost more time, taking them below the surface. He lost his grip on her. His chest ached. The urge to breathe was almost overwhelming. He reached out for her. Felt her leg. She kicked. The boot was off. He climbed through the water, grabbing for the surface; his chest felt ready to explode. Her hand gripped him. Pulling him. He surfaced next to her face. They gasped together. Slapping the water, kicking, kicking. Kicking.

Something grabbed them. Spinning them. Spinning. Taking them lower. Taking them away from precious air. The water was darker, colder. They could feel themselves going deeper.

Whirlpool!

The spin grew faster. Nauseous. Lights exploded in their eyes. The ache in the chests was like razor cuts. Needle pricks spread over their bodies. Blackness filling their minds. The urge to breathe, the desire was becoming overwhelming to release the dead air wanting to explode from their lungs; to inhale. Knowing to open their mouths and inhale would kill them, but ready for it to happen to escape the torture in the chest. The spinning stopped, released them.

They exploded at the surface, gasping, rasping, coughing. Delicious air. Delicious. The water washed over them. They kicked again, treaded water, fought the power. Felt the confusing push and pull of the currents. The flood and the river fought over them, taking them up the river, then down it, then across it. The turbulence was confusing. Something punched into the back of Ben's head. A piece of wood. Lumber. Big. It was a cured beam floating in the flood. Ben helped Sonja put her arms over the shaft to let it hold her at the surface. It would not support both of them. The sky was lighter. The clouds thinning, but the wind blew hard, filling the air with spray. Ben kicked, trying to raise his head farther. There was another beam close by, almost spinning in the melee.

Maybe if I put them together?

Sonja rested her head on the beam, her eyes closed, still catching her breath. Ben turned away, reached out toward the other beam, kicked toward it. Sonja slipped unconscious from her beam. Ben reached the other beam then glanced back at Sonja's to begin his pull toward her. He saw her head sink under the surface.

"Sonja!"

His arms and legs ached, leaden and reluctant to respond. In a panic, he clawed and kicked his way to her. Grabbed her hair. Pulled her to the surface. Managed to droop her arms over the beam again. Slapped her face to awaken her. She gagged and coughed. She gasped.

"Hold on," he said. "Another beam close. Have to get it. Hold on."

She nodded her answer.

Ben kicked up again to raise his head in search

of the other beam. It was too far away. He sank low in the water, then kicked up again. Closer by was a wooden box with a brass clasp floating high in the water, twisting within the contesting currents.

"Maybe," Ben said.

The angry floodwaters threw a second canal boat from the basin. The wall separating the canal basin from the river was deep underwater, now nothing more than a muddy shoal below the hulls. Mickey had climbed a tree through the driving current, barely having sufficient air to make the struggle above the water. The tidal wave ripped through bushes shoving the barge's bow between Mickey's tree and the next. The force of the water shouldered the stern, pushing it out into the river while the bow wedged against Mickey's tree, threatening to snap it like a giant pry bar. Mickey jumped from the tree to the barge's deck, then dashed toward the stern, pushing the tiller to bring the face of the rudder into the current. The stern's increased leverage pulled the boat's bow from the trees, whipping the boat around in the floodwaters like a wooden toy, spinning it away from the basin.

Out in the river, the other barge rolled precariously onto its side tossing two people into the water. Each barge was nothing more than a wooden bucket, shaped like a boat for its journeys up and down the canal but always pulled by mules. Mickey was helpless, as were the remaining people on the other barge and the two hapless souls thrown into the water. Ben and Sonja. Mickey sank to his knees, clinging onto the tiller, a useless spectator to the death of his friends.

The water around Mickey's barge was thick with debris of all description, tree limbs, crates, lumber, sawdust, garbage. Back toward the shore, where the shore had been, the Pulaski horse kicked in a frenzy to keep her head above water, but the leather traces chained to the buggy below kept her from escaping. Her whinny was a damnation to any observing her useless frantic struggle. The leather straps cut into her flesh as she tried to pull free of the buggy below her until she finally slipped under, unable to fight on, condemned to drown. Still, flaring nostrils taking one final breath of air before she was gone. Mickey had to look away. He felt at his waist, finding his revolver still in its holster, the hammer loop held it in place.

"I'll not go like that poor damned horse, Mr. Colt," Mickey said. "I will require your services if it comes to that."

The barge rocked ungainly in the currents, signaling empty cargo holds and a barge riding high in the water as it drifted helplessly within the competing currents. The tide overpowered the river current one second, then the river slammed it back the next. Mickey gripped the low sides' edges, peering at the water, and spat into it, yelling at the river below the flood.

"God sent you something meaner than you, didn't he, bitch? You took my wife and son, and I hope the devil in this flood drives you to hell...with a never-ending current that runs up your ass for eternity!" Mickey spat at the water again.

"All right, Doctor O'Grady, get to your senses and do something worthwhile."

He gazed out at the waves seeking the other barge. It was farther away, moving in the center of the floodwaters. Two people were still on deck, huddling near the cabin. Among the debris behind their barge, slightly farther from him, Mickey caught a glimpse of two heads in the water.

It must be them.

"Please, God, let that be Ben and Sonja. Please don't take them too."

The edges of a whirlpool slipped toward them, and then the heads disappeared.

"No!"

The river gnawed at the edges of the tide, trying to hurt it, to push the tide out of its kingdom. The powerful forces fought in a churning liquid battlefield of tremendous pressures and explosive waves. The tide was winning against the island in the center, driving its water high onto the shore and into buildings there. But the river was attacking it from the sides, making its offensive drive through the narrow channel on the eastern side of the island, where it was more potent than the tide. There the river slammed into the tide with killing body blows, creating vicious whirlpools and volcanoes of spouting water.

Mickey glanced around, searching for something to do, something that might help...someone. His barge twisted within the confused currents. He noticed the tow rope tailing from the bow.

"At least that's something."

On hands and knees, Mickey crawled to the bow and grabbed the end of the rope knotted to the iron ring, pulling it in a foot at a time. The cold air only made the wet rope harder to handle, and

Mickey's fingers less able to do his bidding. The forward cargo hatch cover had been torn away, leaving a jagged wooden strut at the coaming around the edge of the hold. As he pulled in enough line, he looped it between the coaming and the tiller post, so he could stop to warm his hands with his breath without losing the rope back into the water. His hands were turning blue, and his knuckles throbbed, unable to bend.

Mickey crawled to the cabin stairway and made his way down. The erratic motion inside the cabin was soon nauseating as he searched through storage boxes. No one had been living in the barge's cabin, and few supplies were to be found. He pulled a folded wool blanket from one of the bunks and then shrieked with joy when it unrolled onto the cabin floor. Inside the blanket roll, he discovered a pair of musty wool gloves. Soon the entire one-hundred-foot tow rope was on deck, dripping water.

When Mickey returned to the deck, he noticed his barge had moved nearer to the other one. He could recognize faces. The Haneys with their baby appeared unharmed. Like him, they had elected to stay on the deck, on hands and knees, rather than endure the nauseating motion in the cabin. The two barges were moving closer to the center of the tidal flow, closer together. Both barges were outfitted with large hemp rope fenders to prevent them from hitting against docks or piers – or each other. All of the Pulaski barges had fenders, but none of the canal company's boats. When the barges moved close enough to shout to each other, Mickey noticed that the other barge had its tow rope on deck. Mickey suggested they bring the two barges side by side to stop the rocking or at least the worst of it.

Claude was quick to understand and urged that all the fenders from both sides be brought between them.

As the barges came nearer, Claude suggested tossing towropes to draw the barges together rather than relying on the unpredictable current to do it. The ends of the tow ropes were thrown in turn with the tiller post as both snubbing post and mooring point. The eight hemp fenders earned their keep as the turbulent water was less than cooperative when the men pulled the barges together. There was a shuddering thud when the boats merged along the fenders. But the grinding and even hull damage that could have occurred was prevented by the hemp. The dramatic stomach-churning rocking that had cursed both barges since leaving the basin, at once subsided to a milder motion, not placid but tolerable. The Haney deck was spotted with small pools of vomit.

Mrs. Haney was ecstatic, "I think it's safe to build a small fire in the cabin to warm the baby."

Mickey stayed on his barge to watch over the tow rope at his tiller post. "Have you seen Ben and Sonja?"

"They came out of that whirlpool. Must have pushed them closer to the other shore—"

"You think they made it to shore?"

Claude shook his head. "I haven't seen anything pushed to shore. The middle seems to be moving faster than the edges. Still, Mrs. Pulaski was holding on to a piece of wood, and he was swimming for another one when I saw them last...There just wasn't anything I could do for them. It was all we could do to hold on to the baby and the boat."

Mickey shivered in his wet clothes, glancing up to the troubled sky. "Have you nothing for me to do?"

He went down into the cabin with a heavy sense of guilt to wrap himself in a dry wool blanket. Sonja clung to the bobbing wooden box in the battlefield tempest where the river charged from the eastern side of the island into the tidal flood. Ben had one arm looped over the beam, with the other hand gripping the belt he had buckled around her waist, as numbing cold water pummeled them both.

The three men crammed into the *Jester's* rowboat took turns bailing water. The rowboat was designed for two people in calmer waters, but tidal waters constantly splashed over the low sides into the boat's bottom. The thole pin on one side gave way in the old wood, and they had lost one of their oars.

"Up ahead," Jimmy said. "One of the oyster boats is up there."

They fixed their eyes on the larger boat.

"We're not getting any closer," Garrett said.

"That boat will hold four hundred pounds of oysters and two men," Tobias said. "We need to get there."

"We need to get to the center of this flow," Jimmy said. "We need to paddle farther out."

"Away from shore is deeper," Garret said.

"It's deep everywhere," Jimmy said. "If we don't get to that boat, we'll be in the water, and I can't swim."

"Me neither," said Garrett, who began to paddle with the single oar in a near frenzy.

Tobias bailed the water from the bottom of the boat, using the wooden scoop that had been tied to one of the thole pins when they piled into the rowboat. Luckily, it was connected to the thole pin that did not pull out from rotten wood. He met Jimmy's glance. They both knew the rowboat was rotten in several places.

"I can't swim either," Tobias said. He thought of Rebecca, imagining the sweet taste of her lips kissing his before they closed his casket.

When Garrett tired from the awkward pull with the single oar, Tobias took the oar and dug into the water, pulling them toward the abandoned oyster boat as Jimmy bailed. More water seeped in between the hull boards than came over the gunwale at the top of the sides. The old boat was sinking through her wood, not from floodwaters splashing into the bottom.

"We're getting closer," Garrett said.

"There's her painter, floating behind her," Tobias said. "Get to that line. It's closer. Then we can pull her to us."

Water in the rowboat was over the tops of their shoes, even though bailing was constant.

"We need to hurry, men," Garrett said, "We're sinkin fast."

"Jimmy, you've got one good arm. You bail." Tobias said. "Garrett, you're strongest. You paddle. I'll push with my hands."

None question him. They became demons at their tasks.

"Got the line!" Tobias said, yanking the oyster boat to them. The little rowboat was only an inch above the water when the two boats met.

Tobias pushed Jimmy. "Get in."

Tobias pulled on Garrett, "Now you."

Garrett stood to step into the oyster boat, but the rowboat spun onto its side, going underwater and hitting Garrett in the head as it flipped. He fell into the water unconscious. Tobias rolled with the rowboat, wrapping the painter line twice around his wrist, grasping the knotted end in his hand, and then threw himself after Garrett. The line went taut behind the oyster boat, then straight down. Jimmy grabbed the rope with his good hand and leaned back, pulling with all his weight and strength. At the end of his pull, he wrapped the line around a thole pin to keep it, then pulled at the rope again, slipping his injured arm from its sling, grabbing the line with both hands. He groaned in pain as he pulled the rope. Lightning bolts of pain shot through his shoulder and up his neck. He cursed and yelled and grit his teeth, wrapped the next loop of line, then grabbed it again, pulling. Tobias's head came to the surface, gasping for air.

"Pull," Tobias called.

"What th'hell do you think I'm doing?" Jimmy answered.

With another pull from both men, Garrett's face came above water. His face was pale, and a fleshy gash on his forehead seeped blood. Cold hands and reluctant fingers managed to get Garrett into the oyster boat. With additional struggle, Tobias climbed into the boat to collapse exhausted on the boat's floor, next to Garrett. There was a storage compartment in the stern containing a canvas tarpaulin against the rain and a rubberized rain parka. Jimmy covered the two men with the canvas and donned the parka, huddling within it, trembling from the cold and wincing from the thunderous pain that seemed to inhabit his entire body. The boat passed between Shad and Battery Islands. The few structures on Shad Island had been washed away. In the distance, outlined by the Havre de Grace dock lamps, tremendous flooding swept into town.

Garrett stirred underneath the canvas, sitting up in a panic, gasping for breath.

"You're in the oyster boat," Jimmy said.

Garrett touched his throbbing head. "What happened?"

"Rowboat capsized. Gunnel hit you in the head. You went into the water."

"Why ain't I dead?"

Jimmy pointed at Tobias. "He went after you."

Garrett gazed at Tobias, lying next to him. He poked at him. "Hey. Hey. You there?"

Tobias groaned, then stretched, remaining on the oyster boat's plank flooring, peering up at Garrett.

"You went in after me." It was both a statement and a question.

Tobias only nodded, saying nothing.

"Why? Five years ago, I would have killed you."

Tobias sat up next to him. "Five years ago, I would have killed you."

"It wouldn't have been on you if you let me drown?"

'Yes, it would have. War and murder are different things."

Garrett nodded his head in agreement.

"Besides," Tobias said. "I'd hate for another scar to be added to that beautiful face."

Garrett bellowed in laughter, slapping Tobias on his back and pulling him close. It was a moment only comrades will ever understand, even among those who had once faced each other on the battlefield.

Sonja's grip on the wooden box relaxed, letting one hand slip into the water, touching Ben's cheek as it went down. Half-awake, he pulled up on her belt.

"Um, what?" He asked. "Oh, here...put your arms over the beam."

Ben shifted his weight to the box as she moved. The cold water swirled around them as they changed positions, finding little spots that had momentarily escaped some of the cold and stabbed at them renewed.

Her voice trembled; her words slurred. "Don't want my hands in the water, Ben. So cold."

He moved her arms. "Then try this. Your hands under your chin, just your elbows in the water.... Like that. Like sleeping."

Her eyes were closed and she allowed a faint smile on pale shivering lips. "Isaac used to sleep like this."

Ben pulled the box closer to the beam to rest more of his weight on it and still hold her belt. "Yes, I remember," he said, fighting to hide his own trembling."

"Tell me more" she said. "What you remember."

"You smiled when I came home...We rented the cabin on Saint John Street...not there long. Couple months." He shivered. "A woman was with you...didn't know her. You smiled at me. The afternoon sun lit your face. I knew."

"Mmmm. She was...midwife." Her voice was fading. "Was with you and me again when Isaac came. You would not leave."

"I had seen births before."

Her eyes opened an instant, then drifted closed again. "Cows and pigs, Benjamin."

"But...at the instant...similar. A miracle from your belly. My son."

Darkness filled the mind's eye in both of them.

The woman wiped off the infant and laid him on his mother's belly. He suckled while the woman cut and tied the cord. She frowned at Ben for staying and took the bloodied cloths away because Ben didn't. He was afraid to touch the baby until Sonja pulled his hand to the matted head. The name was chosen long before, one of two, in case it was a girl. Ben thought it would be a girl, but it didn't matter now. She placed her hand on his.

"Name him, Ben. Say his name."

"Isaac," he said, and she had repeated it.

The blackness swirled. The cold went deep into their bones.

Together, they saw his first step. A surprise. He wiggled on his belly across the blanket on the floor. The coffee pot boiled in the kitchen, and Sonja went to set it aside. She dropped a ladle onto the floor, and Ben glanced toward the sound. Ben's eyes went back to Isaac, but he was already standing. On his tiptoes before Sonja's chair, gripping its edge with his tiny hand and eyes sparkling.

Ben had yelled to her. "He stood up."

The loud voice startled Isaac, who lost his grip, plopped down on his bottom and cried. Ben was mortified and ashamed, but she laughed when he told her what happened.

Something tugged on his hand. Something was wrong. He forced his eyes open, but there was no daylight, only swirling gray water. They had both slipped away into the depths. He kicked and pulled. She joined him clawing to the surface, to the blessed air again. Cold, harsh, biting blessed fresh air. Their flotsam was not far. The water was turbulent, but the currents were confused, doubling back on each other, keeping them from both the center of the river and the shore, trapped in the twisting currents.

We will die on this spot. Too far to swim. Too deep to breathe.

Again, holding the floating wood. Again, cold, wet skin exposed to the frigid wind.

Her lips trembled with her shiver. "You were so terrified that you had made Isaac fall...the first time he stood."

"You were remembering that too?"

"I laughed at you, my bullheaded man. Brought low by the cry of a baby."

"We had the same dream, Sonja."

"We share the same memories...about some things."

Deputy Alexander came into the house. She pushed him away. Ben was on the Osprey far away. She was in her nightgown. He grabbed at her, threw her to the floor. His breath stank of alcohol and laudanum. She hit at him. He punched her ribs. It took her breath. He pulled up her gown. They struggled on the floor at the doorway to the bedroom.

She could see the split wood stacked near the front room stove. It wasn't far. She let him grope her body as she reached for the wood. His lips were on her nipples when she kicked him back and smashed the wood onto his head. Catherine came. Her neighbor. Sonja sent her for Mac, the blacksmith up the hill.

The man on the floor breathed. He wasn't dead. She punched at her attacker, but he did not awaken. She went to the kitchen. Brought back the knife and knelt on the floor beside him. When Mac arrived, Sonja had already castrated the man. Mac sewed him up like the hogs he raised behind his forge.

She jerked awake, driving her hand off the beam into the water. Ben coughed.

"I was remembering Aaron's birth," Ben said. "Were you dreaming that?"

"No."

"It was odd," Ben said. "Deputy Alexander was in the room."

Sonja gazed into his eyes, then slowly let her lids close, tucking her hand back under her chin. Her ankles hung in the water, and the throbbing pain was less. They were going numb.

Ben kicked his feet in the water. Making them work. But some toes no longer had feelings. Ben and Sonja were freezing to death. Loose lumber and another beam bumped against Sonja's beam. Some of the lumber still retained the line that had tied them together before the flood took them.

"We can use them," Ben said.

Sonja focused her eyes on the lumber. "Yes. We put the boards across the two beams. Tie them."

She slipped into the water.

"No, Sonja."

She held one arm looped around her beam, reached for a board with the other hand.

"Will take both. Save us both."

Ben pulled the new beam parallel to Sonja's. "Put your other arm over this one."

As she held on to the beams, Ben pulled the boards over the top of them, laying a platform a few inches above the water. The rope still tied to one board was knotted. Ben's fingers could not untie it. He clawed at the rope. His fingers were stiff with cold, aching, and throbbing. He managed to loop the line around four planks, securing them to the beam between each board, but none remained to hold the other beam. He shifted in front of Sonja.

"I need the belt." Warm vapor from his lungs followed his words in the air between their lips. She closed her eyes, reveling in the meager gift.

She nodded in agreement. Ben removed his belt from her waist and slipped around her to the other beam, where he could only secure the two inner boards to the beam. He walked with his hands along the edge of the boards back to Sonja.

"Once we get up on it, we will need to lay at the end with only two boards held by my belt. We will have to be the tie for the ones on the end."

He pushed the beams apart several feet, Sonja held on to the closest, but the boards still extended two or three feet beyond each beam.

"You go first," he said.

"No. You go. Then pull me up."

"Don't think I can, Sonja. I can hold on to the outer board, slip down, wrap my other arm around your legs and lift you, pulling us up by the board.

That should put your waist above the boards. Then you swing your legs over. I can push them from below."

"How will you get up?"

"I'll push the box under my feet. It will help push me up to the planks."

The struggle was more difficult than Ben expected and took more time, but Sonja lay on the boards, out of the water. Ben pulled the wooden box close by his side and forced it below the surface to his feet. The buoyancy that had kept him afloat fought him hard to stay on the surface. He finally managed to get his feet on the top of the box, working it under his body. He could feel the strength of the captured air in the box fighting to push him up. The instant he felt the box directly under his body, he pushed his legs down on it and pulled at the board with his remaining strength. Ben rose from the water, passing the platform's level with his waist, and rolled onto his back, almost falling between two boards, but caught himself by his hand on the beam, straddling the first board. Below Ben, as he pulled onto the raft, the box exploded from the opposing forces of resisting air and compressing water. The little chest so coveted by Bolton and still holding shards of Lydia's bones imploded. The water frothed with the release of captured air, splitting the chest into pieces, finally freeing the bone fragments into the dark water. The heavy base sank toward the bottom, and the side pieces joined nearby flotsam on the surface, released from their onerous chore.

Sonja straddled two boards, one knee holding the distance between them and her hands holding the boards near her head to the beam. It was a difficult position but required far less strength and energy than fighting the water. They relaxed as best they could on the makeshift platform, out of the water at last and exposed to the wind. The cold grew fierce, gnawing at their skin.

When the floodwaters crashed into the southern end of Watson's Island, Franklin and Rebecca were inside the church cooking stew. The water rose up from the short pebble beach and dashed to the buildings, flooded through spaces around bared doors and weathered boards. The little church shuddered from the force of the wave. Water ran shin-deep among the chairs and rough-hewn pews, up to the altar, then into the kitchen, hissing as it kissed the bottom of the iron stove. There was no back door to the church. Built as a storage shed to support the massive annual fishing, the only doors face the shore. Franklin and his daughter crept through the cold water to assess the depth outside. The water was not above the lower edges of the two front windows, but more water poured between the doors and their frame. It was not river water, but the stale salt aroma of brackish water pushed far up the bay. The water frothed and foamed, squeezing into the church.

Rebecca's eyes were wide open in fear. "Where can we go, Papa?"

"Stand on the pew, daughter. It will not rise above that. Get your feet out of the cold water."

He pointed out through the window, "It is not above the window yet. When it goes back down, we can open the doors and let it out from here."

"What if it gets higher?"

"We will use the back window. The ground rises steeply there. We'll climb up to the crest of the island."

Steam hissed from the kitchen, and a cloud of burned water drifted into the sanctuary. The cooking fire had been extinguished. Franklin peered out the window at the water surging around the building.

"The boat is gone."

"Maybe that man got untied and took it," she said.

"Maybe. But maybe if we have to climb up to the peak, we will find him there."

"Oh, I hope not, Papa. He is an evil man."

Franklin chuckled. "Yes, evil...but not much of a boxer. We won't worry about him."

More water poured in between the door, but the water outside the window did not rise. Franklin sloshed through the water in the church, then almost knee-high, gazing out the window.

"The surface is filled with debris of every kind. It seems to be dividing directly in front of the church, going east and west around the island, floating farther upriver. How is that? I have never seen such a thing. It is floating UP river–and there are canal barges out there! Out in the river."

Rebecca trembled. "Oh, Papa...Is this the end of the world? Are we going to die?"

Franklin moved quickly to her and wrapped his arms around her waist. "No, daughter. Remember, after the great flood, the Lord promised to never drown the world again."

She cried and rested her cheek on his hand. He lifted her up from the pew and carried her to the kitchen. The table there was higher. Then he picked up a ladderback chair and set it on top of the table for her to sit on. He pulled out an old wool blanket from a nearby storage locker not yet touched by the rising water and wrapped it around her legs.

"The air is warmer up here," she said.

"It will be warmer there a few minutes longer," he said. "Wrap up in that blanket."

Franklin lifted the lid from the cast iron pot sitting on top of the stove and poked his finger into the stew. "It never did get hot, but it's warm."

He walked back to the front of the church, peering again at the canal barges floating in the center of the current. They were still hundreds of yards from the island but appeared to be moving directly toward the church.

Franklin mumbled to himself. "But I don't recall reading a scripture where the Lord promised not to hit us with canal barges." He then spoke to the barges. "When you get close, a one-legged man and his daughter may have to climb the hill behind this church, so don't be in too much of a hurry to get here."

Back at the Watkins Mansion, Wallace assisted Lester Watkins return to his office to examine the damage. Lester walked about the room, tsking and muttering to himself, then sank into his chair behind the desk.

"So, both Mr. and Mrs. Lister were killed?"

"Yes, suh. It was horrible what that Bolton man did to them."

Lester glanced up, then grabbed his neck.

"Please. Please, sit down, Wallace. It pains me to look up."

"Yes, suh."

Lester leafed through the papers he had readied for Sonja Pulaski's signature. "And you saw Bolton leave with the wooden box from my cabinet."

"Yes, suh."

Lester crumpled the Pulaski papers. "Well, these are useless. Please put them in the fireplace and set fire to them. And add some wood as well. It's freezing in here."

When the flames lit the fireplace's interior and Wallace stood, Lester pointed to the liquor cabinet. "Kindly pour me a brandy."

Wallace stepped across the room to open the cabinet. Lester added another command. "Get two glasses. Fill them both."

Wallace presented both glasses to Lester, the unspoken question blatant on his face. Lester took one glass and motioned for Wallace to take the chair in front of the desk. "The other is yours. Do you drink brandy?"

Wallace settled onto the chair. "Never had any, suh. But I do like a whiskey from time to time."

Lester smiled. "It has alcohol in it, Wallace." Watkins raised his glass in a toast, "To being alive, Wallace."

Wallace sipped from the glass, then took in half of it, licking the taste of it on his lips. "I like this, suh."

The lawyer pointed at the fireplace with his glass. "I had expected those burning papers to bring me a considerable amount of money, but it will not happen now, thanks to Mr. Bolton. Nor will I have the opportunity to sue Mr. Benjamin Pulaski for some of his money since I no longer have a complainant, also thanks to Mr. Bolton. Furthermore, since Mr. Bolton is now a fugitive from the law, he will no longer provide me an alternate avenue to Pulaski money."

Wallace and Lester drank the remainder of their brandy. Lester examined his empty glass. "Kindly bring the decanter over here, Wallace. It may well be the last excellent brandy I have in the house, assuming I stay in this house."

Wallace returned to the desk and set the decanter before Lester.

"You lettin me go, suh?"

Lester motioned to the chair again, then leaned forward to refill both glasses. A half-smile grew on Wallace's face as he picked up his glass and held it up to Lester in salute, then they both sipped.

"No, not at all," Lester said, "but I may need to take in a lodger or two for a while. Would that be acceptable to you?"

"Work is work, Mr. Watkins. Long as I get paid and can feed the children my wife and I have."

"You have children?"

Wallace chuckled. "Yes, suh. Two girls and a boy."

"And...you are married? Have a wife?"

Wallace laughed quietly. "Yes, suh."

"Have I met her, Wallace?"

Wallace released a belly laugh, shaking his head. "She's your cook, suh."

Watkin's face was crimson, but it may have been due mainly to the brandy.

"Well, Wallace, I am in your debt for going for the sheriff's deputy instead of just going home and letting me die in this room." Then Lester refilled their glasses with the last of the brandy. "I suppose we should ask your wife if she will accept boarders to cook for."

"Work is work," Wallace said, draining his glass.

White men and black men still made most family decisions in the year of the lord, 1870.

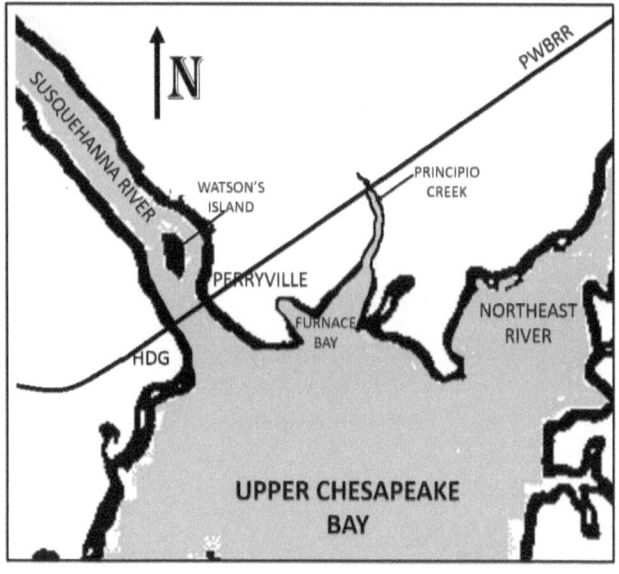

The windblown sky was still overcast but getting lighter as the morning advanced. The three castaways in the rowboat could make out the uppermost Chesapeake Bay shoreline in the distance, getting closer. The tidal surface was peppered with debris and flotsam. Ahead, the debris was separating into different flows, on the west into the Susquehanna's mouth, on the east into the mouth of the Northeast River. Straight ahead, the tide flowed toward Furnace Bay at the southern shore of Perryville. Without paddles or oars, their direction would be decided by the tidal force. The boat slipped among loose lumber, and small crates pushed from Spesutie and Battery Islands.

"Grab the boards," Jimmy said. "We can use them as paddles."

With three boards in hand, the men splashed at the water, digging into it, pulling it back. They managed to move the boat into the current headed for the Susquehanna River. The boat spun in the stronger current, tossed like a toy by the power. Garrett fell back against the stern, hitting his head on the transom, dropping his makeshift paddle with a clatter onto the bottom of the boat. Jimmy and Tobias checked their comrade then struggled to pull the boat closer to Havre de Grace. However, out from the center, the current was more powerful, and they could not break free. Farther ahead, in the mouth of the Susquehanna, several whirlpools sucked in debris, pulling it under. Even a floating barrel could not escape the grip of the swirling vortex as it slipped below the surface.

"We can't go that way," Tobias said. "It could tear this boat to pieces. We need to paddle back to where we were."

Garrett sat up, shaking his head to clear his thoughts, then joined them, paddling back toward the center current.

Jimmy spoke through clenched teeth. "All right then. Furnace Bay it is."

"I know some good people in Perryville," Garrett said.

Once again, they bent to pulling the rowboat

through the water toward their new destination and managed to achieve the success of riding the center current into the mouth of Furnace Bay.

"It's time we had some good luck," Jimmy said as he slumped on his knees and brought his board across the tops of the sides where he rested his elbows on the plank.

The tidal current there slalomed more to the east beyond Perryville toward Principio Creek, where the floodwaters were racing inland over a pasture and into a dense stand of pine trees. Like a bobsled on icy snow diving down a steep slope, the rowboat rushed ahead on the wave toward the trees. Tobias quickly assessed the rowboat's width and the spacing between the trees they approached, as was Garrett.

"This is gonna hurt," Garrett said.

"Jimmy," Tobias said, "Get your board in the boat or throw it away."

Jimmy glanced ahead as the boat dashed toward the trees, shoving his plank away just before they entered the trees. The board smacked the trees, turning to splinters, and the boat shot between the first two. The next tree was dead ahead, but they scraped the one on their left side, pushing the blunt bow of the boat toward the right, scraping the next tree on their left, and shooting toward three more trees standing close together.

"Lean left," Jimmy called out.

The boat tilted up on the right, giving it a slightly thinner profile as they came at the trees. The boat's bottom edge caught the bark of the outer tree on the right, and the boat catapulted between two more sets. More trees were ahead. Brush and vines grew between them, but the water was lifting them higher.

"Left again," Jimmy yelled.

The thud of the boat's right-side hull and the force ricocheting away threw all three men to the bottom in a pile of bodies. The boat shot over the tangle of brush and vines, launching into the air between the last pair of trees in the stand, then fell back within the charging water over the railroad tracks. It rode the thinning water through a cow pasture up a slight grade, running aground just short of the Post Road to Philadelphia. The fading waves splashed up the slope several more yards to slap the earth in their dying effort to continue, then retreated back to lower ground, finally succumbing to gravity. Nervous cows crept close to the boat to sniff at the disheveled passengers.

Garrett sat up to look around. "Good God a'mighty. Where are we?"

Tobias stood up and looked around, then rested his hand on the head of a cow to step out of the boat.

"Looks like we're a couple miles northeast of Perryville," Tobias said. "We were pushed up a hillside above the flood crest. God knows what it's doing on Watson's Island to Rebecca."

Jimmy moaned from inside the boat. The force of the boat motion had re-injured his shoulder.

Tobias pointed down the slope where the water had returned to the creek bed. "We need to get back to the water."

Garrett scanned the nearby ground. "This field's covered in mud and cow shit. Shouldn't be hard ta slide her back down."

Jimmy made an effort to rise in the boat, but Tobias laid a hand on his back. "You just stay where you are."

Garrett and Tobias strained and grunted, turning the boat around so the bow pointed downhill. Once the boat was moving, it required little force to keep it toward the creek. Water was draining from higher ground on both sides, adding to the water flow in the stream back toward the bay. A broken sapling served as a steering pole to keep them near the center of the water flow and avoid obstacles. Within minutes they had returned to the bay. Among the debris cast over the surface, a badly damaged rowboat offered them much-needed oars. Pulling with all their strength, Tobias and Garrett drove the boat out of Furnace Bay.

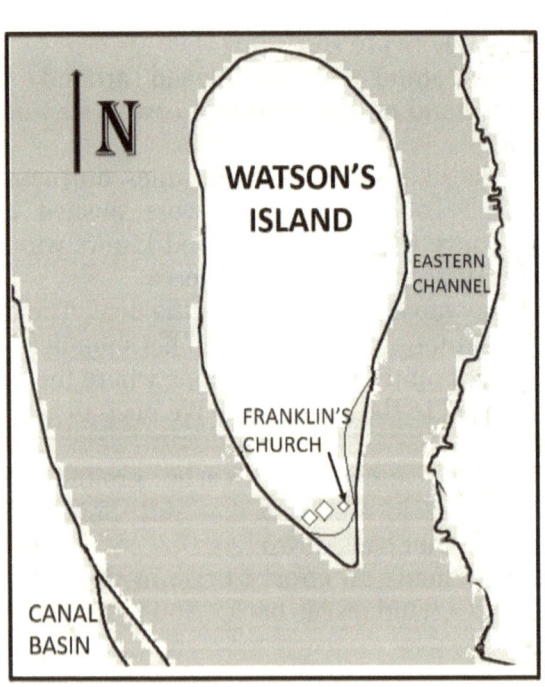

The struggle of great forces between the tidal flood and the Susquehanna River continued within the watery battlefield surrounding Watson's Island. Whirlpools arose and faded. Currents dashed against and across each other, seeking weaknesses to overpower. The river retained ownership of the flow within the eastern channel around the island. Still, the tide bashed against it as the river attempted to rush out from the channel. The cross currents and resulting turbulence created a maelstrom of crashing waves no less than an ocean hurricane.

Ben and Sonja were tossed about on their fragile raft within the churning cauldron, trapped between the struggling forces of river and tide, while safety was less than two hundred yards away. Spinning among the swirling waves, Ben had glimpses of shore when the makeshift raft peaked on swells.

"It's not far from us," Ben said, "but we can't get there."

His voice stuttered amid shivering spasms in his muscles. The rope holding the four boards together was unraveling, his knot poorly laid by stiff fingers hampered with cold. Water continually splashed up between the boards—icy slush formed at the ends of his and Sonja's hair. The raft drifted uncontrollably in the troubled waters, a weightless leaf in the raging storm. They neared another whirlpool. Several had formed near them then faded away as the raft was pulled toward them. Now another was opened close by, more extensive than the other ones.

"Not another," Sonja said.

She gripped her boards with failing muscles, hands, and fingers that no longer closed into grips. Ben peered at her, unable to help her. His own hands nearly useless, his legs holding his two boards together, his knees and feet dangling in the icy water. He forced his hand out toward Sonja; it was nearly numb. Ben's only retained control was to bend it at the wrist, use it as a hook to add a modicum of his fading strength to help hold it in place. The whirlpool widened. The raft was pulled apart. They rolled into the water, spinning along the edges of the vortex, glancing a final time through the wall of spinning water, their eyes open, seeing each other's faces in shades of blue. Their fingertips touched one last time, but there was no feeling left. The darkness overcame them.

Little Aaron had fallen among the rocks and pebbles on the shore at the end of St. Clair Street. He was always dashing off to investigate different directions when Sonja's back was turned. She had sent Isaac to help find him when a neighbor woman said he went toward the water. In a panic, she ran toward the water's edge. A ship had tied up at the dock ahead, and Ben walked up the steep bank, his head and shoulders appearing first as he rose with a giggling Aaron on his shoulder and Isaac's hand in Ben's. Sonja stopped, relieved, happy to see her children safe and her husband returning after several days. Aaron's face and elbows showed fresh scratches, but he smiled and giggled with his father despite them.

Isaac yelled to her, "I found Pa, too."

She stood there in the street as they approached. Ben yanked Isaac up into the crook of his left arm, keeping Aaron snugly held on his right shoulder, and bent to kiss Sonja as he stood before her.

"I am made first-mate," he said. "Jenkins took to a larger ship sailing away, and the captain said I could have the position."

She placed her hands on his cheeks and returned his kiss. "I am proud of you."

He set the boys down and pulled her to him. "A man doesn't need to read and write if he has skills with his hands."

"Will you be gone longer now?"

He laughed. "Same schooner. Same business. Just more money."

"Oh, Ben. Will it be much more?"

"I was thinking about those new houses they are building up on Pearl Street."

"I would love to live there, Ben. Can we do that?"

"Captain Rodgers knows the owner of a bank on Oyster Street. Binterfield. The captain says he could help us buy a house of our own."

The spinning darkness and the cold drove them deeper into their lingering thoughts and memories.

Isaac carried the planks from the barn down the slope to the canal. Sonja watched him from the porch, smiling. All of his chores were finished, and he would spend the rest of the daylight working on the little dock. Ben would be back from Wrightsville the next day, and Isaac wanted it finished to surprise him. So severe and determined at sixteen. She felt a pang of sadness. He rushes to become a man, she thought, he will follow his father on the canal.

"The banks are closing," Ben said. "They call it a depression. Work is stopping. I have to find another way to make money. I will be back soon."

"How long will you be gone, Ben?"

"Eight or nine months. No longer."

"No!!"

It was wrong, Sonja thought. That wasn't how it happened. Sailing away happened before the Canal. I can't do all that again.

Ben helped Isaac remove his Union Army coat. Isaac's left sleeve hung empty. His arm was gone. Ben turned to hang the coat on the wall. Fighting the tears welling up in his eyes. Sonja placed her hand over her mouth.

"Mickey is a doctor now, Pa," Isaac said. "He had to take it off at Fredericksburg."

Sonja watched from the shadows as Ben and Isaac sat before the fire outside Isaac's cabin in New York. Isaac folded onto his knees. Ben wrapped his arms around him.

The blackness went deeper, darker, colder.

Isaac stood before them, smiling. His arms were by his side, then he raised his hands to them. "I am all right here. Don't worry about me. There is no more pain. I am so sorry I brought you so much sadness."

Sonja ran to him, grabbed him in her arms, sobbed on his shoulder.

"I am here," he said. "I am always here for you, waiting. I will meet you when it is time."

Ben pulled at Sonja. "We must go back."

"No!"

Ben pulled again. "We have to go, Sonja. We cannot stay here."

"I will stay," she said, pulling Isaac's face to hers. "Let me stay with you, son."

"I will always be here for you, Ma."

"Then let me stay."

"It is not time for you, Ma."

Ben pulled at her arm. "Not yet, Sonja. Not yet. Come back with me."

Isaac gently pulled down her hands and turned her to face Ben. "It is not time for you, Ma."

Ben pulled her away, stepping into the darkness, trying to leave Isaac in the light. She hesitated to go, pulling away from Ben, turning back toward Isaac.

Cold blackness bit at their skin. Their joints ached and throbbed. The pain in their chests was immense. The blackness expanded to consume the world, to fill it with nothingness, except the cold, the bitter cold.

———⊸∽◯◯∾⊷———

Mickey stood at the bow of his barge. Claude stood across from him on the other barge. The floodwaters pushed them toward the tip of the island ahead. They raced toward the buildings on the island's shore, where the water was already pushing up inside the buildings. Black gaps in the fronts showed where water had broken down the doors of the larger two buildings, but the smaller building's doors appeared to be holding. The barges sped forward faster than a locomotive.

Claude called out. "Maybe we should untie the barges."

"I agree. Maybe we will go between some of the buildings if we are separated."

The knots in the rope were soaked and nearly frozen. Mickey ran down into the cabin to grab a hand ax he had seen. The barges raced on toward the buildings on the shore. Mickey chopped at the heavy towropes tied between them as the barges charged ahead. Claude had brought up a hand ax to chop on the lines from his barge. The water carried them on, closer and closer to impact. The surging flood slammed into the island, throwing a massive wave into the air over the buildings' tops, sending cold spray in all directions. The lines snapped away between the barges, and they separated, but the current kept them side by side. The barges were trapped within the forces of the flood. The buildings loomed ahead. Mickey and Claude dove behind the cabin roofs for protection. Claude screamed into his cabin for his wife to hold on.

The barges rushed at the buildings, grinding their hulls on the rocky shore, gouging out sand and earth plowing toward the smallest building. The barges growled, digging into the beach, shoving into the ground, thrusting themselves ahead, driving into the island, ramming at the buildings. In the window of the building ahead, a black man stood watching them propelled to where he stood, then he closed his eyes in prayer.

Water crashed over the little building, and geysers shot high into the air as the barges embedded into the earth before the structures, grinding to a jerking halt. The waves fell back over the barges, returning to the river, as other waves slipped up onto the island then fell back to join their herd. The flood had crested, throwing the last of its anger against Watson's Island. The wave collapsed. Its remnants slid back down the slope, leaving a sand-covered beach where the bottom of the Susquehanna Flats had been scooped up and thrown upon the shore. The barges settled. The man in the window moved to open his front door, letting the water run out onto the sand.

Mickey slid off the bow of his barge and met Franklin.

"My friends were swept away from the canal basin," Mickey said. "Did anyone wash up here?"

⟿⟾◦⟾⟿

Mickey stood on the shore of the island, transfixed, gazing out onto the water. The Haneys climbed down from their barge for the welcoming heat of the fire that Rebecca had re-started in the kitchen stove. Franklin placed his hand on Mickey's shoulder.

"Doc, I am afraid we have lost Ben and Sonja."

"No."

"You said you saw them go into the water when the flood hit the basin, even before you managed to get on that barge. That's over two hours in ice cold flood waters."

Mickey kept his attention on the water. "They are out there."

"What do you see?" Franklin asked.

"Nothing," Mickey said, "but this is why I am here. I know it now. She is close. I can feel her."

Franklin pulled gently on Mickey's shoulder. "Maybe you should come to the church to get warmed up."

"No. They need me. I need to be here. This spot."

Mickey shrugged his shoulder from Franklin's hand. Something floated to the surface several yards out into the water.

"There," Mickey said, then rushed into the

water. Franklin followed but his artificial leg stumbled, causing him to fall.

Mickey waded deeper into the water, reaching out to the form, shoving his hand into the water, pulling a form to the surface.

"It's Ben!"

Franklin was up, grabbing at the form, pulling the body toward shore.

"His face is all screwed up," Franklin said, "like he's still holding his breath, but his skin color says he's dead. Blue as a catfish."

Franklin peered over the water. "Maybe we can find Sonja's body, too".

They strained to pull Ben's body to shore, encountering heavy resistance.

"He's caught on something," Franklin said.

Mickey reached into the water, feeling down Ben's lower arm to free him, groaning as he pulled. Franklin pulled at Mickey's waist. Together they brought another body to the surface.

"Oh my God," Mickey said. "It's Sonja! He's still holding her hand. Pull Franklin, pull."

They strained to get the bodies to shore.

"Rebecca! Rebecca," Franklin called out.

As they came to the shallows, Rebecca and Claude joined them to help pull the bodies onto the sandy beach. O'Grady managed to separate their hands and roll them onto their sides.

"Slap their backs."

"That won't bring them back, Dr. O'Grady."

"They've been in ice-cold water, Franklin. I've seen men come back from that. Keep slapping their backs."

Franklin gave Ben's back a mighty slap, causing a plug of mucous to fly out. Ben groaned, releasing a long rasping breath of fetid air, then began spasmatic coughing. Franklin's eyes were wide open.

Rebecca gasped. "It's a miracle."

Ben continued to cough and pull in breaths through deathly wheezes. He was still rasping like the dying as he rolled onto his back and grabbed Franklin's arm. Ben spoke, but it was unintelligible. He squeezed his grip on Franklin and forced the sound out again.

"Sonja."

"She's here, Ben," O'Grady said, "but she's not moving."

Ben rolled up onto his side, but his arm gave way under his weight, and he fell face-first into the sand. Franklin helped him sit up. Ben leaned to Sonja, grabbing her shoulder with one hand, shaking her.

"Sonja."

O'Grady's face was solemn as he peered at Ben, shaking his head. "Ben...I don't–"

Ben sat up. "No! No. Keep doing that. What else?"

"Her lungs are full of water, Ben. Not enough is coming out. It may be too late." He motioned to Franklin and Rebecca. "Let's turn her, so her head is lower."

"What??"

"That will put her head lower. Turn her head to the side, pat her back."

O'Grady pushed them aside, straddling Sonja's body in her new position, and began massaging her back, rubbing toward her head.

Ben lay his face close to Sonja's. "Some water is coming out of her mouth."

"Her color is still bad," Franklin said.

Ben pushed O'Grady aside. "Let me do it."

He began pressing and squeezing Sonja's waist then pushing up toward her shoulders. A minute passed, and nothing happened.

"Ben," O'Grady said.

Ben repeated his efforts. "No! What else? What else? Something else you know. Something else you've seen. What else, dammit?"

"A Scotsman, Tossach," Mickey said, "blew into the mouths of rescued coal miners. It was a long time ago. No one does it here."

"Did they live?"

"Some."

"How? Show me!"

"I've only read about it. Put her on her back."

All three worked to turn Sonja onto her back.

Ben whimpered, seeing her face, grabbing her shoulders, pulling her limp body to him, shaking her.

"You get back here! You hear me? I need you." Then faced O'Grady. "Now what?"

O'Grady shrugged his shoulders. "Blow into her mouth."

Ben blew several times onto her face.

"I think..." O'Grady said. "I think you should press your lips to hers...like kissing."

Ben met with her lips and blew deep into her lungs, but air escaped from her nose, spotting his cheek with blood. Rebecca reached down to squeeze Sonja's nose shut.

"Try it again," Rebecca said.

Ben molded to her lips again and blew into her throat. Her chest rose as if she took in a breath. He rose up to smile at her and stroked her cheek. "All right, woman, we have work to do."

Time and time again, Ben blew into her lungs. Moments passed with the sound of air being forced into her lungs and pressed out, but no response. Rebecca's eyes filled with tears. O'Grady leaned forward to pinch Sonja's nose and release Rebecca to rest.

Again and again, Ben blew into Sonja's lungs.

"I heard a gurgle," O'Grady said. "Let's roll her on her side to let some water out."

They rolled her up, Ben massaged her back, forcing less than a cup of liquid from her. O'Grady felt her arm and leg.

"Her body is too cold." O'Grady said, then glanced at Franklin, "We need to take her into the church."

"I'll go poke the fire in the stove," Rebecca said.

The three men lifted Sonja from the sand. Ben's wet trousers knees were soaked with blood. Walking toward the little chapel, Ben began to sink to the ground, his skin pale. Franklin took Sonja in his arms and carried her alone as O'Grady helped Ben back onto his feet.

Inside the chapel, Franklin glanced around for a place to lay her body. Only the wet floor was available, but then he gazed at the altar under the cross. Franklin's wooden leg thumped on the floorboards as he approached the altar. Examining the chalice and candlesticks set out on the tabletop, he peered up at the cross.

"Forgive me, Lord, but this woman needs that table."

He swiveled his body to bring Sonja's feet near the tabletop, then swung her feet in an arc, clearing everything off of it and onto the floor. Rebecca's eyes were wide with surprise as the holy objects clattered on the floor but said nothing as she grabbed some nearby blankets.

Ben and O'Grady entered and moved beside the table to continue breathing for Sonja. After another minute, Ben wobbled and stepped back, sinking to his knees. Rebecca dashed to the table to resume breathing for Sonja. Franklin brought Ben up on his feet. Ben grabbed Franklin's neck and whispered frantically into his ear.

Franklin gazed into Ben's eyes.

Ben's voice was still raw and rasping. "Not for me. For her," Ben said. "Tell him. Tell him. That's my promise."

Ben returned to Sonja, machine-like, repeating and repeating and repeating.

Breathe.

"Isaac told you to go back," Ben said.

Breathe.

"Isaac told you."

Breathe.

"Come back to me. Come back to me."

At last, Sonja coughed.

Ben rolled her onto her side and patted her back, then messaging her waist and back, some color returning to her face. She took in a rasping breath, coughing again and again. O'Grady, Rebecca, and Franklin gathered around the altar, smiling down at her. Sonja gazed about her unseeing, confused, gasping more breaths. Her mouth hung open, fighting for each breath. She reached out, unable to focus, grabbing a sleeve. It was Mickey.

She spoke, but the word was little more than a deathly moan. She gripped the sleeve and forced the sound again, pleading.

"Ben?" she said. "Ben?"

Ben leaned close to her, his nose touching hers. She took his face in trembling hands and smiled. "I heard Isaac," she said, then slipped into unconsciousness, breathing softly.

Breathing.

Breathing.

Ben lay on the floor beside the altar.

Outside, a man's voice barked commands. Bolton had come down from the hill. He had found the rowboat in the thickets on the far side of the island. His face was severely bruised, and his nose grotesquely swollen. There were broad black circles under his eyes. He brandished his knife toward Franklin, as Ben emerged ungainly from the church

"I know you've got supplies in there. I smelled you cooking."

Franklin scoffed. "I'm surprised you can smell anything."

Ben lunged at Bolton, knocking the knife to the ground. Claude and Mickey grabbed Bolton's arms. Ben snatched up the knife and held it before Bolton's throat.

"I should kill you. You tried to kill my wife and me."

Bolton gulped; his eyes wide open. "No. No. Just your horse. I wanted you to know what it felt like to lose something."

Ben put the tip of the blade against Bolton's throat.

"Ben," Franklin said. "Ben, is this what you want for you and Sonja now? Is this what her life is worth?"

Ben hesitated, the fire in his eyes still hot. He

glanced at Franklin, then blew out his breath. He lowered the blade only an inch, then brought the blade down, handing the knife to Franklin. Ben stumbled back into the church, where he stood beside Sonja, watching her sleep.

Franklin addressed O'Grady and Claude. "This man held my daughter and me at gunpoint last night. I think we should tie him up and present him to Deputy Hopkins as soon as we get back to Havre de Grace."

After Bolton's hands were tied and he was locked in a shed, Franklin reheated the stew. When most had eaten, Franklin took a cup of stew out to Bolton. Mickey ambled out to the shore, watching the sunrise, its light sparkling off the modest waves, then glanced up at the clearing sky.

"You never take the easy way, do you?"

The sun was halfway to its zenith when Sonja awoke, still lying on the altar, wrapped in blankets. Mickey stood from the rickety front pew where he sat with Rebecca and Tobias, turning to face Sonja. She met his eyes and then sat up, the blanket slipping from her shoulders. Mickey and Tobias spun around to face away as Rebecca rushed to her side, pulling the blanket up over her naked body.

"I took your clothes to dry them near the stove," Rebecca said.

"Where is Ben? Did he?...is he?..."

"He is outside with Papa," Rebecca said.

"I want to see him." She looked down at the floor from the high table. "Help me down, please."

"Your shoes and stockings are drying as well."

"Please help me down."

On her feet, Sonja pulled the blanket snugly

around her and walked to the door. Tobias stood near Rebecca. Mickey came to her, offering his hand. She smiled.

"Sweet Mickey. I think we found our darkness," she said but gently pushed him away, then stepped outside into the cold morning. The sky was nearly clear again and bright blue above cotton white clouds drifting south in the chilling wind from the north.

Before the chapel stood the two massive barges, like buildings that had always been there, sitting on dry land towering above her head, blocking the view of the river. Barefoot, she took awkward steps across layered sand that had spent years covering the bottom of the Susquehanna Flats. Beyond the barges, the new beach sloped to the water's edge yards away, where the water had always rested, now laced with thin ice growing thick. She heard the voices of men drifting in the air.

To her left, two boats were run up onto the sand. The smaller boat appeared to be one of Tobias's oyster boats. The larger one was a ferry, where a sulking man she knew as Harris Bolton sat with his hands tied, frowning at her. Deputy Hopkins stood near the boat, holding Turner's shotgun and tipping his hat to her with a smile.

Sonja stepped further down the beach, drawn by voices but not understanding the words spoken. One voice was Ben's. Out in the frigid water, two men stood almost chest-deep, exchanging a mellow but serious conversation. She neared the shoreline of the little beach, recognizing Ben and Franklin facing each other. Franklin was asking questions. Ben listened, then when Franklin had finished the question, Ben nodded in agreement. She tilted her head in curiosity.

After more questions, Franklin brought his hand onto Ben's back and his other hand to Ben's forehead, then she heard the sound of Franklin's voice, but not the words he spoke. Ben nodded his head then Franklin lowered him under the water, noticing Sonja watching as he did. Franklin raised Ben from the water, hugged him tightly, saying a few brief words, then nodded in Sonja's direction.

Ben turned toward her, his face lit by the rising sun and a joyous boyhood smile she had not seen for many, many years.

Mist filled Sonja's eyes, and tears streamed down her cheeks.

"Oh, Ben."

ROBERT F. LACKEY

CLIPPINGS FROM THE AEGIS INTELLIGENCER,
BEL AIR, MD. JANUARY 7, 1870

HIGH TIDE.—The highest tide known for years, flowed into Bush and Gunpowder rivers, on Sunday afternoon last, caused by the prevalence of the south east wind on that day. At Otter Point, in this county we are informed the water rose above the wharf at Messrs Michael & Son's, and flowed into their wharehouse, causing some damage to salt and other articles stored therein. The water also broke over the embankments at the ends of the railroad bridges over Bush and Gunpowder rivers, causing thereby a detention of trains on the Philadelphia, Wilmington & Baltimore railroad.

At Havre de Grace there was a perfect flood, owing to the high tide, which was higher at that point than it had been known to be for many years. Two canal boats, in the basin of the Tide Water Canal, were floated over the tow path and into the river, and finally lodged high and dry on Watson's Island. At Mr. DuBois' lumber manufactory, the water carried off some 40,000 feet of lumber. Also Messrs. Woodruff & Richardson ber. Also Messrs. Woodruff & Richardson and Smith and others lost quite heavily in lumber. At Spesutia Island, Messrs. Green & Williams, in the fishing business, lost some two hundred barrels of salt stored in buildings at that place that had stood there for many years, but which were flooded and carried away by this tide.

Samuel Smith lost to the amount of $1,000 in fishing materials and buildings, at Spesutia Island. Coale & O'Brien, at the same place, lost $500 worth of property, and $300 worth at Watson's Island. Amos Osborn lost all of his buildings, at Shad Battery, valued at $2,000. At Carpenter's Point, on the Cecil shore, Mr. Geo. W. Barnes lost property to the value of $3,000. Also much damage was done to property at the fishing shores along North East, in the same county. Considerable damage was also done to the wharves of Messrs. Simmons & Co., Hilles & Co., and others, at Havre de Grace.

Altogether this tide was unparalleled in the memory of the "oldest inhabitant."

ROBBERY AT HAVRE DE GRACE.—On Sunday night last, during the storm that prevailed at that time, a thief or thieves broke into the clothing store of S. Bachrach & Co., at Havre de Grace, and stole therefrom fifty dollars' worth of clothing and four watches. Their entrance was effected by breaking open a shutter and removing a pane of glass in the window. The upper part of the building is occupied by John B. Coale, Esq., as a residence, but neither that gentleman nor his family were alarmed by any noise made by the thieves. No traces of the rogues have yet been discovered.

ROBERT F. LACKEY

EPILOGUE

OCTOBER 22, 1909.
THE UPPER CHESAPEAKE BAY

Aboard the steamboat *Susquehanna*, the fifth hull to be given that name, three generations of women enjoyed an annual pilgrimage up the Chesapeake Bay. The red and gold of an Indian summer autumn speckled from maples and oaks standing proudly among the pine trees on the shores. The smooth water mirrored an inverted tree line, except where the bow wave of the steamer rippled the image. A little girl with golden hair and bright blue eyes leaned on the railing, bouncing on tiptoes in her laced dress. She gazed at the shore slipping by, her coat abandoned in her deck chair in the warm sunshine. She glanced over her shoulder to where her mother sat.

"Are we there yet, Momma?" Little Polly asked the question yet again and pointed to a spit of land with a wiggly finger. "Is that Havey Grace over there?"

"Lord, child," her mother, Rachel, said, "how many times are you going to ask me that?"

Cathy, the child's grandmother, chuckled from her deck chair beside Rachel, patting her daughter's arm.

"Relax, Rachel, you were a busier child than

that at her age. Polly's a little girl, all excited about her eleventh birthday tomorrow and her first visit to Havre de Grace."

"Yes, Momma, I know," Rachel said. "But between Polly's excitability and her cousin's non-stop running around this steamboat, I'm a nervous wreck. William's mother should have come with us instead of sending him alone."

"Odie and Lenz would have come, Rachel," Cathy said. "But my Uncle Aaron is frail. He's eighty-two now. He still lives in those mountains of Virginia, and Cousin Lenz wanted to see his grandfather before winter set in. And, please remember, we all agreed to take Billy on with us so his mother could get off in Tolchester to visit her own mother."

"I know that, Momma, but any second William Benjamin could—"

A child's wail punched the air. Rachel leaped from her deck chair and dashed in the direction of the cry. Seconds later, she returned, dragging her reluctant nephew by his hand. Cathy examined the boy as he came close.

"You look all right to me, Billy..."

"Momma, please don't call him Billy..."

Cathy frowned at her daughter. "You can't really mean that, Rachel. He's a nine-year-old boy. William Benjamin is far too old a name to call him yet."

Rachel paid scant attention to her mother as she inspected her nephew for damage. "What hurts, William?" She asked.

Billy scowled and stuck out his lower lip, then showed her his right hand. His palm was without a mark, but his knuckles were bright red.

Rachel's eyes widened. "You were in a fight?"

Billy pushed out his chin. "He started it."

Rachel blew out her breath. "Then, why did you cry out?"

"I didn't. He did. Then he ran away."

Rachel pointed a stiff finger at a nearby deck chair. "Sit, young man."

Polly came back from the railing and whispered to Rachel. "Momma, here come's great granny."

Slender with spry movements, barely relying on her cane, the old matriarch made her way across the deck to her chair just beyond Cathy.

Cathy pushed the deck chair around so it would be easier for the old woman to sit. "Have a seat with us, Momma,"

The woman dropped into the chair and blew out her breath. Cathy frowned.

"Momma, were you drinking?"

The woman pushed back stray strands of silver hair and returned the frown, almost hiding her crystal blue eyes in the shadow of the afternoon sun from her wide-brimmed hat.

"I am seventy-one years old, young lady. I can have a brandy when I wish it."

Cathy rolled her eyes. "Momma, it's only two o'clock in the afternoon."

Cathy's mother ignored her and pointed out beyond the railing, speaking to Polly. "That's

Spesutie Island," she said.

She pushed herself from her chair and headed to the railing, thumping her cane and calling the youngsters. "Come to me, children."

As soon as she reached the railing, Polly and Billy came to her sides like bookends. The woman let her cane fall onto the deck and put her arms around the children, leaning over each to kiss the tops of their heads. Then she pointed to the island.

"That is where my first momma was born," she said.

"Your first momma, great-granny?" Polly asked.

The old woman scoffed. "Don't call me that. Call me...hell, if we're talking about Spesutie Island, you must call me Moses."

"Moses?" Both children spoke in unison.

"Yes. My first momma, who named me Moses, was born on that island, on this side." She looked down at their faces. "And the other side there was once a pirate ship anchored in the narrows there. The pirates were stealing black folks to take them away, but your great-great-grandfather and great-great-grandmother fought them. They led people from Havre de Grace to fight the pirates and then captured the pirate ship for themselves."

Billy peered at her from the corners of his eyes. "Awww, great — Moses. Did they really?"

Polly stared up at Moses, her blue eyes sparkling and her mouth wide open. "For true?"

Moses pointed to another island, a smaller one the steamer approached next. "When I was little, I lived there a while. It was called Shad Island, then. It didn't have a lighthouse, like it does now, just that old rickety house, where me and my first Momma lived."

"Were you born there?" Sonja asked.

Moses smiled. "No. I was born farther north, in Havre de Grace, where we are going."

"And then you moved there?" Asked Polly.

"No, child. When I was just an infant, I floated on a chunk of ice in a great flood and landed on the shore of Shad Island."

Polly stared at her with wide eyes. Billy peered askance from the corner of his. "Awww..."

"That's where Momma Rachel found me," Moses said. "She was the first Momma I knew and the woman your momma is named after."

Polly's mouth was still open as she and Billy turned back to face Rachel. Polly's mother released a heavy sigh, gave them a weary nod, and then shared a knowing smile with her own mother, Cathy.

Moses kept her attention on Shad Island. "We lived all alone there. My first momma became very sick when I was a little younger than Billy's age, so I rowed a boat from the island to find help, but it turned over."

"What happened?" Billy asked.

Moses kissed their heads again and pulled them close to her. "Just when I thought I would drown, my real Momma and Papa rescued me on that pirate ship. It was theirs then."

The children giggled with excitement. "More.

Tell us more, Moses."

"Well," Moses said, "since now the story moves to my real Momma and Papa, you'll need to call me by my birth name, Alisha. That's the name I was given the day I was born. December 19th, 18 and 39."

"Your Momma and Papa had a pirate ship?" Billy asked.

"Yes, they did," she said. Tears filled her eyes. "It was named the *Raven*. Benjamin and Sonja Pulaski were something else." She gazed smiling at Polly. "You are the spitting image of Sonja. I had blonde hair in my youth, as well. And eyes the color of yours."

"Then what happened?" Polly asked.

"A lot happened before then that I need to tell you about, too. But I should tell it to you from the very start...when a widow who thought she was all alone in the world received a telegram from a dead man."

Rachel and Cathy shared smiles and held hands, watching the children with Alisha.

Polly and Billy nearly squealed. "What? What? Tell us the story."

"Tomorrow, children," Alisha said. "Tomorrow, we will spend the day in Havre de Grace, and Polly will be eleven years old. We will walk the streets your ancestors did, and I will tell you about them. Havre de Grace is always the best place to start a story, the story of Ben and Sonja Pulaski."

PULASKI'S REDEMPTION

ROBERT F. LACKEY

PULASKI'S REDEMPTION

Dear Reader,

If you also read volumes 1-9, then you have reached the end of this series. I hope our journey together has been enjoyable for you, despite the struggles, dangers and sadness I have heaped upon the Pulaskis in the nearly 3,000 pages of this saga. I tried to write each novel in the series as a stand-alone story, throwing the Pulaskis into the shifting historic periods faced by America during the 29 years of the saga. My wife says otherwise and insists you read it in sequence of the years. Many readers agree with her and tell me that the saga is best savored from the beginning.

You and I began this series in the canal era and the moral awakening of the Pulaskis to the harsh reality of slavery. Maryland was a slave state until the Civil War, and it was years before that when we began with 'Pulaski's Canal', the first volume, in 1841. Since then, we have peeked into other historic moments, slavery and its economic poison, the underground railroad, the war with Mexico, Bleeding Kansas, the American Civil War, and its devastating aftermath.

With this novel, I have left the Pulaskis in 1870, but I prefer to think that they go on, just without my prying eyes watching them and telling you.

THE PULASKI SAGA

PULASKI GENERATIONS

**PULSAKI
GENERATIONS**

BEN AND SONJA

ISAAC AND HARRIET	AARON AND BERNADETTE	ALISHA AND JESSE
SONJA	ARRY	CATHY
HERBIE	TILDY OPHELIA	
CAROLINE	SIMON PATRICK	
	LENZ	RACHEL
	BILLY	POLLY

ROBERT F. LACKEY

In developing this 10-book series, I invented 172 characters. For those series readers who like to track characters and volumes, I offer a list of those characters, a descriptive comment about most, and the book in which they were introduced.
Also, for those who are determined to separate the history from artistic balderdash in my books, I offer a bibliography of related books I read in developing and writing this historical fiction series. You will find it on the Pulaski's World page of my internet web site: www.rflackeybooks.com
Enjoy the hunt.

LAST NAME	FIRST NAME	DESCRIPTION	BK
ALEXANDER	BRANDON	Past detective in Baltimore and Washington, DC. Fixated on Pulaski Family as crimicals and murerers. Becomes Deputy Sheriff in HDG beginning 1852.	BD
ANIOSTROZ	MARTIN	Paternal owner of Courland Plantation on Waccamaw River. South of Plametto Haven	BP
BARNES		lst officer of the Star of Phjiladelphia	
BARNES	William Henry	8 yp black boy in 1848. Errand boy at Madison's Tavern in Great Mills	
BARRET	CHARLES	Argyle man in Kansas (AA)	SC
BARTLETT	DAN	Skipper of Canal Barge 26, brother of John Bartlett	PC
BARTLETT	JOHN	Lock Tender at Lock 9, Brother of Dan Bartlett: murdered by Randall Hoagg	BOTC
BARTLETT	MARGARET	Wife of John Bartlett	PC
BINTERFIELD	HERBERT	British(Tory) descent banker in Havre de Grace. Owns Tidewater Bank and Trust Co. Owns papers on Barge. Tries to defeat Benjamin wherever possible. Is infatuated with Sonja. Murdered by Sam Briscoe.	PC
BINTERFIELD	LYDIA	Suspect mixed Negro heritage. Both are pro-slavery. Wife always intent to show royal white heritage.	PC
BOND	TOBY(TOBIAS)	Little boy from PC. In SC leading slaves through Md to north.	PC
BOND	BENNY	Son of Simon and Lettie	SC
BOND	LETTIE	Simon's betrothed	RR
BOND	SIMON	Barge "crew" is Simon Bond, a run-away slave from southern Maryland. He is very educated and teaches the family reading, writing, and cultural --------. Simon works to buy his wife from Sotterlee. Has difficulty hiding from slave owners. Has false papers showing as free black. Also has false papers showing him as property of Benjamin - as needed for situation. Becomes Canadian with Lettie, moves north. Returns in SC.	PC
BONNEAU	FREDERICK	Editor of Capital Telegraph Newspaper in Washington. Age 43 in 1849. Uncle of Bernadette Washford, Brother of Bernadette's mother.	SC
BOOKER	DAVID	KITM & SC. Lives in Jundt/Pulaski farm in York Furnace. UGR station	KITM
BOOKER	HELEN	Wife of David	KITM
BOOKER	ISAIAH	Father of David and Matthew. Matthew killed in KITM.	KITM
BOWMAN	CARL	Owner of Oyster Street Tavern	BOT

282

LAST NAME	FIRST NAME	DESCRIPTION	BK
BOYD	ALICE	Wife of William Boyd	PC
BOYD	WILLIAM	Canal Superintendent. Died April ? (before 4/8 report) 1841. Informal History HDG p37. Served in Florida Army with Pulaski 1829 ??	PC
BRISCOE	SAMUEL	Real Estate agent working for Joseph Binterfield.	PC
BRISCOE		BLACKSMITH at HDG Canal Basin Barn	BOT
BROWN	NATHANIEL	Clerk at Binterfield's bank. Helped pull Brandon form the river in 1839	PC
CALVERT	EMMA	Wife of John	PC
CALVERT	JOHN	Lock Tender at York Furnace; friend of Burl Jundt	PC
CANKER	WARREN	Cousin o William, Confederate Prisoner in Point Lookout	BGS
CANKER	WILLIAM (BILL)	Enrollment Assistant to Major Alexander	BGS
CARDWELL	ROBERT	Georgetown SC Lawyer (Mansfield Debt - KITM)	KITM
CARMICHAEL	RICHARD	Ex Major, Adjutant, durng Spanish Florida war. Suspicious of James Yount.	BD
COBB	JOSEPH	Con man, fake major, husband of Lucy	BP
COBB	LUCY	White House Mistress. Pardon broker woman	BP
CREW	OSPREY	1849 CREW: Captain: Horatio Cuttingham, First Mate: Edward Leonard (Ben's half brother), Alistair (Atlantic Sailor), Warren (Cook), Daniel (Atlantic sailor, Black), Wyatt (Bay sailor from Annapolis). END OF BD, first of SC.	KITM
CREW	RAVEN	1847 CREW: Edward (Ben's half brother), Alistair (Atlantic Sailor), Warren (Cook), Daniel (Atlantic sailor, Black), Wyatt (Bay sailor from Annapolis). END OF KITM & FIRST OF SC.	RR
CUMMINGS	WILBUR (Will)	Railroad detective investigating murder of union soldier in HDG 1861.	BGSG
CURRIER	MATTHEW	Co-owner of Currier Ferry between HDG and Perryville. Brother of William. Lives on Lafayette St,	DH
CURRIER	WILLIAM	Co-owner of Currier Ferry between HDG and Perryville. Brother of Matthew Lives on Market St,	DH
CURTIS	ARCHIE	Black boy working the mules for Pulaski barges. Becomes crewman on Jester, then Barge Captain (BGSG). Then hired away by Sonja to work on the Sloop Jester	SC. Name
CURTIS	FRANKLIN	Ex Union Seargent Major, New owner & Cook Oyster Street Tavern, Father of Rebecca. Newly ordained baptist preacher, has small chapel on Watson's Island.	PR
CURTIS	REBECCA	DAUGHTER FD FRANKLIN, WAITRESS AT OST, BETROTHED TO TOBIAS.	PR
CUTTINGHAM	HORATIO (Ory)	Previous ensign of the small steamer Lydia. Manager for Palmetto Haven RR and KITM. Returned to England in BGSG	KITM
DORSEY	PHILLIP	Sheriff of SMC 1866	BP
DREW	JONATHAN HENRY	(irish) NY Actor helping Eric Little Con DC Police Commissioner	BD
DUTTON	ANGELA	Black girl working days for Mamie at Pink House starting 1854. Same age as Alisha	SC
DUTTON	MATTHEW	Cousin of Archie Curtis	

LAST NAME	FIRST NAME	DESCRIPTION	BK
EVANS	TILDY	Tildy Haller Evans. Aunt of Bernadette, Sister of Uncle Fred's deceased wife, Thelma. Lives near Wytheville, Va, (Fort Chiswell) birth place of Tildy and Thelma Haller Bonneau. Owns apple orchard.	DH
FINLEY	JIMMY	Young waterman of HDG, crewman on Jester for Sonja.	SC
FORRESTER		Captain of the Star of Philadelphia	
FREIDMAN	ABRAHAM	Maggie's brother, who has been in NY where he withdrew from rabinical school	KITM
FREIDMAN	DELBERT	Co Owner of Hardware, Husband of Mary ,Father of Maggie	BOT
FREIDMAN	MARY	Wife of Delbert, Mother of Maggie, Sister of Margaret Bartlett	BOT
FREIDMAN / PULASKI	MAGGIE	Named for Margaret Bartlett, Mary's sister and husband of John; Deceased wife of Aaron (KITM)	BOT C
FREIZE	JARROD	Crewman on the Raven. Put off for being a trouble maker wanting to work slave ships.	RR
FRIEZE	JAMES	Crewman on the Raven, From Philadelphia	RR
GRAY	GEORGE	Farm Co-op Member at Grayrocks 1866	BP
GRAY	LETTIE	Old woman from Grayrocks, dies in forrest with Simon.	
HANNAH	ABIGAIL	Widow of Robert. HDG Dock Fee Collector.	BOT
HANNAH	ROBERT	Early friend of Ben's. Killed by Sam Briscoe	BOT
HARPER	LUANN	Wife of Dr. Harper	PC
HARPER	WALLACE	Doctor	PC
HOAGG	RANDALL	Bosun of the Star of Philadelphia; Enemy of Ben	PC
HOLDER	JUSTIN	Private in Company E, 18th Connecticut Regiment	BGS
JAH	OTIS	Union veteran returned to Palmetto Haven as a pacifist	BP
JOHANNSEN	ADDISON	Younger son of Jacob	BP
JOHANNSEN	AVERY	Older son of Jacob	BP
JOHANNSEN	JACOB	Quaker at York Furnace	BP
JOHNSON	MARTHA	Midwife in HDG, Lives above Peral lane, Knew Pulaskis; husband built bench at Alisha's tree; thrift. (PC, KITM, SC)	PC
JUNDT	BURL	Burl Jundt, Sonja's Father has a farm in York Furnace, PA. He lives with evil step daughter, Liza, from second marriage. He is an abolitionist. She is pro-slavery and suspects Simon of being runaway slave. Sonja's grandfather (Warner Jungt) served under John Paul Jones with Joseph Pulaski. The grandfathers' friendship tied the two families and brought Sonja and Benjamin together.	PC
KANE	GEORGE	Marshal of Police for Baltimore 1860. Pro South.	

LAST NAME	FIRST NAME	DESCRIPTION	BK
KENLY	JOHN	Just before daybreak on June 27, 1861, soldiers marched from Ft. McHenry on orders from Major General Nathaniel P. Banks, who had succeeded Cadwalader as commander of the Department of Annapolis, and arrested Marshal George P. Kane. Banks appointed Colonel John Reese Kenly of the 1st Regiment Maryland Volunteer Infantry as provost marshal to superintend the Baltimore police; Kenly enrolled, organized, and armed 250 Unionists for a new police. When the old Board of Police would not recognize the new police, and tried to continue the old police, they were arrested and sent to Fort Warren in Boston Harbor. On July 10, George R. Dodge, a civilian, was appointed as marshal of police.	DH
KINCAID	ABIGAIL	Mother of Harlett and Wallace	BD
KINCAID	HERBERT	Father of Harriet and Wallace	BD
KINCAID	WALLACE	Brother of Harriet, Borther-in-law of Isaac Pulaski	BD
LAMBDIN	ROBERT	By 1840 Robert Lambdin had severed his partnership with Butler. Samuel Butler continued to operate a yard in Baltimore, and Lambdin returned to his native St. Michaels. He leased the waterfront land at the foot of Mulberry Street, immediately adjacent to his house, for use as a shipyard. For forty-five years, Lambdin constructed vessels at his small Mulberry Street yard ranging in type from small, flat-bottomed oyster tonging boats to the schooners, pungies, sloops, and bugeyes of his day.	RR
LANDRY	WILSON	Asst Supt, Dept of Justice Clerks	
LEONARD	BELLE	EDWARDS WIFE	RR
LEONARD	EDWARD	Ben's half brother	RR
LEXINGTON	PARKER	Manager at Gray Rocks 1866. Fired for embezzelment by Sonja	BP
LISTER	BARTHOLOME	HDG Undertaker	RR
LISTER	NADJA	Wife of Undertaker	RR
LITTLE	ERIC	Owner of Andrew Jackson Tavern	BD
MADISON	JOHN	Overseer at Gray Rocks in 1848. Brother of Matthew Madison, owner of Madis on Tavern in Great Mills.	BD
MATTINGLY	ALBERT	Farmhand at Yount Farm, Leonardtown.	BD
MATTINGLY	LYLE	Deputy Sheriff in Havre de Grace	PC
MCGRAW	STEPHEN	Lambdin trained several shipbuilders by taking on apprentices. He taught all five of his sons the shipbuilding trade and took other apprentices as well, including Thomas H. Kirby	RR
MCMALLERY	FORREST	"Mac", Blacksmith in Lapidum	BOT
MCMALLERY	JEREMY	Son of Forrest	BOT
MEECHUM	WYATT	Bowdoin College, Brunswick, Maine. Joshua Chamberlain was Rhetoric Professor. New York Times while it was in the field reporting the war; works at Capital Telegraph	BP
MILTON	GEORGE	Lawyer	PC
MITCHELL	"MITCH" (JOHN)	Works for Canal. Helped pull Brandon from river.	PC
MORRISON	ANNA	Determined mature widow of Union Sergeant. Cook and Housekeeper	BP
NAYERS	MATTHEW	Sheriff of York County, Pa.	
NONE	Jimmy	Mule tender for Henry Scott	
NONE	Lilly	Jimmy's mother	
NONE	THOMAS	Young Male slave at Grayrocks. Friend of Lettie & Simon	RR

LAST NAME	FIRST NAME	DESCRIPTION	BK
O'GRADY	Michael Patrick (Mickey)	Irish stone mason, lost wife in flood of 1839, told Ben how to find 2nd Barge when he began working for Ben. Becomes Physician Medicia Doctor in Union Army during CW. Meets B&S at Gettysburg. Finds Jesse's grave for Alisha.	PC
PENN	ABNER	Manager at Palmetto Haven, hired by Robert Cardwell from Rhode Island	BP
POOSHEE	ACME	House slave of Leland Washford	
PRICE	CATHERINE	Wife of Jesse Price Sr.	KITM
PRICE	CATHY (CATHERINE)	Catherine Rachel Sonja Price , CATHY , Daughter of Alisha AND Jesse , Jr.	SC
PRICE	JESSE	Lock Tender at Lock 9, After death of John Bartlett	KITM
PRICE	JESSE JR.	ROUGH FRIEND WITH ALISHA, LATER HUSBAND	KITM
PRICE	MARTHY	SPECIAL NEEDS WOMAN DAIGHTER OF CATHERINE	KITM
PRICE	PATTIE	PEER FRIEND OF ALISHA	KITM
PRICE	TAMMY	FACE SCARRED BY POX DAUGHTER OF CATHERINE AND JESSE SR.	KITM
PULASKI	AARON	Born 1826. Wants to be a painter. Late teens. One year younger than Alex.He plays the dulcimer, inherited from an uncle in western North Carolina. Has girlfriends in several ports and towns. Drawn to inns and alehouses. This worries his parents (mostly Sonja)	PC
PULASKI	BEN	Polish and from Baltimore. Benjamin and Sonja are middle aged with unusually warm relationship. Boys offer experiences and viewpoints of 19th century America. Ben was crew on ship to Pacific, later in Chesapeake Bay schooners; traveled well. Was also in Army (Where? What?). Knew lighthouse keeper in Havre de Grace. Predicts Polish empire will swallow Germany--running lighthearted feud with Sonja Had proposed to Sonja after getting out of the army, but she turned him down. He had grown up in fishing villages and on ships, so he signed on with a ship in Baltimore, heading for the Pacific. When he returned he had gained a small amount of gold and asked Sonja again to marry him. After a tumultuous courtship, she married him, and he bought the barge Rockfish and renamed it the Sonja.	PC
PULASKI	CAROLINE	Caroline Elizabeth Pulaski, Daughter of Isaac and Hariet, Born during the bombardment of Fort Sumter. April 12, 1861	DH
PULASKI	HARRIET K.	Wife of Isaac Pulaski	BD
PULASKI	HERBERT BENJAMIN	Son of Isaac and Harriet	SC
PULASKI	ISAAC	**Born 1825.** Wants to be an engineer. Late teens. He frequently produces diagrams of imaginative mechanical devices. Believes human flight is possible. This worries his parents. BUILDS WHARF FOR BARGES IN LAPIDUM. GOES TO WEST POINT. WOUNDED AT FREDERICKSBERG LOSING LEFT ARM. SUICIDE IN 1869, ALBANY NY	PC
PULASKI	LELAND	Arry, son of Isaaron and Bernadette, born 1861	DH
PULASKI	LENZ	Ben's father (Lenz Pulaski) was a powder monkey under John Paul Jones and a U.S.Navy Lieutenant late in the War of 1812. Knew Francis Scott Key. When British invaded Washington DC, he ran through the British blockade at the mouth of the Chesapeake and took his clipper the "Osprey" to Charleston. Ben went along. Ben's mother stayed in Baltimore.	PC
PULASKI	SARAH	Deceased daughter of Aaron, Granddaughter to Ben & Sonja	KITM
PULASKI	SIMON	Son of Isaaron and Bernadette, born 1865	BGS
PULASKI	SONJA	**Sonja** Jungt Pulaski is Germanic blond with blue hazel eyes. She is described as: "the sun rises in the east just to show the world her smile".	PC
PULASKI	SONJA ABIGAIL	Daughter of Isaac and Harriet, "Little Sonja"	SC
PULASKI	TILDY	Tildy Ophelia Pulaski, Birn Dec 25, 1869 to Aaron and Bernadette Pulaski in Fort Vhiswell, Va.	BP
PULASKI PRICE	ALISHA	Baby girl lost in the flood of 1839; Discovered alive on Shad (Battery) Island; Wife and widow of Jesse Price Jr. who died at Gettysburg	PC

PULASKI'S REDEMPTION

LAST NAME	FIRST NAME	DESCRIPTION	BK
PULASKI /TATUM	Mos / Alisha	Alisha, daughter of Sonja & Ben; Sought by Ramona Tatum (SC)	RR
QUENTIN	JOHN	SC Plantation owner, Murdered Jonah	BP
RENOWITZ	ANTHONY	Anthony and Camilla Renowitz own competing Barge and frequently try to prempt or share in Ben's successes. Friendly rivalry with Ben, Anthony sailed with Ben in the Pacific.	PC
RENOWITZ	CAMILLA	Wife of Anthony	PC?
RODGERS	HARRY	Crewman on the Raven, from Baltimore	RR
SCOTT	HENRY	Barge Captain for STC, Owner of slaves Lilly and Jimmy	
SCOTT	OTHO	Owner of Battery Island, Fishing Island	BD
SILONA	HERNANDO	Spanish aristocrat, once a boarder at the Pink House, who assists Mamie in the pretense that Lydia is a resident at his estate north of seville.	SC
SIMPSON	GARRETT	Canaller living in Benls barges during winter of 1870.	PR
SMILIES			PC
SMITH	Albert	Lost son of slaves Deborah and Saul	
SMITH	Deborah	Mother of Albert, housekeeper of Berl in NC	
SMITH	Saul	Father of Albert, farm hand to Berl in NC	
STANNER	SAMUEL	Harford County Secessionist	BGS
STANNER	WALTER	Harford County Secessionist, BIGGER BUT OLDER BROTHER OF Stanner	BGS G
STEWART	Mamie	Widowed owneer of Pink House Boarding House	RR
STEWART	William	Dead Husband of Mamie Stewart	RR
TATUM	RACHEL	Alisha's adoptive mother	RR
TATUM	RAMONA	Sister of Rachel, from Dundalk?, claims Alisha (SC)	RR
TRUMAINE	ATTICUS	Staff reporter at CapTel, Graduated with honors at William and Mary College in Williamsburg, Virginia. At CT since 1840; works at Capital Telegraph	BP
TUCKER	DANIEL	Self taught DR on Plantation NEAR Palmetto Haven	KITM
TURNER	ROBERT	English friend of Cuttingham, starts mercantile business in HDG. Fond of Sonja, even though she is married.	SC
LAST NAME	FIRST NAME	DESCRIPTION	BK
TUTTLE	JACK	Nephew of Adam Tuttle. Father was eastern shore farmer that never liked Adam. Jack doesn't know why. Jack ran off to sea at 12. Becomes crew on the Jester.	
TUTTLE	ADAM	Boatwright; Good friend; Killed in Bermuda (RR)	PC
UNKN	MARGARET	Maid; Black woman married to Ex-Union Sergeant carpenter	BP
UNKN	SADIE	Maid; white widow of Union Sergent-major killed at Fredericksburg.	BP
WALLACE	RALPH	School teacher at Grayrocks 1866	BP
WALTERS		Subscription clerk at Capital Telegraph	BP
WASHFORD	BERNADETTE	Love interest for Aaron	DH
WASHFORD	DANIEL	Benradette's Uncle, Planter in SC, Charleston, co-owner of	DH
WASHFORD	JANE	Wife of Daniel Washford	DH
WASHFORD	LELAND	Bernadette's father, Cotton Lobbyist	DH
WASHFORD	OPHELIA	Wife of Leland, Bernadette's mother, Brother of Fred	DH
WATKINS	LESTER	Lawyer for Binterfiled & Tatum; Later for Mamie Stewart	KITM
WILLAIMSON	JUNIE	Lydia's slave, gift from Gray Rocks father, mother of Sissy	PC
WILLIAMSON	FATU	Daughter of Nadine and Bala (Gulah man)	BP
WILLIAMSON	GRANNY CELESTE	Oldest slave on Palmetto Haven, Nursemaid to Lydia for Ruth; carried on homemade chair left	
WILLIAMSON	JAMES	Owner of Grayrocks & Lettie, father of Lydia	PC
WILLIAMSON	JAMES,JR.	Son of Master James Williamson	PC
WILLIAMSON	JASON	Master James Williamson's younger son. Hateful. Spiteful. Gray Rocks Master 1844-1860	BD
WILLIAMSON	JEREMIAH	Brother of James Sr Father of Lydia's sister-daughter	RR
WILLIAMSON	NADINE	Lydia's sister/daughter. Sired by Jeremiah through Lydia. Murdered by Lydia at Palmetto Haven.	KITM
WILLIAMSON	RUTH	Lydia's mother. Murdered by Nadine at Palmetto Haven.	KITM
WILLIAMSON	SISSY	Daughter of Junie, working for Mamie	PC
WOOLSIE	LLOYD	Worked under Pollard at Richmond Times until Union occupation; works at Capital Telegraph	BP
ZENOBI	EMILIO	Ben's replacement in prison	BD

ROBERT F. LACKEY

SO, WHAT IS NEXT FOR US?

There are still two more projects flitting about in my mind that will touch upon the Pulaski story. I am considering going back to the Pulaski earlier years, when Ben and Sonja arrived in Havre de Grace in 1825. Only 11 years after the devastating raid by the British in 1813, many buildings still languished after the burning when Ben and Sonja rent a house on Market Street from kindly Mr. Greene. The working title is "Havre de Grace – A Novel". Look for this one in Spring 2022.

"1825. The country was new and the sleepy town sitting at the top of the Chesapeake Bay with its feet dangling in the bountiful waters was on the verge of a rebirth. Languishing after the devastation from the British attack of 1813, shipping and new opportunities brought a bright future and people who would awaken the town in search of fortunes and daring undertakings. Young and eager, Ben and Sonja Pulaski join the excitement and forever connect their hopes, dreams and nightmares to Havre de Grace, willing to risk everything, even themselves."

Additionally, and you might already suspect something was planted in the epilogue, I want to visit Havre de Grace in 1920. That was an exciting time for the little town sitting at the shore of the Chesapeake Bay with its toes dangling in the mighty Susquehanna River. It was a time of returning doughboys, prohibition, whiskey smuggling, flapper girls, horse racing at the nationally known racetrack, and gangsters. It will be a time for Billy and Polly to meet again.

"Returning soldiers from France during the Great War, find the nation in the midst of Prohibition. A small town hosting a nationally recognized racetrack, called "The Graw" by those who played the ponies. Rivers of illegal whiskey, speakeasy bordellos visited by mob and gangster bosses staying at the local hotel, and young men looking for a fast buck, trying to stay alive in a country flooded with surplus submachine guns. What could possibly go wrong?"

The working title for this one is "The Graw". Look for it in Winter 2022.

Until then, be well and be safe. And if you ever have an opportunity to visit Havre de Grace, you must come. The lockhouse and the iconic lighthouse are still there, and the swing bridge works to get you over one of the last remaining canal locks. Havre de Grace is a lovely place with delightful shops, wonderful bed and breakfasts, restaurants and taverns. It is a place where today whispers in your ear of yesterday.

Thank

The author now lives in Murrells Inlet, SC, with his wife, Sandi.

Rflackey.author@gmail.com
http://www.rflackeybooks.com

PULASKI'S REDEMPTION